Earl Grey with a Hint of Murder

A Le Doux Mystery

Le Doux Mysteries
Book 9

Abigail Lynn Thornton

Le Doux Mysteries #9

"Earl Grey with a Hint of Murder"

Le Doux Mysteries #9

By Abigail Lynn Thornton

To my eldest.
I'm so proud of the man you're becoming.
Your kindness and vision for life will
always be an inspiration.
Thank you for teaching me how
to be a mother. I love you.

Acknowledgments

No author works alone. Thank you, Mariah.
Your cover work is beautiful!
And to Laura, for your timely and thorough editing!

Prologue
"No Matcha For Murder" chapter 31

The room was uncomfortably quiet as Wynona began her work. As if they were each holding their breath, unsure of the outcome. If Wynona's heart hadn't already been about to burst through her chest, the heavy tension in the room would have squeezed it into oblivion.

Violet's tail flicked against her neck. *One step at a time, Wynona. Just get started.*

"Easier said than done," Wynona whispered back. She was currently walking around Lusgu, looking for a piece to begin with, but the curse around Lusgu was much sleeker than the barbed wire around Tag. "We're going to start with the one that stops you from speaking," Wynona said softly.

Lusgu nodded. He, at least, looked unafraid.

Wynona wasn't sure if that comforted her, or made it worse that he was putting on a false front. She didn't want to hurt him, but she did want to help. One would more than likely not come without the other.

Her fingers were like ice as she tugged at a strand of the curse just below Lusgu's ear.

He flinched, but held his silence.

"Sorry," Wynona murmured. The chain was much more substantial than Tag's and Wynona could already tell it was going to drain her further than before.

Rascal growled at her thoughts.

She gave him a wan smile and went back to the curse. Using one finger, she ran it under the magical thread until she found a linked beginning. "I need to untie this...then I think we can begin."

"Tell us what you're seeing," Celia said, her voice tangible with curiosity.

"There's a thick...thread or chain...for lack of a better word," Wynona explained. She used her nails to dig at the knot. "I'm working to find a beginning so I can unravel it from Lusgu's neck, but this one has been tied off. Tag's wasn't quite so complicated."

Lusgu's throat moved as he swallowed.

"Ah-ha!" Wynona cried in triumph, then yelped when the end of the thread shocked her.

Rascal was there immediately, reaching out to steady her.

"It's okay," she assured him. "I'm fine, just surprised." She rubbed her fingers, noting that Lusgu still wouldn't look at her. "I need that piece of wood now."

Rascal grudgingly handed over the stick they had decided to use.

Until Wynona knew more about the curses, she figured wood was probably her best bet, since it wasn't living and shouldn't affect the curse in any way. Careful not to touch the very tip of the curse again, she began to slowly wind it into a spool. The process was tedious and the curse was far longer than Wynona would have predicted.

By the time she finished, she was trembling and her fingers felt raw. "Daemon?" Wynona held it out. "Can you?"

Daemon gave her a sympathetic look, gingerly took the spool and concentrated for a moment until the glow of magic faded. "It won't last," he explained. "Only while I'm using my powers."

Wynona nodded, wiping at her forehead. She smiled when

Earl Grey with a Hint of Murder

Rascal handed her a cool glass of water, gulping it down with a decidedly unladylike manner.

"Can you try healing yourself now?" Rascal asked. "Before you do the second half?"

Wynona pinched her lips. "I'm afraid to use the magic on that and not have enough to handle the big curse."

"Do it," Lusgu said, causing everyone to jerk toward him. His voice had gone from low and gravelly to baritone smooth, almost silky in nature.

Wynona's eyes widened. "What did you say?"

The brownie's lips quirked. "Heal yourself. It will be better for everyone in the end."

"Please tell me that some old crone cursed you because she was jealous of your singing voice," Prim said with a laugh.

Lusgu scowled. "I don't sing."

"You should," Celia said with a smirk.

Wynona caught Rascal rolling his eyes in her peripheral vision and she laughed a little before coming to a realization. "Did it hurt to talk?"

Lusgu's mouth snapped shut and all humor fled. He didn't answer.

Wynona hung her head. "I'm so sorry."

Lusgu shrugged, but stayed silent.

Rascal put a hand on her lower back and Violet nuzzled under Wynona's ear. *Get your energy back and let's take care of this once and for all.*

Wynona nodded. Closing her eyes for a split second, she used her magic to take away the aches, pains and weakness in her body. Just like she'd predicted, however, she could feel that her magical supplies were lower than she was comfortable with.

We'll deal with that later, Violet said. *I'm here and can lend a hand, and so can Celia if it comes down to it, though she'll probably act like a diva about it.* Violet sniffed and Wynona couldn't help but smile a little. *But I think she's curious, so we'll use that to our advantage.*

"Why does it sound like we're going to war?" Wynona asked her familiar.

Violet gave Wynona a deadpan look. *Everything is war. Where have you been the last two years?*

Laughing softly, Wynona walked back to Lusgu, grateful her joints no longer ached, but still worried. This thread was infinitely thicker. In fact, it was more like a chain than a thread. "A stick isn't going to cut it," Wynona murmured absently as she walked around the brownie.

"What about a bucket of some sort?" Daemon asked.

"A bucket?" Prim scrunched her nose. "Whatever for?"

"This one is too thick to wind," Wynona responded, indicating Lusgu. She stopped in front of the brownie. "I have a feeling this is going to hurt. Badly. Are you sure you want to try? I don't even know if I'm strong enough to pull it off."

Lusgu clenched his jaw and nodded.

"How long have you been cursed, Lusgu?"

His black eyes glittered in anger. "Too long."

Sighing, Wynona nodded and knelt down. Without allowing herself to think on it further, she reached out and grasped the chain. Pain immediately shot up her arm and Wynona grit her teeth. Violet was right. Everything was war.

A plastic tub landed at her side and Wynona began the arduous task of unwinding what felt like miles of chains from Lusgu's tiny body. His face was contorted in torture with each pull and Wynona noticed that he was bleeding from several locations, as if the curse had been attached to his skin.

Her chest heaved and her body felt on fire. Instead of just her hands, which had struggled with the previous curses, this one was pulsing through Wynona's entire system. Every tug felt heavier than the one before, but slowly, the chain in the bucket began to build up.

Wynona's head was buzzing so badly from the magic she was

dealing with that she had no idea what was going on in the room around her. She couldn't hear Rascal anymore and she was struggling to keep her arms moving.

Violet's tail tightened. *Let me help.* She sent a few pulses of magic through Wynona, enough to have her opening her eyes.

"Thanks," Wynona whispered hoarsely. A few more minutes went by and Wynona could finally see the end. Another four to five feet was wrapped around Lusgu's legs, but she could barely stay upright.

Get your lazy sister over here to share some of her magic.

Wynona shook her head. Celia would never go for it.

Do it, Wynona. You won't finish otherwise and who knows what the curse will do if left like this.

Wynona leaned back on her heels. It took a few blinks to make everyone in the room not look blurry. "Celia?" she croaked.

Celia lifted her chin.

"Will you..." Wynona coughed and gasped for breath.

"She needs your magic," Rascal ground out. His hands hovered over Wynona's shoulders.

"Don't touch me," Wynona warned him. "I don't know what will happen."

"Oh sure..." Celia drawled. "But it's fine if I do."

"Celia, I..." Wynona coughed again.

Celia pinched her lips and she glared at Lusgu. "This had better be worth it," she snapped. Marching over, she put a hand on Wynona's shoulder.

A surge of magic went through Wynona's chest and she obeyed as quickly as she could, trying to capitalize on the energy before it waned. Crawling on hands and knees, Wynona continued her tugging, even knowing each pull was hurting her and Lusgu. They were so close. She just couldn't stop.

Finally, the last loop lay around his ankle.

"Hang on, Lusgu," Wynona rasped. "This is going to be the worst part, I think." Climbing clumsily to her feet, Wynona grasped the curse with both hands and braced herself. Thin arms came around her and she startled, looking over her shoulder.

Celia made a face. "Someone has to keep you from killing yourself," she muttered. "I still want that tea reading, after all."

Her strength warmed Wynona more than the magic flowing between them and Wynona nodded gratefully. "One...two...three!" The two women fell to the floor as Lusgu bellowed in pain and collapsed.

Wynona couldn't move. Her body shook with residual magic and her skin felt as if she were being burned from the inside out.

Voices were screaming and shouting and she couldn't respond to any of them. A heavy thud to her left and a deep growl told Wynona Rascal was there. His hand landed on her forehead.

"Hold on," he ordered. "You're going to be fine." His thumb rubbed against her skin and Wynona didn't have the energy to tell him how much it hurt with her raw nerves trying to out-do each other.

She gasped when the heavy weight of the chain in her hand disappeared.

"I've got it," Daemon told her, referring to the curse. His voice was strained and she knew that he was struggling to keep the magic contained.

"What...are..."

"Don't," Rascal interrupted. "Don't talk. We'll figure it all out."

"Out of my way."

Rascal's head jerked up and his eyes flashed with a warning. "If you think I'm letting you near her, then you better think again."

"I can heal her," the smooth voice said. "Let me in."

Rascal's skin rippled and Wynona knew he was about to lose it to the wolf. But she had no way of stopping him.

Trust him, Violet said, her voice uncharacteristically soft.

Rascal's head jerked down to the mouse. "Why?"

"I owe her everything," the male voice said again. "And her work isn't done yet."

Earl Grey with a Hint of Murder

Rascal's hands flexed and he looked at Wynona, obviously torn with indecision.

Rascal, Violet said again. *Trust me.*

Shaking with anger, Rascal stood and backed off.

Wynona's eyesight was blurry and still slightly purple around the edges. The weight of the curse was gone, but her body was still suffering all the ill effects of having handled and dealt with a magic so dark. She shook against the hardwood floor, her body screaming in pain and her brain crying for relief of any kind.

A dark shadow landed over her and she couldn't tell who it was. She'd never seen the man before as he laid a cool hand on her forehead. Unlike Rascal's warm touch, there was a slight abetting to the pain when the man's hand reached her skin and Wynona sighed without meaning to.

"That's it," the voice cooed. "Relax."

Slowly at first, then with increasing speed, Wynona found her body relaxing. Contorted muscles stop twitching and pain eased. Her joints felt normal again and soon her breathing had calmed down as well.

When the hand came off her forehead, she blinked, not having realized she had closed her eyes, and took in a deep breath. "Thank you," she whispered.

The man stood and held out a hand for her.

Wynona allowed him to help her to her feet, then immediately leaned into Rascal when he wrapped his arms around her, but she couldn't quite take her eyes from the newcomer. "Who are you?" she asked.

The man smirked and adjusted the cuffs on his perfectly tailored suit. He stood taller than Rascal, but with a thinner build, though there was no denying the power that emanated from every pore of his being.

Confidence, even arrogance, were written in every line of his face as he turned black eyes that felt oddly familiar to Wynona.

Abigail Lynn Thornton

"I suppose introductions are in order," the man said, that grin still tugging at his mouth. He inclined his head slightly, as if he were royalty come to visit. "I never expected to greet not only one, but two family members at the same time." His eyes went from Wynona to a gaping Celia and back. "Hello, my dear nieces. I'm your Uncle Arune."

Chapter One

"My...what?" Wynona whispered, her knees giving out. Rascal tightened his hold and his chest rumbled with anger. A few choice words slipped through and Wynona didn't even have the energy to scold him.

"Liar," Celia spat.

Arune raised a single eyebrow. "That's a serious accusation, Celia, dear."

"Don't call me that." Celia marched up and pointed a sharp fingernail to his chest. "Uncle Arune died. He's been dead for ages."

Arune tilted his head back and forth. "I did die...of a sort." He sighed. "Can we take this conversation to the couch? I haven't sat down as a full grown man and without pain in decades."

A high-pitched giggle caught everyone's attention and Wynona turned to see Prim covering her mouth. The fairy shook her head, her pink hair flying. "This is all just so...crazy!" She turned wide eyes to Wynona. "How did I get so lucky as to have a front-row seat to this? Your family is insane!"

Rascal's growling grew and Wynona rested a hand against his chest. "Easy," she whispered. "She means well."

Daemon huffed and shifted the bucket and wood he was holding. "If you'll promise not to kill Prim, I'll excuse myself for a moment." His black eyes went to Arune, then to Wynona. "Be careful," he said in a deep tone.

"Kill me," Prim grunted, putting her hands on her hips. "They can't kill me. I'd miss everything."

"Prim," Daemon warned, his voice strained.

Prim's shoulders fell. "I know. Too much." She looked up at him, her face sorrowful. "I can't help it," she said with a shrug. "Every fairy loves gossip."

"You're not every fairy," he whispered back. "And Wynona is your best friend. Think of this from her perspective." He leaned forward as if to kiss her, but stopped, wincing and shifting the curses again. "Excuse me."

Wynona had cast her eyes to the floor, feeling as if she were intruding on a private moment.

Then they shouldn't have had it here, Rascal grumbled through their link.

Wynona just shook her head and gave him a small smile. "Daemon, are you going to be alright?"

Daemon shrugged as best he could. "I plan to try."

"Where are you putting them?" Arune asked, his voice suddenly serious.

Daemon's eyes narrowed and he didn't respond.

Arune straightened his shoulders. "You trusted me as Lusgu," he pointed out.

"No," Rascal growled. "Wynona trusted you as Lusgu. The rest of us knew to be careful."

Wynona jerked a little at the remark. "I'm not some naive damsel you have to take care of," she snapped back before thinking better of it.

"I never said you were," Rascal argued.

Wynona could feel her frustration building, but Celia beat her to the punch. "Children," Celia said loudly, putting her hands in the air.

"Enough is enough. The tension in this room is thick enough to strangle a dragon." She pierced Arune with a look. "And we have a bigger problem than your petty newlywed squabbles."

Wynona snapped her mouth shut.

Dang it, the nincompoop is right.

Wynona nearly choked and looked at her familiar. "You can't say things like that."

Violet smirked and raised her eyebrows. *Why not?*

Rascal's chuckle only had Wynona scowling harder.

She shook her head and walked away. "Daemon, seriously, do you need help?" The front door closed and Wynona realized her little chat had taken her out of the loop long enough for the Black Hole to escape.

Prim was watching the door, wringing her hands, but then she turned to Wynona. "I'm sorry. I...I know I get carried away at times."

Wynona smiled and held out her arms, hugging her friend tightly for a moment. "It's fine. I know you don't mean it maliciously."

"Still..." Prim pulled back, wiping at her eyes. "I'll do better. I promise."

Celia snorted. "This is all very touching, but it doesn't get us any closer to solving the problem at hand." She eyed Arune. "Have a seat, slick guy, and let's get this figured out."

"Not a very respectful way to speak to your uncle," Arune muttered, but he walked to the sitting area, settling himself in an armchair. His face relaxed and he closed his eyes, sighing in bliss. "I'd forgotten how good it felt," he said softly, settling himself deeper into the chair.

Wynona watched him as she walked to the couch, perching on the edge. "I don't understand," she said. "How could you possibly be my uncle? I remember reading about Arune in Granny's grimoire, but he was only mentioned once, then disappeared."

"That's because he died," Celia pointed out. She stood next to the couch, her hip cocked and her arms folded. "This guy's a quack."

Arune glared. "Careful, little one. The stories you were raised on are not all they seem." He leaned forward, his eyes glittering with intensity. "If you truly trust your parents so much, why are you not living with them? Why hide behind your sister's power?"

Wynona frowned and grabbed Rascal's hand when he sat down beside her. "What do you mean, hide behind my power?" She turned to Celia when Arune didn't respond. "Celia?"

Celia's nostrils flared and her pale face was whiter than normal. "I don't know what you're talking about," she said through clenched teeth.

Arune chuckled, the sound dark. "Would you have me be the one to explain it then?"

"How did you know?" Celia rasped.

Arune's smirk grew into a grin that was anything but friendly. "There's a reason they cursed me," he responded. "Sometimes you can't get rid of power, you can only...redirect it."

"Stop!" Wynona jumped to her feet as she shouted. "Enough with the riddles!" she cried. "I have spent the last two years trying to forgive and show trust to each and every one of you, despite how horrible you are at times."

Celia made a noise and Wynona shut her up with a glare.

"I've offered friendship and trust when no one else would," she said pointedly to Arune. "I've let you in when you had nowhere else to go," Wynona offered, turning to Celia. "I've been to purgatory and back and through it all I've still given you everything I can." Her chest was heaving at this point, but Wynona's righteous anger was still rising. "Would someone, just ONCE!" she shouted. "Actually offer me the truth without vague parables or hints that will take me another two years to figure out!"

Prim clapped excitedly when Wynona finished, then stuffed her hands behind her back when all eyes turned to the fairy, only to clap again a moment later. "That was amazing," Prim gushed.

"Prim," Rascal grumbled, though Wynona could tell he wasn't really that upset. In fact, he was leaning back easily on the couch, grinning like a fool. His smile grew when she turned to him. "That's my wife," he whispered.

"Gross," Celia muttered, planting herself more evenly between her two feet. She studied her nails.

"What did he mean about hiding behind my power?" Wynona asked, point blank.

Celia's eyes flashed at Arune, then came to Wynona, two high points of color on her cheeks. "He means that I've been using your magical signature to hide my own so that our dear parents don't know where I am."

Wynona's jaw dropped. "You can do that?"

One side of Celia's mouth curled up, but Arune cleared his throat and whatever remark had been about to come out must have died in her throat. Sighing long and loud, Celia rolled her eyes and threw her hands in the air. "Obviously, I can, or I wouldn't have done it."

"How exactly does it work?" Wynona asked, then put up her hand. "Wait, never mind. I want to know, but there are other more important things currently." She paused. "But do you really believe you're in that much danger? When you moved out, I assumed it was because you felt safe."

Celia shrugged, looking much less sure of herself than usual, and flipped her hair over her shoulder. "If you recall, I didn't exactly ask Mumsy if I could have those grimoires," she said with a bite in her tone.

Wynona rubbed her forehead. "Why does my life just have a way of getting more and more complicated?" she muttered.

That would be a very good question, Violet added.

Rascal grumbled under his breath and Wynona didn't bother trying to decipher it. "Okay...so Mom is on the rampage," Wynona clarified. "And you've been using me as your shield without my permission. That about sum it up?"

Celia huffed. "Probably, but it's not quite as bad as a family member hiding his identity while living with you for a year." She sent a pointed look Arune's way.

"Oh, so now I'm family?" he said with a laugh.

Prim shook her head. "Wynona, I don't know how you came from this bunch. Seriously. Drama to high heaven. Every fairy's dream, but…" She tsked her tongue. "But I feel bad for you," she whispered, making a face.

"Truthfully, I'm starting to feel bad for myself as well," Wynona responded. When Celia and Arune both began to argue…loudly… Wynona held up her hand again, but it wasn't enough this time. Pinching her lips together, Wynona concentrated, then followed her instinct and sent a pulse of magic through the room.

The shift from annoyed arguing to dead silence was almost enough to make Wynona's head spin. Rascal stood up and placed his hand on her back.

"Well done," he whispered, kissing her temple. "I think it's time you sent the guests home."

Wynona looked up at him. "We don't have any answers yet."

Rascal's jaw tightened. "I don't think we're going to get any until everyone's had some time away from each other."

"For Wynona's sake," Arune said slowly, raising a questioning eyebrow at Rascal, "I'll cooperate."

Rascal's lip curled. "I still don't like you."

Arune leaned back comfortably in his chair. "I don't care. My only concern is my niece. You're lucky I ever let you near her."

"He's your nephew by marriage," Wynona pointed out. "You don't get me without him."

"Pity," Arune grumbled.

"Wynona," Rascal said tightly, his skin rippling. "Either you kick them out, or I will and I won't be as nice about it."

She rubbed his arm, trying to calm down his wolf. "Celia, I still want that story, but I have questions for Arune first." After making sure Celia wasn't going to run, Wynona turned her attention to Arune. "Can you prove to us that you're our uncle? Right now all you've done is offer us a name and anyone could claim it."

Arune nodded slowly, his lips pursed. "I suppose that's fair." He tilted his head and narrowed his eyes in thought. "Old photos would be at the palace, so they'll do you no good. But ask me any question about the family. I can answer them all."

"So could anyone with a good internet connection," Celia shot back.

Arune chuckled again. "Very little of what I can tell you about our family can be found on the internet, dear niece."

"Stop calling me that," Celia hissed.

Arune put up his hands as if in surrender, but Wynona knew he was only placating them.

"If you're our uncle, why change your name?" Wynona asked. "I understand you were cursed, but why change your name and hide it?"

Arune rubbed his chin. "That's a very good question…"

"I thought you could answer any of them?" Celia asked sweetly.

Arune ignored her. "But the answer is far more complicated than you would think."

"Why?" Wynona pressed.

Arune leaned forward, intensity on his face. "To truly understand, we would need to go back to your grandfather's murder."

Wynona paused. "The one you claimed my father committed?"

Arune nodded slowly. "Yes, dear one. Rayn and I told you a bit about it, but his death and Saffron's visions were the start of it all."

"That's it!" Rascal shouted, snapping his fingers.

Wynona blinked, his cry catching her off guard. "That's what?" she asked.

Rascal put his hands on his hips and looked at Arune triumphantly. "I know how we can tell if he's lying or not."

"And?" Celia asked, her tone bored.

"Mama Rena would know."

Wynona almost smacked her forehead. How could she have forgotten about the werewolf grandmother who watched over Rascal and had helped Granny Saffron in her plan to bind Wynona's powers?

Arune looked like he'd eaten a rotten prune.

"I'm guessing that Rascal's right," Wynona ventured. "She'll know who you are."

"Oh, she'll know," Arune agreed. "But wanting to know badly enough to deal with the old bat is another matter."

Before anyone could respond, the house shuddered and Wynona immediately sent a purple shield over the inhabitants.

"Daemon," Prim whispered.

Wynona shook her head. "No...that wasn't the curses." She frowned, concentrating on the movement. "It's a creature, I think."

Violet's tail twitched.

Wynona looked at the ceiling. "In fact, I'm pretty sure it's a—"

"Dragon," Arune breathed, his eyes wide with delight. "She came for me."

"Excuse me?" Celia asked as Arune bolted for the door.

Wynona dropped her shield just in time and, as if pulled by a single string, the whole group ran out into the front yard just in time to see a large orange and yellow dragon land, flash into a woman and fall into Arune's arms with a kiss that should have had every hair on Wynona's head going up in flames.

Chapter Two

"I can never unsee this!" Prim shouted, covering her face and bending over.

I was thinking the same thing, Violet grumbled, tucking further into Wynona's hair.

"What in the paranormal world is going on here?" Wynona whispered, her eyes glued to the scene, even as a feeling of intrusion simmered in her stomach.

"You knew they liked each other," Rascal said with a grunt.

"Yeah...but this?" Wynona waved a hand at the display. Her cheeks were starting to burn with heat at how long it had been going on.

"If I wasn't afraid of getting singed, I'd break it up," Celia muttered from Wynona's other side.

Wynona cleared her throat and tried to gain their attention. "Um...Rayn? Lu-I mean...Arune?"

It still took a few moments, but eventually they pulled back, both of them breathing heavily and staring into each other's eyes.

Wynona paused before speaking. There was something about the way they were looking at each other that caught her attention.

"No way," Rascal breathed.

Way, Violet offered cheerfully, coming out into view again now that the kissing was over.

"You're soulmates!" Wynona blurted out before she could think to stop herself. As if the air was just as shocked as the guests, everything went still. Too still. Wynona looked around, the heat in her cheeks for an entirely different reason now. She winced when both Rayn and Arune turned her way. "Sorry," she whispered. "I just… wasn't thinking?"

Rayn blinked a few times, the yellow in her eyes fading as she slowly straightened herself out of Arune's arms. "It would seem our secret isn't so secret," she said in a wry tone, giving Arune a side glance.

Arune snorted and rested his hand on her lower back. "It's not as if we could have kept it that way for long anyway."

"But…" Wynona turned to Rascal. "I thought it was mostly a wolf thing."

Rascal shook his head. "It can happen to anyone, it's just more common among wolves because we tend to believe in those types of pairings anyway." Rascal's eyes narrowed and he turned to the couple on display. "But I wonder if maybe animal shifters in general are more prone to them."

Rayn grinned. "Very good, Wolf. We'll make a scientist out of you yet."

"I'm fine where I'm at, thanks," Rascal growled.

"So when he was cursed, you…" Wynona pointed a finger between the two of them. "I'm so lost." She rubbed her forehead and looked at Arune. "Please tell me this is part of that long story you said I'd need to hear."

Arune nodded, though it looked reluctant. "I do believe that would be best."

Celia flipped her hair. "Then let's do this because I think it's gone on long enough."

Earl Grey with a Hint of Murder

"Hold on," Rascal said. He raised an eyebrow at Rayn. "Who is this man?"

Rayn frowned. "What do you mean? Hasn't he told you?"

"They're trying to corroborate my story," Arune said with a sigh. "Go ahead, sweetheart. Tell them."

Rayn made a face. "This is Arune Iroqe. Brother to Saffron and Uncle, or rather *great* uncle, to Celia and Wynona."

"Thank you for the reminder of my age," Arune said sarcastically.

Rayn chuckled.

He turned to Rascal. "Is that enough for you?"

"I'll feel better after we've talked to Mama Rena, but for now...yes."

Arune shook his head and straightened the sleeves of his suit. "Fair enough. Now..." He paused and took a few breaths. "How much do you remember of our chat in the police station?"

"Enough," Wynona responded, folding her arms over her chest. She was suddenly feeling a little protective, as if her life would never be the same, and she was really starting to get tired of these kinds of moments. She'd had her fair share of them, after all. "Grandfather and Granny Saffron used to rule. You were all cocky, but things were going well."

Celia laughed...loudly...and Violet chittered. By the smirk on Rascal's face, he'd also enjoyed her little dig.

Wynona worked hard not to apologize. She'd been bowled over too many times in the last couple years to let herself feel bad about one little comment.

"Then Grandfather was killed, you believe it was an assassin witch hired by my father, who proved too much for you all to handle and somehow you all got cursed in the deal, leaving Arune to become Lusgu the brownie, and Rayn eventually was exiled because of her company and unable to speak of the incident because of a curse." Wynona closed her eyes and tilted her head back. "Then Granny saw me coming, cursed me before my birth, arranged her own death to allow me to escape before my powers broke free on their own and my parents got a hold of them. And now I've been living a slowly unraveling lie for the last two years and every time I stand back up, something knocks me flat on my back." She looked at the couple and tilted her head. "Sound about right?"

Rayn grinned as she elbowed Arune. "She's got more spirit than I gave her credit for."

Arune gave his soulmate a sharp look. "I suppose we'll see if it helps when it really counts." He cleared his throat. "That does sum it up, yes," he stated. "But now…you broke my curse, which means I can tell you more." He paused. "Perhaps when I'm done talking, you could do the same for Rayn?"

Wynona nodded. "Of course. But answers first this time. Unfortunately, Rayn will simply have to let you do the talking."

Rayn's smile grew and she leaned her head on Arune's shoulder.

"Understandable, I suppose." Arune stuck his chin in the air. "We did confront the witch, but she wasn't alone. I never saw your father or mother, but one witch, even a black one, against two powerful witches and a couple of shapeshifters shouldn't have been enough."

Rascal growled low. "And yet you were the ones who were cursed."

Arune nodded curtly. "Exactly. We were the ones cursed."

Rascal spread his feet and folded his arms over his chest. "And what makes you think that Wynona is the answer to your problem? If her parents and the witch were enough to overcome all of you, why would she be any different?"

Arune scoffed. "Have you seen her powers? The extent of them?"

Rascal shifted uneasily, his challenge fading. "No," he finally responded.

Arune's smile was completely mercenary. "Exactly," he said intently. "None of us have. Her powers not only haven't reached their limit, but they keep emerging."

Rayn laid a hand on his arm. "Watch yourself," she warned. "Your hunger's showing." She looked up at Wynona apologetically.

"Sorry. Your family's desire for power didn't exactly skip his generation, he's just a little less insane than the rest of them."

Wynona couldn't bring herself to laugh at the joke, and apparently, neither could anyone else. Celia grunted, and Rascal let out another growl. Even Prim only made a face. "So the plan all along has been to use me to take out my dad, just like I've said."

Arune's eagerness faded a bit. "You're the only one who can," he said simply.

"You've forgotten one thing," Wynona said, her breathing feeling stuck in her throat. "I have no desire to rule."

Arune threw up his hands. "So you would let the whole of Hex Haven suffer at your dad's hands? You'd let him abuse his position of power and hurt creatures just because you want a simple life without complications?"

Rascal stepped forward threateningly. "Back off," he growled, his jaw clenched. "You have no say here."

"I absolutely have a say here," Arune argued, stepping forward as well. "I've been a part of this longer than she has." He pointed to Wynona.

"She didn't ask to be brought into this," Rascal snapped back. His voice was low and gravelly. "You can't force her into your machinations."

"We're not trying to force her into anything," Rayn inserted, smoke trickling out of her nose. "We're trying to make her see. We've *all* sacrificed to get this far and even though things haven't gone exactly how we've wanted them to, she's the only hope we have. If she doesn't help us, then we're doomed."

Prim laughed, stepping up next to Wynona's side. "Now who's being dramatic?" she taunted.

Rayn's eyes flashed yellow. "Careful, fairy. My kind used to eat yours for midafternoon snacks."

Prim's fingers twitched and the rose bushes in front of the small cottage began to slither along the ground like a snake. "I'm not concerned," Prim said airily. "I have ways of protecting myself."

Abigail Lynn Thornton

Wynona's eyes were wide as her vision shot from one creature to another. Speaking of a fight...one was about to break out on her front lawn at this very moment. Silver sparks were dripping from Celia's fingertips, Arune looked a little too smug, Rayn was nearly breathing fire at this point, Prim was bouncing on her toes, the roses gathering around her like a thorn-sprouting army, and Rascal was sporting fur on the back of his hands while his eyes glowed so brightly they could probably be seen from half a mile away.

Before Wynona could figure out how to stop it all, pandemonium nearly took her off her feet. Fire shot out of Rayn's mouth, incinerating Prim's roses. Prim screamed like a banshee and her arms began weaving through the air, bringing the ashes back to life.

Before Wynona could process what exactly she was seeing, Rascal lunged at Arune, flashing into his wolf, only to freeze merely a foot away from the witch. An angry bellow echoed through the forest as he struggled midair to move, but didn't budge. His anger and frustration nearly brought Wynona to her knees with the power of it.

Celia raised her hands, a wind strong enough to be a tornado following her movements.

Wynona covered her eyes to keep the dust and debris out even as her mind spun to try and catch up with it all.

With a scream of rage, Celia sent the magic toward Arune, who simply held out one hand and caught the wind as if it were a rope. He smirked easily as the funnel shrunk until it was spinning on his palm like a child's toy.

Wynona couldn't move as she watched Arune's smile grow and slowly, he brought his fingers together, pinching out the wind. As he did so, Celia silently collapsed to the ground, completely unconscious.

"Stop!" Wynona screamed. "Stop it now!" Her heart was in her throat and she felt close to throwing up, but she couldn't seem to figure out how to stop anything without hurting those she loved the most.

Another roar joined the fray and suddenly all the magic disappeared. Rascal fell to the ground, back in his human form. The roses dropped and shrunk, Prim's hair stopped its gravity-defying dance. Celia groaned and put a hand to her forehead, while Rayn's fire snuffed out and Arune scowled.

Wynona almost collapsed with relief when she saw Daemon standing just beyond the house. Every vein in his arm was pulsing black against his skin and he looked larger than normal. The lack of color in his eyes was as dark as the universe and Wynona realized with a start that they were shifting like molten lava, another aspect of his magic she'd never seen before.

"It would appear our black hole has found another level of his abilities," Arune said cheerfully. "He has the potential to be extremely useful."

Prim stepped forward again, then stomped her foot when she realized she had no magic to back her up. "You can't have him," she said through clenched teeth.

"When are you going to understand that we're all in this together?" Rayn argued.

"Maybe when you stop trying to kill us all!" Prim screamed.

"Then perhaps you shouldn't have used your flowers to try and strangle me!" Rayn responded calmly.

When Daemon grunted and his knees began to buckle, Wynona realized that he was about to lose his hold on the situation. The magic would only stay gone for so long and with the tempers still flaring, the fight would be back on immediately. She didn't pause to think this time. Instead, she brought her hands high above her head and clapped them loudly.

The sound was like thunder, surprising her as well as the others with its intensity. But the purple domes that spread over each individual, keeping them from attacking each other, were the real shockers.

Almost in unison, every face slowly turned to look at her with wide eyes.

Daemon, meanwhile, fell to his knees and his eyes went back to normal. His palms landed on the ground and his breath came in great heaves of air.

Wynona swallowed down the bile in her throat and stared at him, waiting to make sure he was alright. She hadn't considered what her magic would do to him when she brought it out and he was already at his max.

Still panting, Daemon looked up and met her gaze. He nodded, assuring her all was well.

Forcing herself to take control, Wynona faced the crowd.

"Are these…cages…really necessary?" Arune asked. He poked it with his finger, then scowled.

Wynona, unbeknownst to anyone else, had felt his surge of power as he tested her strength. She wasn't sure how long she could keep them contained, but right now she would pretend her strength was limitless. "They are," she answered. "Until I know that you can all handle this like adults and stop throwing around your magic as if we're on different sides of this issue."

"As long as you refuse to take your place," Arune said slowly, "then we are on different sides."

Wynona stuck her chin in the air. "I disagree. I don't like my father in charge any more than you do, but where we differ is the solution."

"Sweetheart," Rascal said in a soothing tone. "Let me out, huh?"

Wynona shook her head and pointed a finger at him. "Right now you're just as willing to harm others as they are. Not until this is settled."

Rascal sighed and put his hands in the air. "You're right. I lost my temper and I'm sorry. I won't do it again."

Wynona hesitated, wanting to let him free, but worried he would still be angry.

"I promise," Rascal added.

Wynona nodded and let him out. He walked to her side, grabbing his cell phone out of his back pocket and scrolling the screen as he did so.

Earl Grey with a Hint of Murder

"Me too," Prim offered, though she glared at Rayn one more time. "Like it or not, these two are family. If I can keep myself from killing sissy-poo, I can keep the roses to myself." She sniffed and put her hands on her hips.

Wynona let her out. She knew full well that was the best she was going to get from Prim, plus she could tell the fairy wanted to run over and check on Daemon, which she did as soon as she was free.

"Excuse me?" Celia snapped.

Wynona raised her eyebrows. "Yes?"

"I'm your sister."

"And he's my uncle."

Celia scowled. "Fine. I promise not to hurt anyone."

Wynona nodded again and the third cage disappeared. She then turned to Rayn and Arune.

Arune was watching her a little too closely for Wynona's liking.

"I promise not to *start* anything," Rayn said. "But I don't promise not to harm if I'm defending myself."

Wynona let her out. "I think that's fair." She turned to Arune, but he still didn't speak. Without overthinking it, Wynona walked over to his dome. "What about you, Uncle Arune? You've sworn in the past not to harm me, but by harming my friends and family, you're harming me in other ways."

He stepped up until they were practically nose to nose, with only a thin layer of purple between them.

Rascal was immediately at Wynona's back, his heated presence palpable, but true to his word, he wasn't growling or threatening.

Arune continued to stare, searching Wynona as if trying to see into every corner of her mind.

She allowed him to stare. Wynona knew that she couldn't back down. She didn't like her father. There was no lost love between them, not anymore. But she was serious when she said she wasn't the solution. She'd make a terrible president. They'd have to find another way.

Arune's eyes narrowed and he finally tilted his head ever so slightly. "You're even more than we expected," he whispered. "Saffron will be sad she missed it."

"Arune," Rayn warned.

He straightened. "I promise not to harm those you love," he said simply. "But I will *not* promise to stop trying to teach you who you are."

Wynona swallowed hard and forced a calm look to her face. "I know who I am."

Arune slowly shook his head. "No...you don't. Because when you do, you'll be begging to fight."

Chapter Three

Wynona watched Rascal throw several T-shirts into a ratty suitcase without folding them. She raised an eyebrow at him. "Am I going to become a glorified maid?" she teased. Her grin widened when he gave her a look and sauntered across their bedroom.

Rascal's thick arms caged her into the wall and his eyes flashed gold as he smirked at her. Slowly, he leaned in until their mouths were only a centimeter away. "I guess it's a good thing you figured out how to use your magic, huh?" He laughed when Wynona slugged him in the stomach, holding a hand there as if she'd actually hurt him.

"Gee, I'm so looking forward to married life," Wynona said sarcastically. She narrowed her eyes at the corner where Violet was snickering.

Rascal went back to his suitcase, stuffed the clothes down and zipped it up. "Then I suppose I'll just have to spend the next two weeks convincing you it was worth it."

"Are you going to tell me where we're going?" Wynona asked, gathering her own suitcase. "It really would have helped with the packing."

Rascal smiled and left a sweet kiss on her cheek. "Nope. I don't want to risk anyone else figuring it out. For the next two weeks, you're mine. Not Prim's, not Chief's, not even your crazy Uncle Arune's. You're mine and we're going to completely shut out the world."

"Until we get back and Prim throws us our wedding reception," Wynona reminded him.

Rascal scowled. "If she covers everything in glitter, I don't care how much work she put into it. I'm outta there."

Wynona laughed and patted his chest. "She's a fairy. Of course there's going to be glitter."

Rascal playfully growled in her ear, then dropped their luggage and swung Wynona into his arms.

She squealed and held on tightly to his neck. "What are you doing?"

"Leaving the world behind," he stated, giving her a wide smile.

With a flick of her fingers, Wynona opened the front door and then the truck door as Rascal deposited her on the passenger side. He reached across, buckling her in, then leaned in just high enough to kiss her breathless. "Ready?" he asked.

Wynona shook her head and wiggled her fingers, bringing the suitcases out of the cottage and into the back seat. "Okay. Now I'm ready."

"That's my girl."

I thought that was my line, Violet pouted from the front door.

Can't I have two girls? Rascal sent back as he got behind the wheel.

"The line itself would imply that isn't the case," Wynona told him. She tried to hold back her smile, but was unsuccessful. When Violet decided to pout it was a sight to behold and Wynona knew that Rascal had put his foot in it this time.

"Eh, she'll forgive me," Rascal said with a shrug. *Especially when we bring her back something nice.*

There was a pause before the mouse answered. *If you think that something flaky and buttery will clear your conscience...you might be right.*

Wynona laughed and waved out the window as they pulled away from the house. Things had been so tense yesterday with Arune and Rayn and the fight in the front yard, but no one would be able to tell by looking at the cottage now. Debris from the tornado was gone and the roses looked perfectly normal. The pulsing magic of the Grove of Secrets was the only magic left in the place and Wynona was grateful for it.

She was also grateful for the wolf at her side. Reaching over, she rested her hand on his thigh and he grasped her fingers, entwining them as he relaxed in the driver's seat, leaving Hex Haven in the rearview mirror.

No one had been happy the couple were leaving, but they also had no power to stop it. Rascal still had time off from work, Arune and Rayn needed time together as well, and Prim and Daemon both still had jobs that required their attention.

When Rascal had stated his intentions, he'd left no room for arguments and had given Arune something to do by assigning him the tea shop. Since he'd run it several times as Lusgu, Wynona knew it would be in good hands, even if Arune wasn't happy about it.

"Can I know now?" Wynona asked after several peaceful minutes of driving. They were working their way down a winding road with forest on both sides. Rascal's phone had been buzzing almost nonstop, but he'd just silenced it and Wynona was ready for some conversation.

It almost looked as if they were moving deeper into the Grove of Secrets, though Wynona could tell by the feel of the magic that this was a separate forest. She'd never been to this area of their region and was looking forward to what was on the other side.

"So..." Rascal hedged, shifting in his seat. "We're making a slight detour before we hit our actual destination."

"Okay..." Wynona turned to look at him. "You're making it sound ominous."

He shrugged and gave her fingers a squeeze. "We're going to camp, in a cabin," he quickly assured her, "for just a few nights."

Wynona blinked a few times. That hadn't been exactly what she'd planned, but still, they would be together...*and most importantly...alone,* she reassured herself.

Rascal winced. "Not exactly."

Wynona shook her head. "I've *got* to remember to close off my thoughts," she muttered. Then she straightened when she realized what he'd said. "Explain, please."

Rascal glanced sideways at her. "We're going to meet my family."

Wynona's mouth opened, then shut. Then it opened again, only to shut once more.

"Surprise!" Rascal said, wincing even as he said it.

Wynona faced the front. Her mind was whirling and she wasn't sure how to handle this right now.

"Well, you figured that out fast," he grumbled. "What're you thinking?"

"I'm thinking that you should have warned me so that I could have brought some proper clothing and been prepared to handle a large family of shifters, instead of putting me in a position where I'm once again the odd woman out because I have no idea what's going on and don't have the slightest clue who your family even is." Wynona snapped her mouth shut. That was far more than she'd meant to say, but it seemed as if the last couple of days had turned her into a better advocate for herself. Only a year ago, she'd have just stuffed it all down and worried about hurting someone's feelings. More and more thoughts were making their way past her lips and though some of them were necessary, Wynona also knew that some things needed to stay where they started. Hopefully, she'd learn to tell the difference.

"You're right." Rascal sighed. "I'm sorry." He squeezed her hand. "I should've told you, but I was worried after everything that just went down with your family that you wouldn't want to talk to mine."

Wynona frowned. "I...am completely lost in that explanation. But thank you anyway and I accept your apology." She straightened

Earl Grey with a Hint of Murder

in her seat. "It's not like I wasn't going to have to meet them at some point." She hesitated. "Is your mother going to hate me because we got married without her?"

"You? Nah..." Rascal pushed his lips to one side. "I might get a verbal thrashing though."

"Do I get any tips and tricks, here?" Wynona asked. "Names? Faces? What should I prepare for? How many are there again?"

"I'm the oldest of six," Rascal told her. "Five younger cubs, though they're all adults at this point. My mom is Sable and dad is Lyall. The pack is pretty big, so be prepared for lots of eyes, but don't worry." Rascal pulled the truck off to the side of the road into a small dirt road, then parked. "They'll love you because I love you." He chuckled. "And I'm afraid that's all you're going to get because we're here."

"What!" Wynona screeched. She let go of his hand and looked around at the wooded area frantically. "What do you mean, we're here? You said we'd at least get a cabin." Her heart was about to break a couple of ribs with how heavily it was thudding against it.

"Whoa, whoa, whoa..." Rascal leaned over the bench and cupped her face in his hands. "Hang on, sweetheart. It's all going to be alright."

"It's not alright," Wynona whispered. "I know nothing about them and you're throwing me into the deep end."

His calloused thumbs brushed her cheeks and his eyes glowed softly. "You're my soulmate," he stated bluntly. "That's all they'll need to know. I realize that you don't understand what it's like to have a large, close family, you've essentially had to make your own since breaking free, but babe...you're about two seconds away from learning that support systems are sometimes as smothering as they are wonderful."

"Two seconds? Ahhh!" Wynona screamed when something slammed onto the front of the truck. A large wolf, almost as big as Rascal's, was standing on the hood, staring through the windshield as he snarled and drooled, looking like he was hungry to eat them both.

Rascal rolled his eyes. "Idiot." Before Wynona could protest, Rascal got out of the truck and started shouting. "Hey! Colb! You've got something right–" He had just started to indicate the edge of his mouth when the wolf leaped.

Wynona screamed again, then fought a battle with her seatbelt before she tore out of the truck and raced around to the other side. Rascal was rolling with the wolf, holding its jaws away from his face and sneering while throwing insults.

Without allowing herself time to consider the consequences, Wynona thrust out her hand. "STOP!"

The wolf froze, along with Rascal, though Wynona knew that she hadn't put a spell on her husband. Lifting his head ever so slightly, Rascal gave her a look. "What're you doing?"

"What am I doing?" she screeched at him. "What are *you* doing? I just barely got you! I'm not going to stand by and watch you be eaten by a wolf! Why did you get out of the truck? Why didn't you change in order to fight?"

Rascal let his head fall back to the dirt and began laughing.

The wolf whined and Wynona felt a sliver of guilt, though she wasn't sure why. What in the world was going on here? That wolf had been angry and had tried to attack them through the windshield! There was no way they were staying with his family after this!

"Sweetheart?"

Wynona turned her attention back to her amused spouse.

"Meet my brother Colby," Rascal said, indicating the wolf. Next Rascal turned to the wolf. "Colby, meet Wynona. My wife...and soulmate."

The wolf whined again and Rascal chuckled.

"Serves you right for coming at us like that. It's like you were raised in a forest or something." Rascal crawled out from under the frozen wolf and dusted himself off as he walked to Wynona, slinging his arm around her shoulders. "You should probably let him go now," he whispered in her ear.

Earl Grey with a Hint of Murder

"That's your brother?" Wynona whispered hoarsely. "Are you sure?"

"Oh, yeah," Rascal answered. His demeanor was cheerful and amused. "I'd know that rotten stench anywhere." His voice rose as he spoke, though Wynona knew that wolf shifters had excellent hearing. There was no way the wolf hadn't heard them. "Go ahead," Rascal encouraged.

Wynona carefully released the spell and the wolf came back to life, shaking his head vigorously. He spun, facing the two of them, his tongue hanging out of his mouth. With one last shake, the wolf rose into a man, who looked remarkably like Rascal. "What gives?" Colby asked, putting his hands on his hips. "You haven't come home in like two years, and now that you're here, you bring a wife?" Golden eyes appraised Wynona from head to toe and a slow smile, a little too familiar, crept across her brother-in-law's face. "And a witch to boot." Colby whistled low. "Mom's going to be so happy and so ticked at the same time that she won't know who to whack first."

Wynona swallowed hard. "I'm sorry," she rasped, wringing her hands together. "I...didn't know."

"Oh, believe you me," Colby said, sauntering their way. "I don't blame you at all." He stepped up and punched Rascal in the shoulder...hard. "I know what a lughead my brother is." Colby winked at Wynona. "If he hadn't said you were soulmates, I'd make a little play for you myself. I can be a lot more accomo–"

Colby didn't get a chance to finish his thought before Rascal threw himself at his sibling.

Wynona quickly stepped back, unsure how to handle the two men scuffling on the forest floor. Pine needles and dirt flew in all directions and within mere moments, the men had become snarling wolves instead of shouting men.

Forcing her fear to calm down, Wynona stepped back even farther, then squeaked in surprise when she ran into something that felt a little too human. She spun, throwing up a purple shield as an automatic reaction.

A man, who looked like an older version of Rascal, stood watching her calmly. His height was maybe an inch shorter than Rascal, but the man's chest was broader, making him more intimidating. His eyes were also golden and glowing with intensity and unless Wynona missed her guess...she had just run into her new father-in-law.

She dropped her shield, though reluctantly. Letting it go was like letting go of a safety blanket and Wynona felt naked without it. "Um...hello..." she ventured. "I'm Wynona. Wynona Strongclaw." She waited, unconsciously holding her breath as she bit her lip, and hoped that the man wouldn't hurt her. She'd purposefully used her married name instead of Le Doux. Her maiden name didn't always bring good results.

The man's face stayed stoic, but he nodded. "I can feel the connection." He glanced past Wynona to the still fighting wolves. "Looks like they're making up for lost time." His eyes came back to hers. "Lyall Strongclaw," he announced, making Wynona's guess correct. Turning, he held out his elbow, waiting for her to take it as if to escort her to a ball, and indicated a rough trail. "But you can call me Dad."

Chapter Four

Wynona glanced over her shoulder again, nervous to be leaving with a man she'd just met, but also concerned about her husband. "Umm...shouldn't we wait for Rascal?" she asked. Her fingers were barely touching Alpha Strongclaw's arm, but he didn't seem to mind her worry.

"If he's more worried about his reputation with his brother than taking care of his wife, I don't think he deserves our waiting for him." For the first time since he'd introduced himself, Alpha Strongclaw smiled a little and gave her an understanding look. "While I'm sure Rascal took the time to woo you as a wolf should, the boy still has a bit of growing up to do."

Wynona smiled back. "I tend to be too serious," she admitted. "He helps even me out."

Alpha Strongclaw nodded. "A good pairing then."

Wynona chewed the inside of her cheek as they walked. A question was sitting on her tongue, but she was worried about opening up a can of worms.

"I hate to tell you this, daughter, but you don't hold in your emotions very well." Alpha Strongclaw glanced down at her. "What did you want to ask me?"

Wynona scrunched up her nose. "I just...you've been very kind since we met five minutes ago, but..."

"But?" he pressed.

"But I'm concerned that your family won't be as accepting of me when they find out I'm a witch," she finally spit out.

Alpha Strongclaw stopped and dropped her arm, then turned and faced Wynona fully. He studied her, tilting his head just like Rascal did, and although Rascal's father had said his son needed to grow up some more, Wynona could see that much of his mannerisms, particularly those he used in his job, were very much from the man standing in front of her. "What was your maiden name?" the alpha asked softly.

Wynona automatically stepped back, her feet shifting on the twigs and pinecones that littered the forest floor. She locked her knees and kept herself upright. Rascal still hadn't shown up and Wynona was beginning to wonder if she would have to defend herself against the alpha. Rascal would be devastated if she hurt his father.

Alpha Strongclaw chuckled and put his hands in the air. "It's a simple question, daughter. Tell me where you came from. I have a strong hunch, but I prefer to get facts rather than make assumptions."

Wynona clenched her fists and forced her lungs to keep breathing. "Le Doux," she whispered, knowing he would hear it.

The alpha nodded. "I thought as much." He folded his arms over his very wide chest. "So tell me...are you truly concerned about us accepting a witch as a mate for my son? Or that we won't accept you because of your family?"

Wynona shrugged. "Both?"

That small smile remained. "On behalf of my family and my pack...we welcome you...officially," he added. "As the soulmate of my son, you will be accepted without question. As the descendant of our president, I cannot guarantee that everything you'll hear will be in his favor, but in this pack, we believe in accepting creatures as individuals. Your father's crimes," he grimaced, "or lack thereof, as he claims, have nothing to do with you, unless you prove otherwise."

A rustle in the woods caught their attention and Wynona realized her wayward husband was finally catching up with them. "Thank you," she said softly before the men arrived. "That means a lot to me."

The alpha's eyes glittered as he nodded. "You're family now. One of our own. Never forget that and understand that as long as you have our trust, you have us at your back. Break that trust, and I cannot promise what will happen." He turned to their upcoming guests. "With the pack or with your husband."

"Dad!" Rascal cried, holding his arms wide with a sarcastic grin on his face. "I never imagined I'd have to take you down for stealing my woman."

Wynona rolled her eyes, though it really served as a way to hide the excess moisture in them. Alpha Strongclaw's words had stung her to the core, in the best of ways. Over the last two years, she'd built a new family, since the one she'd been born into hadn't turned out as expected. But to be accepted so quickly and wholly by a group such as this was equal parts terrifying and amazing. Wynona was still nervous to meet everyone, but she was also eager to understand exactly what it would all mean.

"If you'd put her safety above your pride, I wouldn't have had to," Alpha Strongclaw chided, though there was no hiding the humor in his voice.

Wynona was understanding a little bit more where Rascal's sense of adventure and duty came from.

Rascal wrapped an arm around her shoulders and kissed her temple. "Sorry," he whispered against her skin. "The pup thought he was the big dog since I live in town, and every once in a while I have to remind him who's boss."

Alpha Strongclaw snorted. "Bring her to the house. Your mother's eager to meet her." He paused, his lips twitching with laughter. "And to skin you for staying away for so long."

Rascal hung his head back and groaned. "This was a bad idea. We should just go." He started to turn them, but his brother was in the way.

"Uh, uh, uh, old man," Colby teased. "It's time to get your comeuppance."

"Comeuppance?" Rascal huffed. "Who says that anymore? What? Were you born in the eighteen-hundreds?"

Colby sauntered past them, shoulders swinging. He winked at Wynona as he walked past. "Just because I have a vocabulary that tells people my intelligence level doesn't mean you have to be jealous. I'm sure some woman will find your neanderthal ways endearing someday." He paused midstep. "Oh, wait." He turned and bowed low to Wynona. "You poor thing. I'll bet he hired someone to put a spell on you or something. Shall I break it with True Love's Kiss?"

Wynona couldn't help her laughter as Colby walked toward her, hands out and lips pursed. Rascal, however, took the bait as he stepped forward with his fist clenched.

"Home!" Alpha Strongclaw barked, causing Colby to straighten immediately.

Wynona noticed that Rascal's reaction wasn't nearly as strong and she grew curious when Alpha Strongclaw seemed to catch on as well. A single eyebrow went up, but the older man didn't say anything before turning and walking.

"Yessir, Alpha," Colby said, walking down the trail as if it had been his idea the whole time. "Whatever you say, Alpha! Your word is my command, Alpha!"

Wynona let Rascal hold her by his side as they walked. "Is he always like this?" she whispered.

"Can't turn off all this goodness!" Colby shouted over his shoulder, making it clear that Wynona's whispering wasn't going to be enough for a private conversation.

Gotta use our link if you don't want to be heard, Rascal said wryly.

Earl Grey with a Hint of Murder

And believe you me, they'll listen in on anything they can get their hairy ears on. My siblings are relentless.

Wynona sighed and smiled. This was turning out to be a lot more fun than she thought.

A minute or two later, they came to a clearing and Wynona choked on every word she'd just thought.

A cabin, nearly the size of the castle she'd grown up in, nearly filled the space. A small parking lot with half a dozen cars and trucks was set up on the side, while people milled about the cabin, all of them lean and fit and looking completely unconcerned that a group was walking onto their property.

They can sense my dad, Rascal told her, explaining what was going on. *And I didn't drive us up to the house because my brothers would claim the truck was free property if I did. I parked it just outside our pack lines, which mean we'd have to hike, but it also means they can't touch my stuff.*

Wynona gave him a look. "You've got to be kidding me."

Rascal grinned and kissed the end of her nose. "Old habits die hard."

"HUGO STRONGCLAW!" a shrill voice called, making Wynona nearly jump out of her skin. "YOU GET THAT WIFE IN HERE RIGHT THIS INSTANT!"

Colby turned around and smiled at Rascal with a wild grin. "You're so dead!" he whispered gleefully.

"Colby! The oil needs changing in the four-door. Get on it!" the woman ordered.

Colby pouted and groaned, but obeyed, much to Wynona's surprise and amusement. This woman knew how to get things done and Wynona had a sinking feeling she was about to be the recipient of the kind of attention she'd never experienced before.

All bark, no bite, Rascal assured her, giving Wynona's waist a squeeze.

The closer they got to the front porch and the more Wynona was able to examine the angry look on Mrs. Strongclaw's face, the less Wynona believed her husband.

The woman was quite a bit shorter than Wynona, but strong enough that she had defined lines on her arms, which were currently on her perfectly curved hips. Thick, dark brows were pushed together over light brown eyes that weren't quite as golden as Rascal's or the alpha. Lush lips were pursed and her cheekbones were something Wynona could only dream of owning. The woman's dark skin gave her an exotic air and Wynona's paleness stood out like a beacon in the dark night.

She'd never felt so small.

"How dare you stay away for two years," Mrs. Strongclaw snapped as Wynona and Rascal arrived at the bottom steps of the porch. "You think you can just worry your mother sick and then waltz up with a beautiful wife and think all will be well?"

Rascal grinned, let go of Wynona and began to climb the steps.

Wynona had to clutch her hands to keep from reaching for him. She felt alone and exposed under the eyes of the crowd and desperately wanted the ground to swallow her up. Alpha Strongclaw's declaration that she would be welcome was looking like a placating lie at the moment and Wynona berated herself for believing it.

"Hello, Mama," Rascal cooed before kissing his mother on the cheek. He turned and put his arm around her shoulders, then waved at Wynona. "This is my wife and soulmate, Wynona Strongclaw. She's the only woman besides you who puts me in my place when necessary, so I knew I had to snatch her up the first chance I got."

Just like Alpha Strongclaw, Mrs. Strongclaw tilted her head and studied Wynona. Slowly, she shook her head from side to side and her face softened. "Oh my dear, sweet thing. You haven't had an easy time of it, have you?"

Wynona jerked back ever so slightly, but the movement wasn't lost on the shifters. Body language was second nature to them and Mrs. Strongclaw's face crumpled.

"Now don't you worry about anything," Mrs. Strongclaw said,

bounding down the steps as if she were in her twenties and not the mother of six grown shifters. "I'm loud and bossy because you have to be with this bunch, but it's all for show." She grabbed Wynona and pulled her down into a hug that was as fierce as it was comforting. "You're one of us now. My wolves are a rowdy bunch, but they know how to treat women, or they answer to me." Letting go just enough to grab Wynona's shoulders and hold her in place, Mrs. Strongclaw raised her eyebrows and waited expectantly. "Do you understand? No matter what's happened in your life, you're safe here or my name isn't Sable Strongclaw."

Wynona's mind was whirling. How could a creature be so fierce one moment and so soft the next? "Um...yes?" she squeaked.

Mrs. Strongclaw nodded. "Good. Now." She stepped back and put her hands on her hips again. "I don't know how my pup ever managed to snag a pretty thing like you, but I think it's time we got acquainted. It's too late to talk you out of taking him on, so the least I can do is give you some pointers."

"Mama!" Rascal yelled.

Alpha Strongclaw's chuckle came up from behind Wynona and passed by the two of them. "Again...welcome to the family," he said in an aside, then winked, bent over and kissed his wife's cheek and walked into the house. He slapped Rascal on the back as he passed and Rascal glared.

Mrs. Strongclaw turned around, those hands still at her hips. "And where, pray tell, is her luggage?" She tilted her head to the side. "I *know* you didn't finally come home after this long and not plan to stay for a night or two. Especially after not even inviting me to your wedding."

Wynona was frozen. She felt like she had whiplash from this woman, but somehow, it seemed that Mrs. Strongclaw was on her side, and Wynona was going to be careful to keep it that way.

Rascal stuffed his hands in his pockets. "The luggage is in the truck," he said.

"Good. You and Barry can go get it." Mrs. Strongclaw waved at a man who was waiting beside the house. "This is my second youngest," Mrs. Strongclaw said to Wynona.

The newcomer eyed her, gave her a shy smile and nodded. "Welcome to the family," he said softly. It was clear this sibling wasn't anything like Rascal and Colby. But somehow, that made Wynona feel a little better about standing out herself.

"Thank you," she replied. "And thank you for helping Rascal."

Barry shrugged it off. "It's nothing."

Wynona watched Rascal walk off with his brother, the two of them talking with considerably less energy than Rascal had with Colby. Rascal slapped his younger brother on the back and his words became low and serious. It was going to take her time to figure everyone out, but Barry's soft and kind greeting had helped calm down her flight or fight hormones and made Wynona curious about meeting the rest of the family.

Mrs. Strongclaw put her hand on Wynona's arm. "Come on inside, sweetheart. That talk will do the boys good and I think it's time we got to know each other."

Wynona let herself smile. She could do this. If she could survive being cursed and almost killed several times, then getting to know her in-laws should be a piece of cake...sort of.

"We can commiserate over Rascal's naughty behavior while we have some tea," Mrs. Strongclaw said with a laugh. "I always knew that pup would make a good husband someday, but he doesn't need to know that...yet."

With a light laugh, Wynona went inside. Yes, she was going to be alright. There might be a few bumps and bruises along the way, but Wynona was starting to see what Rascal meant about being smothered and blessed all at the same time.

Chapter Five

Wynona sipped her tea, enjoying the bold flavor of the ginger and subtle hint of lemon. There was nothing remarkable about the combination, but the woman sharing it with Wynona was quickly winning over Wynona's heart, and that made the drink all the better.

"So tell me about yourself," Mrs. Strongclaw asked, waiting expectantly.

Here we go. Rascal, where are you?

Lugging these suitcases through the woods. Why the heck did you pack so much? he grumbled.

Because you didn't tell me what to pack for, Wynona shot back. *I had to plan for emergencies. But now I'm facing your mom alone and no amount of shoes is going to prepare me for that.*

Rascal chuckled. *She won't bite. Not unless she needs to anyway.*

Wynona felt the blood drain from her face. "That's not funny," she whispered out loud.

Mrs. Strongclaw paused in taking a sip of her drink and her eyebrows shot up. "I definitely don't want to know what my son just said to put that terrified look on your face, honey. But you put him out of your mind. Throw up a barrier and tell him to mind his own business." She reached across the space and patted Wynona's knee. "This is just between you and me."

That's what I was afraid of, Wynona thought glumly. "Ummm... I'm not really sure where to start."

"How about your family?"

Wynona closed her eyes. Why was this so hard? Alpha Strongclaw had been nice about it. Surely, his wife would be too?

"Wynona," Mrs. Strongclaw said softly.

Wynona opened her eyes.

"Child...I want to get to know you, not shame you. Rascal didn't just say you were his wife, but his soulmate." Mrs. Strongclaw's eyes were soft as she shook her head. "I don't know if my son has mentioned it, but I've got a small gift beyond that of shifting. My line isn't strictly wolf to wolf. I have the touch of an empath."

Wynona stiffened.

"I can feel your worry and I can sense your past trauma, though I can't translate what I see into words exactly." Mrs. Strongclaw tilted her head consideringly. "But my point is, you're safe here. There's nothing to be afraid of, you're family. Pack. We protect our own and if the fates chose you to be Rascal's partner in life, then there's a reason for it, and it most likely has nothing to do with who your family is."

Wynona forced her shoulders to relax a bit before nodding and giving in. "My maiden name is Le Doux," she responded carefully, still not fully convinced someone wasn't going to kick her out on her ear. "My father is the president."

Mrs. Strongclaw chuckled and took a drink. "Anyone with eyes in their head can see you're the spitting image of your mama," Mrs. Strongclaw said. "I had that much figured out."

Wynona relaxed further. "I just want to say upfront that I'm not necessarily a proponent of their way of life."

Mrs. Strongclaw nodded. "Understood. Everybody should have

the choice to make their own way in the world." She narrowed her light brown eyes. "So what are you a proponent of?"

Wynona's eyes darted around as she gathered her thoughts. "I'm a proponent of making family, rather than accepting what was given you."

Mrs. Strongclaw nodded.

"I'm a proponent of honesty, hard work, and helping others."

"Sounds like a policeman's wife," Mrs. Strongclaw said with a smile. She set her teacup on the coffee table. "I can see why you and Rascal make a good team. Now...tell me about your powers." Her eyes flared. "I can feel that you're hesitant about them and the strength of them overpowers the entire forest around us."

Wynona slumped into the couch. "Then I think you have all the answers you need."

"What do you plan to do with them?" Mrs. Strongclaw pressed.

"I run a custom tea shop in town. Saffron's Tea House," Wynona said. "And sometimes I help the police solve murders."

"Busy woman." Mrs. Strongclaw leaned forward. "But your powers are too strong for making teas. What gifts do you have, child? How do you plan to use them in the future?"

Wynona pinched her lips together. She didn't want to be rude, but she also didn't want to answer the question. Wynona wasn't in the habit of listing the talents she'd discovered in the last couple of years, but she also understood why Mrs. Strongclaw wanted to know who was in her home.

"I was cursed before I was born," Wynona began. "My family wanted nothing to do with a powerless witch and at the age of thirty, my grandmother gave her life so I could escape. I built my teashop in her honor and right before it opened, there was a murder onsite."

Mrs. Strongclaw nodded slowly. "That's how you met Rascal."

"Yes." Wynona set her own teacup down and clasped her hands in her lap. "With my grandmother's death, my powers began to emerge and I discovered she's the one who cursed me, with the intent of saving me from my family. "

Mrs. Strongclaw's eyes flashed. "That must have been difficult to understand."

Wynona gave another curt nod. "For the past two years, multiple powers have emerged, strangers have become friends, friends have become family and I've helped Rascal put several killers behind bars." She snapped her mouth shut and stopped. That was all Wynona really was willing to share, though there was more to the story. At some point, she would need to acknowledge Uncle Arune's arrival in her life and figure out how to move forward, especially with her father's machinations growing stronger in the background.

Mrs. Strongclaw sat still. "I can tell there's more, but I won't press you for it." She gave a deep, respectful nod. "Thank you for sharing what you did. I realize that must have been difficult since we are, in essence, strangers. But I'm grateful for your trust and grateful that my son has such a strong survivor at his side." One side of Mrs. Strongclaw's mouth pulled up. "With his reckless streak, he certainly needs it."

Wynona smiled back and the tension in the room waned. "I'm glad to be here," Wynona responded politely.

"Not yet, you're not," Mrs. Rascal said with a laugh. "Though we'll get there eventually."

Wynona's smile widened. There would be no tiptoeing around this woman. It was a wonder that Rascal had so many stories about his childhood, since it sounded like his mother wouldn't have been an easy one to fool. "Please forgive me for being hesitant," Wynona began, but Mrs. Strongclaw put up her hand.

"You have reason to be," Mrs. Strongclaw assured her. "Don't worry. It'll all work out in time." She cocked her head. "Meanwhile, I'm glad you let the boys carry that luggage. A little hard labor does them good once in a while."

Wynona made a face. "I really probably should have helped."

"Oh no, you don't. Rascal and Barry need to earn their muscles, not have them handed to them." Mrs. Strongclaw smiled. "Besides... the chat did them good."

Earl Grey with a Hint of Murder

When Mrs. Strongclaw turned to watch the front door, Wynona followed suit. It took a moment but soon the sounds of laughter and footsteps were coming up the porch and Wynona felt a huge breath of relief that Rascal was there.

Mrs. Strongclaw laughed softly, but didn't speak again until the boys came in the door.

"Mama! I'm home!" Rascal called out as he rolled Wynona's large suitcase into the house.

"I can see that," Mrs. Strongclaw said, her sass in full swing. "And still dirty to boot. I'm sure that wife of yours loves a man covered in filth."

Rascal brushed at himself, dumping dust into the air and on the floor. "It'll wash off," he said, not the least bit concerned. "Besides, someone had to put Colby in his place. He's starting to get too big for his britches."

"Wonder where he got that from," Mrs. Strongclaw murmured. She stood and Wynona followed suit. "We'll let Rascal take you to the guest house and get settled, but be ready for dinner," Wynona's mother-in-law warned. "Everyone is gonna want to meet you. They've just been too polite to barge in while I was interrogating you."

Rascal stopped. "You didn't say she was interrogating you," he said to Wynona.

Wynona smiled and shook her head. "She wasn't. She just wanted to get to know me."

He rolled his eyes. "And I'll bet you were too polite to tell her to mind her own business."

Wynona raised an eyebrow at him and Rascal had the good sense to blush, the tips of his ears turning red.

Sorry. You're right. I shouldn't have left you alone. But I really did want you to get to know her. My mom's not as scary as she wants everyone to believe.

I know, Wynona sent back. She reached for her luggage, but Mrs. Strongclaw stopped her.

"Let him be a gentleman, Wynona. It's what he was taught." Mrs. Strongclaw put her hands on her hips and waited.

Barry walked back across the room and Wynona spun. She hadn't realized the brother had left the front entrance. A light breeze followed after him and Wynona took a long breath, enjoying the scent of the forest.

Do all wolves smell like that? she asked Rascal.

Nah. Barry just opened the window in the formal sitting room.

Wynona nodded and waited for Rascal and Barry to pick the luggage back up. As soon as they were out of the house and walking down the porch, Wynona put her hand on Barry's arm. "I can take it."

Barry smiled and shook his head. "Mama would skin me alive," he said in a soft, but deep tone.

Wynona glanced over her shoulder but didn't see anyone. She was sure Mrs. Strongclaw was probably watching, but...Wynona snapped her fingers anyway and both suitcases rose into the air. "I appreciate you taking a walk with Rascal," she told Barry again.

His smile widened and he looked over at Rascal. "She's something else."

"Truer words have never been spoken." Rascal kissed his wife's cheek. "It wasn't heavy, you know," he told her, referring to his innate strength as a shifter.

"I know." Wynona shrugged. "But I like to help too."

All three of them grinned at the huff that came from behind the front door and arm in arm, Rascal led Wynona to their small cabin just behind the large family one.

The inside was quaint and clean with a bedroom in the back, a couple of couches, and small kitchen and dining area. Perfect for the two of them for a few nights.

He came up behind her and wrapped his arms around her waist, leaving a kiss on Wynona's neck. "What do you think, wife?" he whispered as he teased her ear. "I've never been given a guest house before." His chuckle went through her back. "I usually just get relegated to a bunk bed upstairs."

"I think your mom is an amazing woman," Wynona said simply.

"Yeah? She didn't scare you off?"

Wynona spun in his arms and wrapped hers around his neck. "No, she didn't." Wynona scrunched her nose. "But she did ask some pretty pointed questions and I'm afraid I was a little blunt back."

"You have to be." He kissed the tip of her nose, then let go and took their luggage over to the bed. "She wouldn't accept anything less."

Wynona folded her arms and pursed her lips. "Why didn't you tell anyone about me?" She immediately wished she could take back the words. They sounded so...needy and Wynona didn't want to be that kind of wife, but she had been curious about it since they'd arrived. Yes, they were busy, but everyone kept mentioning how Rascal hadn't been back in a long time, despite the fact that his family only lived an hour away, and no one even knew he'd been dating her, let alone that they'd gotten married.

Rascal sighed and pushed his hands through his hair. "As trite as this sounds...it had nothing to do with you." He glanced back. "Last time I visited, things were a little...tense when I left."

Wynona raised her eyebrows. "No one seemed upset when we got here."

"They wouldn't be," Rascal continued. "We tend to love just as hard as we fight, but my dad wanted me to move back." He gave Wynona a sideways look. "I guess you could say I have a similar problem to you. Dad wants me to be the next alpha and I don't want to be in charge."

Wynona didn't have an answer to that. What could she say? She knew Rascal had alpha tendencies, it was as plain as the nose on her face, but how could she ask him to consider such a thing when she, herself, was running from the same fate?

Rascal smirked and walked back her direction. "This is our life," he told her. "Yours and mine. No one else gets to tell us what to do. If we decide we want to take on a leadership role, it'll be because *we* want to, not because someone else thinks it's our fate in life."

Wynona closed her eyes when he kissed her. She didn't think she'd ever get tired of it, but even Rascal's nearness didn't stop the whirlwind of thoughts going through her head.

Her family wanted her to take over. His family wanted him to take over. His mom had extra powers. Wynona had extra powers. Did Rascal also have extra powers? Was that why they were soulmates? Had their powers brought them together? Would the rest of the family be as welcoming as the parents had been? Was she going to be the odd witch out all evening? How would she keep everyone's names straight?

Geez, Wy... Rascal intruded on her thoughts, wrapping his arms tightly around her waist and kissing her harder. *Enough already. Put that brain to rest and just enjoy.*

She pulled back and dropped her forehead to his chest. "Sorry," she whispered.

"If they haven't eaten you by now, they definitely aren't planning to serve you up as an appetizer tonight," Rascal teased.

Wynona smiled and relaxed. Rascal was right. Things had been just fine since she'd arrived, despite her fear. Maybe she needed to extend the same trust in the Strongclaws as they'd shown in her so far.

"Darn right," Rascal said before sweeping her off her feet. "Let's just make that phrase a permanent part of your vocabulary, shall we?" He chuckled before kissing her again, obviously determined to make the most of their few moments together.

And Wynona was in complete agreement.

Chapter Six

After finally convincing herself to relax and enjoy, Wynona found a thick tension in the air as she and Rascal went to dinner. She squeezed her husband's hand and pinched her lips. *Is this because of me? What did I do?*

Smiling at his mother, Rascal returned her finger squeeze. *No. I'm not sure what's up yet, but it isn't because of you.*

Wynona tried to relax, but she could feel the emotion of every creature in the large room. The barrier she kept up to handle the animal emotions was barely surviving the onslaught of frustration, anger, jealousy and heartbroken angst that were pounding against it like a sledgehammer. *Something bad has happened,* Wynona sent to Rascal. *I can feel it.*

Rascal grunted and led her to the table. "Wy...meet the rest of my family. You already met my dad."

Alpha Strongclaw nodded calmly. He was the only creature at the table who didn't seem to be angry and Wynona took comfort in that fact. "Daughter," the alpha said in his low tone.

Wynona bit her lip between her teeth. The alpha had called her that since her arrival and Wynona was beginning to realize just how sincere he was in the term, which made her heart beat just a little faster. She'd never had a father figure that was worth noting and Wynona had a feeling that if she allowed it, the Alpha would fill that role very well. "Good evening," she said softly.

"And my mom," Rascal went on. "Here's most of my siblings, in order." Rascal winked at her. "I'm the oldest, of course."

"Bragging about being an old man," Colby teased. "Never thought I'd see the day." He leaned back in his chair, the front two legs off the floor. But when Rascal reached out to kick the chair off balance, Colby quickly righted it and laughed. "You're getting slow, too...pity."

Rascal growled a little, until his mom gave him a look. After clearing his throat, Rascal went on. "My sister, Grecia, or Grey, is married and doesn't live here anymore," Rascal explained. "But I'm sure you'll meet her soon."

"They'll be down on Sunday," Mrs. Strongclaw said as she fussed over the food offerings on the table. She smiled at Wynona. "She's expecting her first pup and–"

"And Mom's about to bust outta her skin," Colby finished, rolling his eyes. "You'd think the rest of us never accomplished a thing with the way she carries on."

"You haven't accomplished a thing," Rascal responded cheerfully. "Mom would just be happy if you could do your own laundry."

A good portion of the table laughed at Rascal's remark and Colby scowled, before a slow grin took his place. "You know...I can feel the power radiating off Wynona. I really think you're just making the whole soulmate thing up. I'll bet she'd like to take a walk, ow!" Colby frowned and rubbed the back of his head that his mother had smacked.

"Keep your eyes where they belong," Mrs. Strongclaw scolded. She nodded at Rascal and Wynona. "There's plenty of time for chatting. Have a seat and let's feed these animals before they come up with any more inane ideas. The fates know there have been enough accusations running through this house today." Her eyes flashed to

Earl Grey with a Hint of Murder

Barry, who was sitting sedately in a chair down the table a little, then back to her work.

Wynona laughed under her breath as Rascal pulled out her seat. The litany of words filtering through their bond was hilarious, if not completely appropriate. Wynona was glad no one else could hear the vocabulary their family member seemed to have picked up in the city.

The table grew loud for several minutes while dishes were passed and called for until most everyone had a full plate. The chaos was almost fun, or would have been, if it hadn't been underlined with so much weight.

Covert glances and flaring eyes were moving around the table like a second glance and Wynona still couldn't figure out what exactly was causing it. The only thing she could think of was her being a witch and showing up so unexpectedly. *Maybe my power is putting them off?* she thought to herself. Her eyes were drawn to Colby as he smacked a hand at Barry, and something small and white dropped into Barry's lap.

Wynona frowned slightly, realizing the brother was passing a note. *None of my business,* she reminded herself, focusing on the food plates being passed around. It wasn't like she was entitled to all the family secrets just because she and Rascal were married.

"Don't you worry about it, honey," Mrs. Strongclaw assured her. The older shifter was sitting across the table from Wynona and pinned her with a look. "It's just an old argument that resurfaced at a bad time." Her eyes went first to her husband, then to Barry, who was quietly eating his dinner. When Mrs. Strongclaw came back to Wynona, she paused and tilted her head. "I can tell you're feeling what's going on. Are you empathic as well?"

Wynona shook her head and dropped her hands in her lap. She wanted to trust everyone here, but she wasn't sure just how much to share. If she spoke of her powers, would Wynona create a wedge that hadn't been there before? Would the sheer amount of them make her an outcast instead of a family member?

"She's got a connection to animals," Rascal grunted, wiping his mouth on a napkin. "Which includes our wolves."

"Ah." Mrs. Strongclaw nodded and Wynona realized the table had gone silent.

Every eye was on her and Wynona sunk back in her seat. Wonderful. The exact thing she was trying to avoid had just landed in her lap. Instead of blending in, she was once again on display and would soon be a source of gossip in this tight-knit community. Wynona could feel their anger turning to fear and curiosity and she immediately began to push her chair away from the table.

Mrs. Strongclaw looked up sharply, obviously having felt Wynona's intent, but she didn't get a chance to speak before her husband did.

"We want to welcome our newest daughter and family member," he said in a forceful, booming voice. His eyes were glowing and moving up and down the large table. "My oldest son has come home, returning with a soulmate who will be a great asset to him in his life and work. We're thrilled at this union and look forward to celebrating it formally in a day or two." He turned to his wife, the stoicism of his face softening. "Just as soon as my lovely wife can throw together enough food for the occasion."

Rascal tucked Wynona into his side as the table broke out in a light applause. He kissed her temple. *Sorry. I didn't realize they'd react that way. We protect our own here, so I assumed it wouldn't be a big deal.*

You forget, Wynona sent him. *I'm not one of their own.*

Rascal growled and held her tighter. *And you forget, you became one of our own as soon as you agreed to be my wife.*

The celebration was interrupted as loud, angry footsteps shook the house. "WHERE IS SHE?" a voice bellowed.

Every wolf at the table was on their feet and Wynona's eyes went wide as she listened to the angry snarling. The only one who appeared to be calm was Alpha Strongclaw, though Rascal wasn't nearly as worked up as his family.

Earl Grey with a Hint of Murder

Alpha Strongclaw stepped forward, cutting off a young man as he marched into the dining room. Wynona had never seen him before, but the angry look on his face and the power of his emotions thrumming against her barrier was giving her a migraine. Behind him were more people. One was a man much larger than any of the other wolves and, in contrast, a young woman who made Wynona feel like a giant.

"Stand down, Boyer," Alpha Strongclaw said firmly. His legs were wide and his stance unyielding.

"I'll stand down when you tell me where my sister is," the young man snarled, his eyes wild and glowing nearly black as he stood up to the alpha.

"Stand. Down," Alpha Strongclaw said again and this time even Wynona could feel the power of his command.

She watched with interest, curious how an alpha from another pack would affect a wolf that wasn't technically his.

The young man winced and his knees faltered, but he stood his ground. "Where's my sister?" he ground out, his voice much less demanding than before.

"She's not here," Mrs. Strongclaw snapped, coming up beside her husband. "We've followed your father's rules ever since he laid them down. So what's this all about?"

Boyer's eyes went to Mrs. Strongclaw, then back to the alpha, as if his wolf knew who the bigger threat was. The large man was still growling, and the young woman looked pale and worried.

Rascal snorted. *He's wrong.*

Wynona felt a tiny smile try to hit her face, but she held it back. This was far from a laughing matter.

"Opal is missing," Boyer said, his nostrils flaring. "She has to be here. She slipped away from Bermin, which means she had to be coming to see Barry."

Mrs. Strongclaw waved her arm around the room. "Well? Do you see her?"

Boyer looked around, his face falling with each moment. "She has to be here," he said again, though the conviction in his voice was gone after he spotted Barry at the table.

"Are you sure she ran away?" Alpha Strongclaw asked. "She's not just in town with some friends?"

Boyer pushed his hands through his hair. "She's not answering her phone and she's been gone since yesterday afternoon, plus she didn't take Sartel with her." He indicated the young woman still hiding behind the large man, a pleading look replacing Boyer's anger. "Where else would she go?"

"Hey, Sar," Colby said with a playful chin tilt. His grin was all rogue. "Long time no see."

The large man, Bermin, stepped between Colby and the young woman, scowling fiercely at Colby. Boyer looked back at Sartel and frowned, obviously not pleased she was getting attention.

Colby's smile only grew. "She's an adult," he taunted. "There's no reason why she can't speak to me." Colby leaned sideways as if to look around Bermin. "You're looking awfully pretty today."

"Colbium," Alpha Strongclaw warned at the same time Bermin stepped closer.

Bermin stood toe to toe with Colby, but nearly a head taller. "Don't talk to her," he growled. "She's off limits to you."

"Not your say," Colby said, clearly unconcerned.

"Hi, Colby," Sartel said softly. She gave him a small wave, then ducked back again, as if desperate to hide from prying eyes.

"You still haven't answered my question," Boyer interrupted. "Do you know where Opal would've gone?"

Alpha Strongclaw shook his head. "I'm sorry," he said. "But I don't."

Boyer's breathing grew louder and louder until he snarled again. "Fine," he snapped. "But if we find out you or your pack had anything to do with this, there *will* be consequences."

"As long as Sartel's the one handing them out, I'll volunteer," Colby said with a laugh.

"Shut up," Rascal growled at his brother, shoving him over.

Earl Grey with a Hint of Murder

Colby caught himself on a chair, but the grin never left his face.

Boyer's threat was followed by a multitude of growls, but Alpha Strongclaw put his hand up and the sounds instantly stopped. "I'll walk you out." With Colby stepping on his heels, Alpha Strongclaw walked out of the room, ushering the guests to the door where it slammed a few moments later.

After a quiet minute, Alpha Strongclaw and Colby walked back to their seats as if nothing had happened. The rest of the family followed suit and Wynona plopped down, her legs shaky. Rascal had a lot of explaining to do.

He snorted and turned to look at her. *Opal is Boyer's sister, she–*

"Let her eat, Rascal," Mrs. Strongclaw said cooly, her eyes on her food. "No one is going to hurt her." Her light brown eyes came up and landed on Wynona, then the shifter raised her eyebrows as if to ask if Wynona was all right.

Wynona took a deep breath and nodded. She'd get the story later. "Thank you, Alpha Strongclaw," she said loud enough to be heard down the table. "Your earlier welcome means a lot to me."

He nodded at her and the table went back to eating, pretending as if the last ten minutes had never occurred.

Wynona frowned at her plate, feeling as if she were missing something, when she realized the creature to her left was gone. Looking over, Wynona saw that Barry had left the table. He had been there during the confrontation...so where was he now?

"Don't worry about him," Rascal grumbled softly. "He'll be fine."

Wynona felt worry begin to churn in her stomach. Barry had been so kind to her. Had Boyer said something to upset Rascal's brother?

Rascal placed a hand on her knee and squeezed. "Seriously, Wy," he whispered. "He's fine. Let it go."

She tried to smile at Rascal, but letting it go was easier said than done. Just what was it that had sent the soft-spoken wolf running away from the table? Why did they think he would have anything to do with Opal's disappearance? And why was Opal forbidden from being there?

She only lasted another fifteen tense minutes before Wynona had to do something.

"Will you point me toward the restroom?" Wynona asked Rascal, setting her napkin on the table.

Rascal sighed, obviously suspecting her intent, but he answered her question anyway. "Across the kitchen, down the hall, second door on the left."

"Thank you," Wynona said, leaving a peck on his cheek. She stood, not making eye contact with anyone else, and slipped out of the room. The kitchen was quiet and full of dishes as Wynona walked across the hardwood floor.

Making a mental note to help clean up when the meal was done, Wynona continued walking, keeping her ears peeled for signs of movement. The restroom was easy enough to find, but it wasn't her actual destination.

Continuing farther down the hall, Wynona peeked into the open doorways, but all she found were several well kept guest rooms and a cleaning closet. Pursing her lips in frustration, she headed back the way she had come. The chatter from the dining room was growing louder, almost shouts at this point, when Wynona realized there was another sound intermingled with it.

She paused and waited. There. A soft sobbing. Forgetting about her mission to find and talk to Barry, Wynona tried to pinpoint the distressed creature. She thinned her emotions barrier ever so slightly, bracing herself against the wall of turmoil that hit her, making Wynona's knees weak.

Wy? Rascal asked immediately.

Fine, she sent back with as much strength as she could muster. *I'm fine. Just give me a minute.* She felt more than heard Rascal's growl, but Wynona ignored it for the moment. He didn't like it, but she knew Rascal would hold off...for at least a few seconds.

Pushing forward, Wynona followed the feeling of despair, hoping to find the creature before Rascal did. He was a wonderful officer, but sometimes his blunt mannerisms were a little too much when a delicate hand was needed. And something in Wynona's tuition told her this creature needed a soft touch.

Coming out of the hallway, Wynona glanced toward the kitchen, but there was no one there. Instead of going across to the dining room, Wynona turned right, heading back toward the front of the house.

The crying turned to whimpering and Wynona picked up her pace. If she could hear this, she knew full well that as soon as one of the wolves at the table grew quiet, they'd hear it too.

"Shhh..." a deep voice soothed. "It's going to be alright."

"How can you say that?" a female voice responded, her emotion thick in her tone. "This ruins everything!"

Wynona paused just outside the front room.

The woman began crying again. "He's going to take me away. Just like before."

"No," the man growled. "We've come too far. There's still hope."

"What hope?" the woman cried, causing Wynona to wince. The wolves would have heard that for sure. She edged forward.

"Shhh..." the man urged. "They're going to hear you." There was a rustling sound and Wynona could hear muffled crying again.

Gritting her teeth, Wynona decided she needed to go in. She didn't know what was going on, but someone was in trouble and she wanted to help, not to mention, she was almost positive the male voice was–

"Barry!"

Wynona's eyes landed on Rascal's brother at the same time Rascal's did, but instead of turning to her husband, Wynona was glued in place.

Barry had his arms around a woman, whose red face told Wynona this was who had been crying. At seeing his brother, Barry's face went pale and he shifted as if he wanted to back up. "It's not what it looks like," Barry said weakly.

It took Wynona a moment, but after stepping a little farther into the room, she realized that Barry and his mystery girl weren't alone. Wynona's heart sank and her eyes nearly popped out of her head when she saw the body on the floor.

A man in a dark suit lay on his stomach, and from the unusual stillness of the body, Wynona had a feeling calling an ambulance wouldn't help them. His head full of blond hair seemed vaguely familiar, but she couldn't see his face.

"What have you done?" Rascal growled, deep betrayal in his voice. He stepped forward, but Barry put a hand up.

"Stop, Rascal. I didn't do this. You know I didn't."

The girl tightened her grip around Barry's midsection and began crying even harder.

"You know I can't let this go," Rascal said and Wynona could feel his pain. It overpowered every other sensation in the house and tears began to track down her cheeks with the weight of it. "Barry," Rascal breathed. "What have you done?" he asked again.

"I didn't do this!" Barry shouted, startling the woman. "You have to know that!"

A loud gasp drew Wynona's eyes and she realized that every wolf from the table was behind Rascal, watching the proceedings. Rascal reached one hand behind his back and then put the other in the air, as if to calm his brother. "We're going to handle this the right way, Barry," Rascal said, a forced calm in his tone.

"NO!" The girl screamed, spinning and baring her teeth and letting Wynona know the stranger was another shifter. "Leave him alone!"

"I'm innocent, Rascal," Barry pleaded, his hands in the air. "You have to know that."

Rascal took another step forward, the crowd frozen in place behind him, all except Alpha Strongclaw. "Listen to your brother," the alpha said and Wynona felt the power of the words.

Rascal twitched, but kept going. Barry, however, stiffened, as if the words had turned him into a statue.

Earl Grey with a Hint of Murder

Wynona stayed still, not daring to draw any attention to herself. She was obviously missing several pieces of the story, but the family seemed to have a better handle on it. Her heart broke, however, at the thought of Barry being guilty of killing someone. Rascal adored his family and this was the type of wound that never healed.

With a grimace of pain, Barry shook himself and stared at Rascal with begging eyes. "You know," he whispered, right before lunging for the open window. His shift into a wolf was just in time for Barry to make it through the small opening, before his furry body disappeared from view.

Rascal cursed and ran to the window while his mother gathered the crying girl into her arms.

Alpha Strongclaw went to the body, squatted down and felt the man's neck before looking up at Rascal.

Spinning, Rascal was barely containing his snarl. "Well?"

The alpha nodded. "He's gone."

"Why would he do this?" Rascal demanded. His glare turned to the girl. "And why is Opal here?" He marched toward his mother and the girl, but Mrs. Strongclaw let go and put herself between her son and Opal.

"Stop," she demanded, putting her hand to Rascal's chest. "I think we have other things to worry about right now, other than you frightening Opal to death."

Rascal growled. "Such as?"

"Such as why Bermin is dead," his mother said in a low tone. "And how that happened in my house when we saw him alive only a few minutes ago."

Wynona's eyes widened. Bermin. The huge man who had come with Boyer. She looked down at the body, noting the size and breadth of the shoulders now that she was looking. Mrs. Strongclaw was right. This death had to be extremely recent and how it occurred in a house full of sharp wolf ears was a very, *very* good question.

Chapter Seven

Wynona leaned against the wall, her arms folded over her chest as she watched the family hash out what to do next. The body was still lying on the floor, but Opal was in the corner, crying into her hands. Colby was standing guard so Opal didn't run away the same way Barry had and the alpha, Mrs. Strongclaw and Rascal were arguing in the middle, while other shifters moved into and out of the room, checking on the situation, but ultimately deciding they didn't want to get involved.

Wynona didn't blame them.

Rascal scrubbed his hands over his face. His eyes were still glowing slightly. "You have to call the authorities, Dad. You can't handle this on your own."

"You *are* the authorities!" his mother cried, her hands back on her hips. "Why don't you handle it?"

Rascal shook his head. "I can't get involved in this. My brother just killed a man, there's no way I can be part of the team."

"He DID NOT kill anyone!" Mrs. Strongclaw shouted, rushing up to Rascal and poking him in the chest. "We don't know what happened."

Earl Grey with a Hint of Murder

"Mama..." Rascal groaned, shoving his hands through his hair. "I walked in with a dead bodyguard on the floor and his charge crying in the arms of my brother. What do you think happened? Not to mention, her brother broke into our house, claiming she had run away. I think everyone here can deduce what happened."

Mrs. Strongclaw threw her hands in the air. "But unless you saw Barry kill anyone, you can't charge him with the murder."

Rascal growled and shook his head again, pacing away before coming back. "Look, I don't like it any more than you do, but we can all see the writing on the wall here. We'll be lucky if the police even bother to look for any other clues. It's too convenient and Barry jumped ship, making it look worse."

Mrs. Strongclaw shook her head, her eyes glowing and full of tears. "You can't mean that. You don't really believe your brother is capable of this?"

Rascal held his ground for only a moment before sighing and hanging his head. "No," he whispered hoarsely. "I don't believe it." His head came back up. "But Mama, I've seen good men do desperate things when they feel they have no choice."

"Why would he have no choice?" his mother argued. "No choice about what?"

You need to talk to the girl, Wynona sent to Rascal. She'd tried to stay out of it all, but they were so caught up in arguing with each other that Wynona felt that they were overlooking an obvious piece of information. That girl probably saw it all, and if everyone would calm down, they could probably calm her down enough to tell them what happened. They also needed to call her father and brother. The brother, especially, might have more information.

Rascal's eyes darted her way, then went straight back to his parents.

Wynona tried not to take it personally, but the quick dismissal hurt a little. This was, after all, supposed to be their honeymoon. She didn't begrudge Rascal his job or taking care of family, but still...she had hoped to be important enough to have him listen to her.

Rascal stopped mid-sentence and turned her way.

Quickly, Wynona realized she must have let her thoughts and feelings out of the barrier and she nearly cursed under her breath. She really needed to do a better job of keeping the wall up.

Rascal gave her a defeated look and left his parents standing in frustration as he walked to her side. "I'm so sorry," he whispered, reaching out and rubbing his hands up and down her upper arms. "I didn't mean to ignore you and this definitely isn't what I had planned for our honeymoon."

Wynona tried to shrug him off, but she couldn't quite contain the hurt yet and it must have shown on her face because Rascal groaned and pulled her into his arms.

"Please..." he begged. "Forgive me." He kissed her temple and rubbed his hands up and down her back. "We'll leave just as soon as they get the authorities out here."

"No!" his mother shouted.

Wynona and Rascal looked over and Wynona's heart broke over Mrs. Strongclaw's tear streaked face.

"You can't leave," she declared. "You can't. You said yourself, they're not going to look at other suspects."

Alpha Strongclaw pulled her into his chest, but his wife refused to be comforted.

"You have to save your brother," she said through her tears. "Please."

Rascal tilted his head back. "I already told you I can't get involved," he explained in a tight voice. "I'm family. It'll look bad."

"Please," his mother begged again. "Please...someone has to save him."

Rascal didn't speak and Wynona didn't know how to respond. She understood why Rascal had to say no. Being too close to the main suspect would make it harder to prove Barry's innocence. But his mother wasn't wrong in wanting help either. Rascal knew the system and the people. No one was better equipped to help Barry than Rascal was.

If he's innocent, Rascal sent to her.

Wynona turned to face Rascal. *You really think there's a chance he's guilty?* She thought of the shy, quite shifter and had a hard time picturing him viciously killing a man, especially one as large as the bodyguard. It wouldn't have been an easy fight and Barry didn't have any blood on him...at least not that Wynona had seen when she walked in the door.

Rascal gave her a sad look. *I've told you before, sweetheart. There's always a chance. Every creature, no matter how soft-spoken, if pushed the right way, will kill.*

Wynona pursed her lips. She still didn't fully agree with that concept, though she understood his reasoning. Rascal had to have seen some difficult things during his years of service.

"Son?"

They looked over and another tug hit Wynona's heart. Alpha Strongclaw was holding onto his normal stoicism...but barely. The tightness around his eyes and mouth and the red rim of his eyes told the real story and Wynona hated to see it. She'd only met the alpha a few hours ago, but he had been so kind and welcoming that seeing him hurt made her hurt.

"I can't," Rascal ground out, not looking at his parents. "I can't do it." He shook his head, and turned to his father. "I'm sorry." Taking Wynona's hand, Rascal pulled her out the back of the house and toward their guest cabin.

Wynona wanted to argue, but she held her tongue. His despair and betrayal was eating him alive and the last thing Rascal needed right now was his wife nagging him to help in a situation he felt was impossible.

She understood where he was coming from, but she absolutely didn't agree with him. Wynona had tried before to stay out of cases she was too close to before, and inevitably, she found that her feelings for the person involved made her better at her job, rather than making it worse.

"They'll just have to understand," Rascal muttered under his breath as he stomped up the steps to their cabin. He paused and Wynona almost ran into his back. Nostrils flaring, Rascal's chest rumbled with a growl before he burst inside the cabin, canines flashing. "What do you think you're doing?" he snarled.

Wynona rushed in after him, skidding to a halt when she realized the cabin wasn't as empty as it should have been. "Barry," she breathed. Wynona's shoulders fell. "And Opal."

Opal sniffled and rested her head against Barry's sternum.

"You have to listen to me," Barry begged, his eyes pleading with his brother.

"Close the door," Rascal said in a low tone and Wynona quickly obeyed.

She glanced out before shutting it fully, making sure they wouldn't have any prying ears or eyes for the next few minutes. She came back to Rascal's side. "It's clear for now," she whispered before nodding at Barry and Opal.

"Why are you here?" Rascal whispered harshly.

"Because we need your help," Barry replied just as quietly. "I didn't kill Bermin. He was dead when we got in the room."

Rascal shifted his focus to Opal. "How did you get away from Colby?"

Opal huffed. "Do you really think it was that hard?" she said softly. "I just asked to use the restroom." She snuggled deeper into Barry's hold. "I thought you would beat me here, but I was able to run straight across the compound because everyone was focused on the house."

Rascal scrubbed his face with his palms. "This is becoming more and more of a nightmare." He shoved a finger in the direction of the house. "I've got a dead body over there and our parents are convinced they can handle it on their own, when their own *son* is the chief suspect. What in the paranormal world do you think I'm capable of doing?"

"Clearing my name," Barry said simply.

Earl Grey with a Hint of Murder

Rascal shook his head. "You know I can't do that. They won't accept my testimony in court. I'm too close to you."

"Clear it before it goes to court," Barry insisted. "Find the real killer and I won't even have to go through the system."

"And in the meantime...what?" Rascal demanded.

Barry didn't have an answer for that and Wynona watched what little confidence had been on the young man's face begin to crumble. "You aren't really going to turn me in, are you?" he asked his brother.

"It's my job," Rascal shot back.

Wynona closed her eyes. Rascal was a good police officer, but this was tearing him apart. If he let Barry go, he could lose his job. If he took Barry in, Rascal would have to live with the consequences of that knowledge for the rest of his life.

Barry's eyes turned to Wynona, a silent plea for help reaching straight to her core. She strengthened up her shield, but it was no use. The emotions in the room were too strong to ignore and she felt her knees begin to shake.

"Don't," Rascal snarled, stepping between Barry and Wynona. "Don't you dare use her to get me to agree." Rascal's shoulders were heaving. "This is between you and me, brother, and if you dare to involve my wife, you won't like where my loyalty will lie."

"Rascal," Wynona breathed. She put her hand on his back, feeling the rippling of his skin as his wolf tried to break free. *He's not going to hurt me,* Wynona assured Rascal. *We'll figure this out.*

"I'm sorry," Barry said, dropping his eyes for just a moment.

Opal sniffled. "If you won't help us," she whimpered, "then who will? We're supposed to be gone already, but Barry wanted to clear his name." She looked up at the shifter she loved, her eyes shining with unshed tears. "We planned this for weeks, working around my father's schedule to make sure we'd be undetected and safe and now we..." Her whimpering grew louder and she was unable to finish her sentence.

With a soft groan, Barry pulled her head into his shoulder and hugged Opal tight to his chest. "Please," he whispered hoarsely.

"Please help us," he directed at Rascal. "You're the only one who can."

Rascal pushed his hands into his hair and tugged harshly. "You're asking me to go against everything I stand for," he snapped.

"I'm asking you to help," Barry clarified. "Since when is helping your family against your moral standard?"

"When my family is the prime suspect in a murder investigation."

Barry blew out a breath and shook his head, his brows pulling together. "What would you have done, Rascal? What would you do to have Wynona as yours? Is there anything you wouldn't risk?"

Rascal stilled.

"Running away from family and pack hasn't exactly been on my to-do list since I was a pup," Barry continued. "I'm not an alpha, you know that. But I'm willing to go rogue and make a go at whatever I need to…just so I can be with her." Barry's head shook slowly from side to side. "I'm not an alpha, but I'm still a wolf and I will do anything I need to to protect and take care of my mate…even go against everything we stand for." He tilted his head. "Tell me you wouldn't do the same. Tell me you wouldn't give it all up."

Rascal waited several moments before replying. "I can't," he finally admitted.

Barry nodded eagerly. "Right. We can't. It's ingrained in us and life without Opal wouldn't be a life at all." His lips twitched in anger. "Her father is wrong and this last situation is just another pitfall in what's been hell on paranormal earth for us."

Wynona could see Barry's knuckles turning white as he clutched the back of Opal's shirt.

"I give you my solemn oath that I didn't kill Bermin. Opal and I weren't even supposed to be at the house, but after her brother showed up, I panicked and we ended up in the sitting room where we stumbled on his body."

The cabin was deathly quiet and Wynona flexed her fingers on Rascal's back. *We have to help,* she sent carefully.

Rascal sighed and his shoulders slumped. *I know, but how do I sacrifice our future for theirs?*

Why is this sacrificing our future? Wynona argued. *If you're worried about your job, I get that. But if you're worried about our financial situation, then don't. We're together, that's more than we can say for them, and our bank account is just fine, with or without your paychecks.*

Rascal turned and raised an eyebrow at her. *Are you offering to make me a kept wolf?*

Wynona smirked. *If it would make you happy.*

He stepped closer and kissed her forehead. *It wouldn't, but thanks for the offer.* He blew out a breath and turned back to Barry and Opal. "You need to be out of sight," he said. "If anyone catches you here, it'll be over before we can get started."

Opal cried out in happiness and Barry's head fell forward, eyes closed and a smile on his face. They hugged for several moments before he looked back up. "I knew I could count on you."

"Yeah, well, don't thank me until it's over because the next few days might not be very pleasant for you." Rascal shook his head and put his hands on his hips. "Now...where to hide you?"

"I've got it," Wynona offered. She gave the couple a reassuring smile. "Tell Arune and Violet I sent you and that you need to lay low for a while. They won't mind."

"Are you sure?" Rascal asked.

"I'm sure. No one can keep a secret like those two," Wynona responded.

"As long as Prim doesn't come around," Rascal grumbled.

Wynona laughed softly. "She won't as long as I'm not there." Looking back at Barry and Opal, Wynona held out her hands. "Come on. I'll port you in, but be warned...I'm not very smooth at it yet."

"Come right back," Rascal cautioned.

Wynona gave him a firm nod, squeezed the hands of her passengers, then closed her eyes and sent a burst of magic through the atmosphere.

Chapter Eight

Wynona didn't bother to orient her guests, simply dropped them in the yard and took off for Rascal again. She was afraid that if Violet or Arune caught wind of her being there, Wynona would never make it back.

She stumbled just slightly after landing back in the small guest cabin, but Rascal's large hand wrapped around her from behind. "You're lucky you didn't land in my lap," he teased.

Wynona smiled at him, after straightening. "Sorry. I was in a hurry."

"Come to think of it..." Rascal's grin grew. "I don't think I would have minded if that's where you landed."

Wynona shook her head and whacked his chest playfully. "We have a murder to solve, Officer Strongclaw. Flirting comes later."

Rascal rolled his eyes. "Retirement may be in my near future." He sighed and let go of her, all playfulness gone. "I guess the first step is to go back to the main house and tell Dad that I'm going to be in charge."

"Do you think he'll let you?" Wynona asked. "It sounded like wolves usually run their own...situations?"

Earl Grey with a Hint of Murder

Rascal nodded. "Because we're outside city limits and the wolves run on a government type entity, they usually handle their own problems, but this one is a bit bigger than normal." He pushed his hand through his hair again, and it stayed put, looking wild and messy. "As far as I'm aware, Dad's never dealt with an actual murder before, at least not one that appears to have happened in cold blood. Years and years ago, they still fought for alpha rites, but that practice has been out for decades."

Wynona couldn't fight the shiver that ran down her spine. Sometimes the stories of older paranormals were frightening. The violence that accompanied their lifestyle was enough to churn her stomach.

Rascal took a deep breath and held out his hand. "Come on. We might as well get this over with."

They stepped outside into the darkening sky and Wynona glanced at her husband. "What are you going to tell them? About why you changed your mind?"

Rascal squished his lips to the side as he considered how to respond. "I guess that I couldn't leave my family hanging," he responded. "We can't tell them we hid Barry." Rascal gave Wynona a wry look. "My mom is good at bossing, but not holding things in."

Wynona gave him a sad smile back. "So noted." She took a deep breath as they reached the back of the house. "Here goes nothing."

They walked inside and discovered the house to be almost too quiet. Rascal gave Wynona a look, then dared to break the silence. "Dad? Mom?"

The sound of footsteps came marching down the hallway and Wynona stepped back as Mrs. Strongclaw wrapped Rascal in a tight hug. "I knew you'd come back," she whispered thickly. She let go of her son and rushed Wynona. "There was no way on this crazy earth that you two would walk away when family needed help."

The petite woman stepped back, wiping at her red rimmed eyes.

Alpha Strongclaw stood in the entrance to the mudroom they were crowded in. He and Rascal stared each other down for several long, uncomfortable moments and Wynona shifted her weight, wondering who would speak first.

"Would you please talk to your colleagues at the station? Are you able to request certain officers?" The alpha's voice was low and strained.

Wynona took notice of her mental shield. It had taken a hit in the guest cabin, but now she was feeling stronger. Yearning, aching and pain were strong in the house, but not as overwhelming as Barry's desperation had been.

Rascal let out a long, slow breath. "I can do that," he said finally. Stepping away from Wynona, he pulled his cell phone out of his back pocket and hit a button. Walking away a little, Wynona watched the tightness of his shoulders and sent good vibes his way. That was bound to be a difficult call.

"Have you moved the body?" Wynona asked, raising her eyebrows.

Alpha Strongclaw shook his head. "I...wasn't sure what to do with it, yet."

Wynona nodded. "Why don't we go back that way while we wait for reinforcements? I can study the crime scene."

The alpha hesitated only momentarily before nodding and turning to lead the way. Wynona followed quietly, but Mrs. Strongclaw continued to sniff and wipe at her eyes.

At the entrance to the room, Alpha Strongclaw paused and looked back. "You're sure you want to be in here?"

Wynona gave him a reassuring smile. "I've been through this before. While I'm sorry it happened, I'm not squeamish."

Liar, Rascal sent through their link.

Wynona stuck her tongue out mentally at him. She really didn't enjoy seeing the bodies, but for the most part, Wynona was able to get through it. The violence was just so senseless and she had a hard time seeing anything be killed, but there were times to set that queasiness aside.

Earl Grey with a Hint of Murder

Nodding his understanding, Alpha Strongclaw stepped aside and let her through.

The first thing Wynona noticed was that the window was still open and she began to walk across the room to shut it, but paused. "Might be important," she muttered to herself before turning back to the shifter.

"They're on their way," Rascal's voice cut in before Wynona could do very much.

She straightened and turned to him. "Should we do anything before they arrive?"

Rascal came up to her side and shrugged, his eyes on the body. "No. I don't have evidence bags and Azirad will fillet me if I mess up any evidence."

Wynona pointed to the man's neck. "Do those scratches look deep enough to kill?"

Rascal squatted down before nodding. "Yeah...though we can't know that for sure until the autopsy. But there aren't any other visible wounds."

Wynona nodded. "That's what I thought."

"Oooh...are we playing detective now?"

Wynona turned and smiled at Colby. The ridiculous shifter was starting to grow on her, though she thought him recklessly bold. His guts in flirting with Sartel had been dangerous, if slightly cute.

Rascal groaned and stood up. "You touch anything," he said, pointing a finger at his brother, "and you'll regret it. Understand?"

Colby put his hands in the air. "I'm not stupid."

Rascal huffed. "Could have fooled me."

"Boys," Mrs. Strongclaw warned. "Now isn't the time for petty squabbles."

"Maybe not," Rascal replied. "But we're taking a serious chance by having me here at all, so everything has to be done exactly by the book. One mess up could ruin Barry's chances of being proven innocent."

Colby snorted a laugh, but didn't argue. Folding his arms over his chest, he leaned against the doorway. "See anything interesting, Wynona?"

Her eyes flared. "Oh my goodness, why didn't I think of that?"

Rascal spun. "Think of...oh." He shook his head. "I think we were too caught up in the shock of what happened." He nodded at her. "Go ahead. What do you see?"

"What's going on?" Mrs. Strongclaw demanded, stepping farther into the room. "What's she looking at?"

"Wynona can see magic," Rascal explained in a low tone, keeping his mother back. "If someone used something odd to help kill Bermin, she'll see it."

Wynona blinked a few times, her world turning purple as her eyes adjusted to her powers. Slowly, she turned in a circle, letting her eyes take in every piece of furniture and space. "There's..." She hesitated, then walked toward the window.

"What?" Rascal pressed.

Wynona reached out, but stopped herself in time. "There's just the slightest trace of something against the bottom of the window." She turned to her audience. "It's gold in color." Scrunching up her nose, she let her mind work it out. "Rascal. Would you shift for just a second?"

Rascal frowned. "What?"

Wynona turned to look at him. "I'm curious if your wolf leaves a trace, since the shift itself is magical? Maybe what I'm seeing is Barry's departure?"

Rascal's frown held for a moment before he nodded. "Okay. But I'm gonna move over here so it doesn't interfere with anything around the body."

Wynona followed him to the far side of the room and watched carefully as he shifted down. "Can you rub your paw on the carpet?" she asked before he shifted back. "That way I have something to look at?"

Rascal followed her directions before coming back to himself. "Well?"

Earl Grey with a Hint of Murder

Wynona crouched down and studied the floor. "I...think that has to be it," she said warily. "It's so slight though. Daemon once said the amount of magic it took to shift was barely noticeable and he's right. If I wasn't specifically looking for things, I would never have noticed it."

Rascal huffed. "So there's nothing here?"

Wynona stood. "Nothing blatant," she admitted. She walked back to Bermin and slowly moved around him. "Again, there's the slightest trace of something on his neck, but I can't tell if there's a color or not." Wynona squinted.

"So what does that tell us?" Colby asked.

"It tells *you* nothing," Rascal snapped.

Colby rolled his eyes. "What does it tell *you*?"

Wynona sighed and snapped her vision back. "Still nothing," she responded. Turning, she shrugged. "All it does is confirm what we were already suggesting...that a wolf caused the scratches."

Colby huffed. "Helpful."

"Watch it," Rascal warned.

"Sorry," Wynona said softly.

Rascal shook his head. "If you could solve cases simply by looking at magic, we'd lose the entire detective department at work."

Wynona nodded. "There's got to be something I can do, though. It seems like such a waste to sit here and do nothing until Chief Ligurio arrives."

Rascal looked at his watch. "Not a waste. It's time to head down and wait for them."

"You directed them to the pull out?" Colby said with a laugh.

"Experience has made me smart," Rascal called over his shoulder. "Come on, Wy. We have a little hike to take."

Chapter Nine

"Strongclaw!" Chief Ligurio bellowed as soon as he got out of his vehicle. The vampire's eyes were shining and his face looked to be carved out of stone as he approached Wynona and her husband. "Tell me what the..." Chief Ligurio glanced at Wynona and cleared his throat, swallowing back whatever he'd been about to say. "What's going on? Why am I in wolf shifter territory? They usually handle their own issues."

Rascal nodded. "There's been a murder."

One black eyebrow shot up. "You're sure it's a murder?"

Rascal nodded and rubbed the back of his neck. "Yeah. We have the body and possible witnesses and suspects."

"Possible?" Chief Ligurio asked.

Rascal took a deep breath. "A wolf and his girlfriend were found in the room with the body, but both have since fled."

Wynona held her breath, knowing that this wasn't going to be an easy conversation for Rascal. She noticed that he stuck to the truth, but the lies of omission would bring their own guilt.

Chief Ligurio paused for just a moment, then nodded curtly. With a huff, he began to walk away, then paused. "Oh...I think this belongs to you." He reached into the front of his pocket and handed Rascal a small, furry handful.

"Violet!" Wynona cried, taking her familiar out of Rascal's hand and cuddling the mouse into her chest. "I didn't hear you."

Violet snickered, her whiskers flickering. *I stayed quiet so I could stay in Chief Vampy's pocket as long as possible.* She grinned. *He hated bringing me, which only made it all the more fun.*

Wynona pinched her lips between her teeth and tried not to laugh. Rascal wasn't as successful and his cough cover-up brought a glare worthy of melting from his boss.

"Tell anyone and I'll drain her dry," the vampire snarled.

Wynona shook her head. "Chief...I'm disappointed that you don't know me well enough by now to know that I would never tease you about something like this. Nor does it look bad on your part as the chief of the station to be seen being kind to a creature smaller than you. The only person who would hold this against you would probably be Celia, but..." Wynona tapped her bottom lip. "Well, I suppose maybe your threat was credible then." She grinned, covering Violet, who was laughing...loudly. "Celia might even find it attractive."

Before Chief Ligurio could react, Rascal wrapped his arm around Wynona's waist, turned her around and began walking very quickly up the trail. "The house is this way!" he shouted over his shoulder, before ducking his head into Wynona's. "You little minx, you shouldn't tempt a vampire like that."

Wynona laughed and set Violet on her shoulder. "I'm not sure what got into me, but after all the things he's said over the years, it felt really good to finally give him a little trouble."

Rascal chuckled low and gave her waist a squeeze. "I liked it."

"Strongclaw!"

They stopped and turned around. Chief Ligurio was as angry as ever as he came up behind them. "Couldn't we have parked closer?" he asked.

"You could," Rascal told them. "But then several of the younger pups would consider the cars fair game. As it stands, you're just off property, which is the safest place to be if you want all the sirens to remain intact."

The vampire stopped. "They wouldn't."

Rascal raised his eyebrows. "You said yourself that the law doesn't interfere out here very often."

"Speaking of..." Chief Ligurio's eyebrows furrowed. "Why is this murder different?"

Rascal opened his mouth, then stopped. Finally he turned to Wynona.

"Because the wolf in the room was his brother," Wynona finished softly.

You've got to be kidding me, Violet grumbled. *Can't anyone in this family stay out of trouble for more than twenty four hours? You guys barely left.*

Hush, Wynona sent back. *I'll explain it all later. I'm positive his brother's innocent.*

Violet grumbled and her tail twitched, but she quieted down.

Chief Ligurio put his hands on his hips and growled. "Has anyone touched anything?"

"They hadn't when we left," Rascal said, his tone flat.

"Who's watching the body now?"

"Several family members are in the room," Wynona provided when Rascal didn't respond right away. "Alpha Strongclaw is there and aware you're coming." She looked at her husband, whose face had lost all emotion. "But we really should get going." She took Rascal's hand, turned them around again and began to walk.

After a couple of minutes, the lodge came into view and Alpha Strongclaw met them on the porch steps. "Chief Ligurio," the large man said, holding his hand out.

Chief Ligurio shook it. "I'm sorry," he said simply. "This can't be easy for you."

Wynona blinked at the compassion in the chief's tone. He rarely showed any emotion other than anger, as displayed by his little threat about Violet. But there was true sadness in the chief's tone when he spoke to the alpha and it made Wynona all the more determined to see that things were made right.

And then you and I will actually take our honeymoon, Rascal grumbled.

We have each other for a lifetime, Wynona responded. *I don't mind giving your family a few days.*

Rascal huffed, but didn't respond.

"I'd like to see the crime scene," Chief Ligurio said bluntly, interrupting Wynona's thoughts.

"Of course," Alpha Strongclaw responded. "Please come inside."

They all trooped up the steps and into the house. The formal sitting room where the murder had occurred was on their left and Wynona stepped aside to allow Chief Ligurio and several other officers through.

Chief Ligurio walked straight over, then knelt down and studied the body. "Are we assuming at this point he bled out?" He looked up at Rascal.

Rascal immediately walked closer, his tone of voice the one he used in his official capacity. "It appears that way."

Chief Ligurio nodded and went back to studying the body. He tilted his head from side to side several times. "How easy is it for a wolf to die that way?" he finally asked. "I know you heal quicker than normal, but how quick?"

Alpha Strongclaw folded his arms over his chest. "Faster than normal means a few days or weeks for big injuries. Not instantaneous or only a few hours."

"So a deep cut through the artery?" Chief Ligurio pressed.

"Would easily take us down, yes," Alpha Strongclaw said tightly.

Wynona frowned. The tension in the room had shifted and she didn't like it. *They were so friendly out on the porch. Why snap at each other now?*

Because now Dad has to give out...trade secrets...is probably the best term. Rascal glanced her way. *Wolves keep to themselves normally. We're pack animals and our alpha tendencies mean we don't like others taking over or being in charge. So having to talk about the weaknesses of our species goes against the grain.*

Wynona nodded, though she found it ridiculous. If the police were here to help, let them help. It wasn't as if Chief Ligurio was going to use it against the wolves that he understood they could die. All creatures could die in one way or another.

Chief Ligurio stood up and made room for his team to move in and work on the body. "Ms...Mrs. Strongclaw suggested that your son was the main suspect." Chief Ligurio looked around. "And he fled?"

Alpha Strongclaw nodded.

"Is there a party out after him?"

Alpha Strongclaw hesitated before shaking his head.

"You're wolves! Track him down!" Chief Ligurio snapped. "Just because he's your son doesn't mean he's immune to the law!"

Alpha Strongclaw began to growl, but he held his ground. "It's not as easy as you think. The best place for a wolf to run is in his own compound. Barry's smell is everywhere. Picking out the scent trail would be nearly impossible."

Chief Ligurio's lip curled with his own snarl. He turned to Rascal. "You said there was a witness? And she's gone too?"

Rascal nodded. "A possible witness. We're unsure yet, since we didn't get a chance to talk to her. She's Barry's girlfriend." He raised an eyebrow. "She's also a possible suspect, though considering Bermin's size, it's unlikely."

Chief Ligurio's red eyes narrowed. "Barry is your brother?"

Rascal nodded. "Opal is his girlfriend and Bermin was her bodyguard." He waved at the body.

"Explain why she's less likely to be a suspect," Chief Ligurio demanded.

Rascal shrugged. "She's a smaller female. Scratches like that," he indicated the body, "would have been caused in wolf form. A large man will be a large wolf, and Bermin, like I said, was Opal's bodyguard. He would have known her wolf and understood her strengths

Earl Grey with a Hint of Murder

and weaknesses. Between the size difference and the knowledge Bermin would have possessed, it's unlikely that Opaline would have been able to attack him like this."

Chief Ligurio nodded curtly. "I'm still keeping her on the list."

Rascal nodded.

Chief Ligurio folded his arms over his chest. "So...you found the couple in here and what? They ran away together?"

Alpha Strongclaw's nostrils flared and his eyes flashed. "No. My son leapt out the window after claiming his innocence."

"Then what happened to her?" Chief Ligurio demanded, stepping up next to the alpha.

Wynona resisted the temptation to tell the vampire to back off. There was a power struggle going on between the wolves at the moment and she wanted nothing to do with it, plus she was also slightly afraid that Chief Ligurio was about to become wolf meat.

Rascal gave her a look, his eyebrow raised. *Wolf meat? Really?*

Wynona widened her eyes and shrugged in a small gesture.

One side of Rascal's mouth lifted, but it quickly disappeared as the tension in the room grew.

"Sable?" the alpha asked.

Mrs. Strongclaw swallowed, but held her ground at her husband's side. "She asked to go to the bathroom, and I had another son watching her. When his back was turned, she left."

"I suppose you can't find her either," Chief Ligurio snapped.

Alpha Strongclaw never looked away from his wife while he shook his head. "Actually, Opal isn't part of our pack. Her trail shouldn't be hard to pick up." He stood a little taller and called a couple of wolves that Wynona didn't know. "Find her," the alpha said simply.

The wolves nodded and disappeared.

"He won't like it," Mrs. Strongclaw said softly.

Her husband gave her a look, but didn't respond to her.

"The odds?" Chief Liguro asked shortly.

Alpha Strongclaw turned and gave the vampire a look. "I don't know," he admitted, his harsh demeanor slightly relaxing. "It depends on a few things."

Chief Ligurio's eyes darted to Mrs. Strongclaw and back to the alpha. "I see."

"I'm afraid you do."

Growling lightly, Chief Ligurio walked back to the body. "Azirad?" he asked.

The redcap coroner, whom Wynona had met a few times before at other crime scenes, leaned back on his heels and pushed his glasses up his nose. "Bleed out," he announced. "The scratches on the neck go clear down to the jugular. I don't know if they were strategic or accidental, but they did the trick."

"Did he fight back?" Wynona asked.

Rascal scowled, but Wynona knew it was a valid question. Barry wasn't the fighting type and he didn't have any visible injuries on him when they'd spoken. If there were signs of a fight, it would help their case.

Azirad huffed. "I don't know."

All eyes went back to Wynona, but she was already neck deep at the moment, so she pressed on. "Is there anything under his fingernails?"

Azirad grunted again and reached over to grab the man's hand. After studying it intently, the redcap reached for his bag. "It's possible," he said to the quiet room. "His hands have light scratches that look new. There might be debris under the fingernails as well."

"There's no sign of struggle in the room," Chief Ligurio pointed out.

"All that means is that it didn't happen here," Wynona responded.

Chief Ligurio folded his arms over his chest and gave her a very familiar look of skepticism. "What are you suggesting, Mrs. Strongclaw? That the body was dragged in here? I don't see dirt or leaves to suggest he was killed out in the woods and brought inside."

Wynona shook her head. "I'm not quite sure what I'm suggesting.

But I don't believe Rascal's brother is responsible, and I think we should examine all possibilities."

"Let me guess," Chief Ligurio drawled sarcastically. "It's too easy."

Wynona gave him a sheepish grin and shrugged. "Sort of, yes, I suppose. I know you've experienced a lot more crime scenes than I have, but something about this one doesn't sit right. I think Barry ran because he was scared. I don't believe he would kill a creature in cold blood."

"You just showed us there might have been a fight," Chief Ligurio stated, his eyes piercing straight through her.

"Yes, but that doesn't mean whatever is under Bermin's nails is Barry's. Barry had no visible scratches or blood on him when we found him."

Chief Ligurio paused and tilted his chin up. "Fair enough," he said finally. "Much as it pains me to say it," he muttered, "your intuition has been spot on several times." Clearing his throat, he straightened. "We will put out an APB on your brother, Strongclaw, but only as a possible witness."

Mrs. Strongclaw cried out, but covered her mouth with her hands to stop the elated sound. Her teary, shining eyes looked at Wynona in gratitude.

"For now!" Chief Ligurio snarled. "If at any point, hard evidence comes up against him, I'll be changing things."

Wynona nodded. "Thank you."

Chief Ligurio raised a black eyebrow at her. "Don't thank me yet. You just lost half your honeymoon in those sentences." One side of his mouth pulled up. "Welcome back from your vacation."

Rascal's scowl deepened. "I'm willing, but do you think it's too much of a conflict of interest?"

Wynona held her breath when Chief Ligurio turned to her.

"Did you know the deceased?" the chief asked.

"No," she responded.

"How well do you know Strongclaw's brother and his girlfriend?" Chief Ligurio continued.

Wynona sighed. "Barely."

Violet shifted. *I hate to say it, but the vamp has you.*

I wasn't trying to get out of it, Wynona told her familiar. *I just want us to make sure it's usable in court.* "I'll help if I can, Chief Ligurio," she finally said softly. "We all will."

Rascal stared at Wynona, gratitude and fear coming through their connection, and Wynona completely understood where he was coming from.

So much was riding on their abilities to solve this case, but if someone found out what they were hiding…their future would be over before it began.

Chapter Ten

"Well?"

Wynona took her locked gaze off Rascal and turned to a very impatient vampire. "I'm sorry. What?"

Chief Ligurio raised that one eyebrow. "Are you going to share that weird, tiny detailed list of things you see at the scene that the rest of us never manage to notice?"

Wynona felt her lips twitch. "I'm not sure I know what you mean, Chief."

He rolled his eyes and muttered something about impossible females under his breath.

Wynona decided it wasn't worth investigating further, but Violet began laughing again. *Hush. He'll hear you.*

I don't understand why that's a problem.

Rascal cleared his throat, but Wynona could see the conversation had lightened the mood considerably, which was a win in her book. "Come on, Wy," he said softly, holding out his arm. "In for a penny, in for a pound."

We'll still go on that honeymoon, she assured him.

He nodded encouragingly.

"Just for the record, Chief Ligurio, I tried looking at the magic in the room, but it was almost nonexistent."

The vampire frowned. "Skymaw's mentioned before that shifters have very little. I'm assuming that's why."

Wynona shrugged. "That was our guess as well. There were slight traces on the window that Barry jumped out of and just enough to hint at magic along the line of cuts on Bermin's neck."

Chief Ligurio grunted. "So noted."

Now get down there and make your weird list thingy, Violet teased.

Very funny, Wynona told her familiar. *You could help instead of laugh, you know.*

I'm here, aren't I? Let me see the body.

Wynona walked over and stood at the body of the man. His size once again caught her off guard. While Wynona agreed with Chief Ligurio that Opal shouldn't be taken off the suspect list, she understood why Rascal said it would be impossible for the small woman to have killed her bodyguard. "Alpha Strongclaw?"

"Hmm?"

"Would you mind going over all the relationships again, please? I want to catch the chief up and make sure I understand everything I've heard," Wynona asked, her eyes still on the body. "Opal is the daughter of your neighboring alpha?"

"That's correct," Alpha Strongclaw said curtly.

"And she's not supposed to be here?"

Chief Ligurio's interest was visibly piqued and he straightened, looking at the shifter.

Alpha Strongclaw's jaw worked back and forth. "Correct."

"But she and Barry have feelings for each other?" Wynona persisted. She walked to the other side of the dead shifter. The scratches down the side of his neck and face were prominent, deep and straight. The cleanness of the lines told Wynona this was no accident.

Alpha Strongclaw cleared his throat and Wynona realized where Rascal got the habit from. "I can't speak to that," he said.

Wynona looked up. "They were embracing when we came in. Is that normal behavior for wolves?"

The alpha's nostrils flared and Wynona shrunk back a little.

"I'm not trying to pull skeletons out of closets," she said softly. "I'm trying to understand the emotional dynamic behind what might have happened here."

The alpha nodded. "Before Alpha Marcel forbade her from coming, they had expressed interest in each other, yes."

"Thank you," Wynona whispered. She took another step around the body for another visual angle. "Azirad?"

He grunted at her and adjusted his glasses.

"Does it appear to you as if the body fell? Or as if it were set down?"

His craggy face frowned. Leaning back a bit, Azirad didn't answer right away, before eventually climbing to his feet and walking around.

"I just noticed that the scratches are very straight," Wynona said. "It made me curious," she explained. "Plus, there's no..." Wynona made a face. "The blood doesn't look like it spattered anywhere, which I guess I assume would've happened if he had fallen while he was bleeding."

Azirad adjusted his glasses and grumbled while he studied the side of the body she was on. "While I applaud your efforts, Ms. Le Doux–"

"Strongclaw," Rascal interrupted. He gave Wynona a smile and she felt some of the tension lighten. "It's Mrs. Strongclaw now."

The redcap straightened and looked back and forth between them. "I see," he muttered. Shaking his head, he went back to talking. "As I was saying, while I understand what you're asking, I believe the skin would have been too slack for the lines to be straight if the body was already down."

Wynona nodded. "Thank you," she responded, still feeling as if something were not quite right. "You're sure he died of blood loss?"

Azirad gave her another disgruntled look. "I won't know for sure until I get him back to the lab, but that's what it appears to be." He huffed and stood up, wiping his pants. "Only further testing will tell for sure."

"I'm not questioning your expertise, Azirad," Wynona explained. It seemed she was upsetting everyone today. "I'm simply putting as many facts as I can in order so I can try to piece together the puzzle."

"YOU SAID SHE WASN'T HERE!"

Wynona jumped and a purple shield spread across the room. A very loud snarl reached her ears and something smacked into the shield before her eyes even landed on Opal's brother and behind him, a large man very similar to Boyer, who had to be the other alpha.

"What in the world?" Mrs. Strongclaw whispered, her eyes wide as she studied the bubble.

Boyer's fist slammed into the shield again. "Where is she?" he snarled. "I believed you. I trusted you!"

Alpha Marcel's hand landed on his son's shoulder and Boyer backed up immediately. The large alpha stepped forward and when he spoke, his voice rumbled from his chest. "Who is this?" he asked, his eyes landing on Wynona.

She swallowed hard, but refused to cower. As frightening as a wolf was, Wynona knew her power was enough to keep herself safe. Her bubble, however, was a little too tuned into her emotions and it flared, pushing him slightly back. Rascal's hand landed on her back and the warmth was soothing, but the anger from Boyer and the undisguised interest, mixed with disgust, from Alpha Marcel were keeping Wynona tense.

Alpha Strongclaw walked up until he was just across the shield from the visitor.

Wynona felt Violet stretched up on her toes. *There's gonna be a throw down.*

Earl Grey with a Hint of Murder

No, there's not, Wynona argued. *I'm just being cautious. Can't you feel all that anger? Boyer's ready to throttle us.*

Boyer's the young guy?

Yeah. Unless I miss my guess, the one trying to melt me with his eyes is Alpha Marcel...Opal's dad. Boyer is his son and Opal's brother. He came in a while ago, interrupting dinner and accusing the Strongclaws of hiding his sister.

Violet snickered. *If they can't keep track of her, then I don't see why we should have to.*

Wynona almost rolled her eyes, but the two alphas grandstanding at each other kept her from it.

"Careful," Alpha Strongclaw said in a low, but steely tone. "You've come onto my property unannounced. You are owed no answers and I would appreciate it if you kept your pup under control."

Slowly, Alpha Marcel's eyes left Wynona and went to Alpha Strongclaw. "I came because I received a call that my daughter was here." He held his hands out. "And that call came only moments after my son came home telling me she couldn't be found." Alpha Marcel tilted his head to the side. "I had assumed the call was an invitation. Do you have my daughter or not?" His eyes flicked to Wynona again and this time Rascal stepped up with a growl.

A small smirk crept onto the alpha's face. "I see," he murmured. His dark eyes roamed the purple shield. "If you felt so unsafe in my presence, Strongclaw, might I recommend not inviting me next time?"

"Wynona?"

Wynona didn't respond until Violet twitched her tail against her neck. "Yes?"

"Please remove the barrier." Alpha Strongclaw looked over his shoulder and gave her a reassuring smile. "We have nothing to fear here."

Wynona didn't completely believe him, she could actually feel the menace emanating from Alpha Marcel, but she didn't want to directly disobey either. None of them would be hurt on her watch. With a twitch of her fingers, she let it down.

Chief Ligurio sauntered next to Alpha Strongclaw. "And who are you?" he asked boldly, though the shifter towered over the much leaner vampire.

Alpha Marcel's lip curled. "First a witch and now a vampire?" He looked at Alpha Strongclaw. "You're keeping strange company these days." He sneered at Rascal. "And wasting such talent."

Rascal didn't bother to hide his eye rolling.

Alpha Strongclaw ignored the dig. "Chief Ligurio, this is Alpha Marcel. His daughter, Opaline, was the witness we had."

Chief Ligurio raised an eyebrow. "I see. You're the one who forbade her from coming here?"

Alpha Marcel growled. "Sometimes pups don't know what's good for them."

Wynona watched Boyer shift uneasily behind his father. She narrowed her eyes and studied him. The indecision radiating from him told her he wasn't as sold on his dad's old-fashioned ideas as the alpha was.

Chief Ligurio grunted. "Your daughter ran off," he announced bluntly. "She's wanted for questioning and is a possible suspect for the murder of..." He looked at Alpha Strongclaw.

"Bermin," Alpha Strongclaw said softly.

Even Wynona heard the soft intake of breath from the other alpha. Apparently, no one had told him about the murder. "Where's the body?" Alpha Marcel demanded after a moment.

Chief Ligurio stepped aside and Alpha Marcel marched in, squatting down at the body. A growl escaped the shifter and he stood quickly, spinning in a slightly crouched position. "We won't let this death go unanswered," he snarled.

"You make a move and I'll have you arrested for impeding an investigation," Chief Ligurio snapped.

"You hold no jurisdiction here," Alpha Marcel argued, his eyes glowing brighter.

"Actually," Chief Ligurio said easily, "the law states that when called in, our precinct takes over the rights of the packs in charge." He put his hands on his hips. "This is Strongclaw land. They called us to investigate, which means I do have jurisdiction and you *will* be arrested if I think it best."

Alpha Marcel's lip curled even higher and Wynona's knees shook. His hatred was so strong, and her emotional barrier was struggling to keep up.

Another hand landed on her arm and she looked down to see Mrs. Strongclaw.

"Imagine it as steel," she whispered, giving Wynona an understanding glance. "Something about that metal works better than brick."

Wynona swallowed, then closed her eyes and shifted her barrier. She hadn't exactly imagined brick, per se. In fact, it was more similar to Wynona's purple shield. But instead of letting her magical bubble block the emotions, she turned it into bright, shiny steel and sighed in relief. "Thank you," she said to Mrs. Strongclaw, Wynona's eyes opening. "That's much better."

Mrs. Strongclaw gave her a small smile. "I'll teach you what I know."

A loud huff broke up their conversation. "This is what happens when you mix bloodlines," Alpha Marcel snapped.

"If you'll wait in another room," Chief Ligurio immediately responded, "I'll be with you shortly."

"Absolutely not," Alpha Marcel said. "I want to see what you're doing."

Chief Ligurio's eyes glowed red. "Now it's my turn to say you hold no jurisdiction here, wolf. Either obey orders, or I'll have you forcibly removed."

"By who?" the alpha scoffed. "None of your men can best me."

Chief Ligurio glanced to Wynona.

You've got to be kidding me, she thought.

Someone has to show him who's boss, Violet giggled. *Ooooh, I like Chief Vampy now. This is getting good.*

"Violet," Wynona scolded.

Alpha Marcel turned to look where Chief Ligurio was looking and his scowl deepened. Before he could speak, however, Rascal stepped between them. His shoulders were bunched and the muscles straining in his neck.

"I'd love the chance to escort you to the dining room," he said in a dark tone.

Protectiveness hit Wynona's steel shelter and she almost welcomed it in. She hoped Rascal could feel her gratitude and how much she loved him in that moment. She was the most powerful creature there, but if there was anything Wynona hated, it was confrontation and she avoided it as much as possible. Having an alpha as a husband helped with that immensely.

The two shifters faced off for a moment, but Alpha Marcel must have decided the fight wasn't worth it. After glaring at Wynona one more time, he turned and stormed off.

Boyer waited by the sitting room entrance. His face continued to show his indecision, but he didn't speak.

"If you stay out of the way, you won't be asked to leave," Chief Ligurio said, his tone still harsh.

Boyer hesitated, then nodded. His eyes went to the body and Boyer paled.

We'll need to question him eventually, Wynona sent to Rascal.

Agreed. Rascal sent her a significant look. *Our suspect list is longer than I thought.*

By my count, we have Barry, Opal, Boyer and... She hesitated. *Your father and Colby.*

Rascal jerked back, then stopped. With another sigh, he nodded. *I can see that, but the time they were gone from the table was short.*

"I know," Wynona reminded him. "But it doesn't take much. We've both seen it before."

Rascal nodded and pushed a hand through his hair. "Looks like the consequences of this just doubled." *And I'm not going to be the one to tell my dad.*

Wynona pinched her lips together. She had nothing to say that would help make the situation better. Right now was a time for clues and work, not placating. Better get to it.

Chapter Eleven

Wynona stood next to Rascal and Chief Ligurio as Azirad walked with the stretcher taking Bermin out of the Strongclaw home.

"Don't tilt him!" Azarid shouted at a troll nearly four times his size. "You'll tear the wounds!"

Wynona put her fist over her mouth and Violet snickered. The situation with the body wasn't funny, but watching the tiny redcap take on the large officer was more than a little humorous.

"You should have seen him talk to Yetu," Rascal huffed. "The creature has no fear."

"Should he?" Wynona asked. "Would they really hurt him?"

Rascal shrugged. "If pushed enough. He oversteps his bounds at times, but mostly everyone ignores him." He turned to Wynona, his hands stuffed in his pockets. "He's kind of a grumpy, old creature that we've all learned to work around."

You mean the kind of creature you're going to be someday? Violet asked sweetly. *Or maybe we're already there?*

Rascal gave a playful growl and reached for Violet, who scrambled into Wynona's hair.

"Ow! Violet! Rascal, stop!" Wynona reached up and grabbed the mouse, pulling her out of the tangles. "Stop teasing each other and let's get to work. This case won't solve itself."

Chief Ligurio gave them all an unimpressed look. "I'm not too eager to work with someone on their honeymoon," he said, "but the sooner we jump in, the sooner we're done."

Rascal's lip curled. "I'll remember this when it's your honeymoon," he snarled.

"Hugo!" his mother shouted.

Wynona shook her head. Those two were going to come to blows some day. Both of them were such strong personalities, it was amazing they hadn't attacked each other yet.

Who says we haven't? Rascal shot her a look, then marched back to the sitting room. He wandered a bit. "Nothing is too out of place, telling me that there really wasn't much of a fight."

Chief Ligurio nodded. "Agreed." He looked at Alpha Strongclaw. "What room can I use for interrogations?"

Alpha Strongclaw sighed, the first sign of his weariness. "I've got an office down the hall."

"Perfect." Chief Ligurio walked toward the room entrance. "We'll start with you, Alpha."

Rascal took Wynona's hand and waited until his father had followed the vampire, to walk behind.

Are you sure we should be in there? Wynona asked.

Too late for that, Rascal sent back. *We're neck deep at this point.* He sighed. *Let's just hope the judge and jury don't throw it all out because of it.*

Unease slithered down Wynona's spine, but she followed her husband and sort-of boss. Something about interrogating her father-in-law, only hours after meeting him, sounded like something straight out of the Do Not Attempt Handbook.

"In here," Alpha Strongclaw said, opening a large wooden door. The room inside followed the same dark pattern. Large wooden bookshelves were on one side, filled to the brim with books.

Wynona had the urge to run her fingers along the spines and sit in the corner for a while...at least she would have if the tension in the room hadn't been threatening to choke her.

"Have a seat, Alpha Strongclaw," Chief Ligurio said. He walked around the large desk and sat in what had to be the alpha's seat.

Alpha Strongclaw huffed, but sat in a wingback chair and crossed one leg over the other.

Wynona stayed near the back of the room and Rascal, with her. As much as she could, Wynona planned to listen rather than interfere.

"Let's start with the basics," Chief Ligurio said, folding his hands together. "Where were you when the murder occurred?"

Alpha Strongclaw took in a deep breath. "As far as I know, I was in the dining room," he stated. "Boyer Marcel, Bermin and Ms. Sartel had interrupted our dinner because they were looking for Opaline."

"And what did you tell them?" Chief Ligurio asked.

"The truth," Alpha Strongclaw said, leaning back. "That I hadn't seen her, which was correct."

"You told me she was here," Chief Ligurio said with a sneer.

"At the point they came during dinner, I had no idea she was on my property," Alpha Strongclaw said tightly. "The chatter at the table was loud and the smells hid that of any visitors. When I said she wasn't there, I knew it to be truth. It wasn't until later that we found her and Baryn in the room with the body."

Chief Ligurio made a few notes on his phone. "How much later?"

Alpha Strongclaw took a moment before he answered. "Probably only twenty minutes."

Chief Ligurio looked up at Rascal and he nodded his agreement. "Are there witnesses to your story?"

Chief Ligurio sighed and rubbed a hand down his face. "The entire table saw me there," he explained. "And when we finally heard voices and crying, we all followed Rascal to the sitting room."

Again, Rascal agreed with a nod.

Chief Ligurio leaned back, his eyes narrowed as he studied the alpha. "Where was Barry during all this? I assume he had to have been at dinner with you?"

Alpha Strongclaw nodded. "He was. He disappeared after we, Colby and myself escorted Boyer and his friends to the front door. I assumed it was because he was upset that Opal appeared to be missing."

"How long have they been interested in each other?"

Alpha Strongclaw shrugged. "I don't know, but they've known each other since they were pups." He grunted. "My wife would know better. She keeps track of these things."

Chief Ligurio nodded. "Understood. I'm planning to speak to her as well." Chief Ligurio grunted. "Is there anything you *can* tell me about your son that you think would be useful?"

Alpha Strongclaw didn't respond right away, but eventually spoke. "Baryn is my second youngest. He and Opaline have been friends for years, and though I don't know when feelings changed, they've expressed a desire to marry." Alpha Strongclaw pushed his hand through his hair. "Her father, who believes only an alpha is appropriate for his daughter's mate, refused the match, then forbade her from coming over anymore." He looked up at the chief. "As you can expect, the young couple were devastated."

"Have they been sneaking around behind your backs?" Chief Ligurio pressed.

Alpha Strongclaw shrugged. "It would appear so. I haven't noticed anything, but if they wanted to see each other, I have no doubt they would figure out how."

"Why was she at the house?" Chief Ligurio pressed.

"That I can't tell you," Alpha Strongclaw responded. "She wasn't supposed to be here and I didn't see her enter the property, let alone the house. Bermin, as I mentioned earlier, came with Boyer, but Opal wasn't with them. I'm not sure when she arrived, if it was planned, or how Bermin ended up back inside my house after I escorted him out." He shrugged and shook his head. "I think I must be getting old because this is making me realize just how much is going on behind my back."

Wynona felt a deep sense of sympathy for the shifter. It couldn't be easy to see so many issues happening right under your nose and have no idea about any of it.

You still think he's a suspect? Rascal asked.

Wynona looked at her husband. *I don't believe he's any more guilty than Barry, but until we DO have a killer, I don't think he can be taken off the list.*

She's right, Rascal, Violet chimed in. *No one's off until more evidence. Gotta play it fair.*

Rascal nodded, though he looked weary at the very thought.

Chief Ligurio pursed his lips. "Who might know? There's no way they were meeting in your house and no one knew."

Wynona's eyebrows pulled together. It was a good question…but who? Rascal's mother hadn't seemed to know either and the whole family had sworn that Opal wasn't there when Boyer had burst in. "Colby!" she shouted as a memory surfaced.

All the men in the room turned to look at her.

"Who?" Chief Ligurio asked.

Wynona shrank back a little. She had no idea if the note she'd watched Colby pass had anything to do with Opal, but it seemed likely. "Colby seemed to be cozy with the visitors. Maybe he knows something?" She decided she would leave it in Colby's hand to tell about the note. After all, it could be nothing of consequence.

Alpha Strongclaw pushed a hand through his hair and growled softly. "He would," the alpha muttered.

"I'll get him," Rascal said tightly. His shoulders were stiff and Wynona hated that she had played a part in that, but she hoped the lively brother would have some answers for them.

"You may go," Chief Ligurio told the alpha.

"I'd rather stay," the shifter said, standing and moving to the side. "If he refuses to answer, I'll interfere, otherwise I'll stay out of your way."

Earl Grey with a Hint of Murder

Chief Ligurio glared, but ultimately didn't fight.

It only took Rascal a couple of minutes to drag his brother into the room.

"Geez," Colby said, shaking off Rascal's hold. "What's your problem?"

"Sit!" Rascal barked.

Colby huffed a laugh and walked nonchalantly to the chair. "I didn't realize I was a wanted man." He brushed his fingernails against his chest. "Wait until I tell the girls this!"

Violet laughed. *I like this one.*

Chief Ligurio stared at the shifter. "Tell me about your relationship with the visitors earlier this evening. It sounds like you know them well."

Colby grinned and leaned back lazily in his chair. "Everyone here knows them. Boyer's a young pup who desperately wants Daddy's attention. Bermin is a brute who has more brawn than brain and Sartel's a beauty who's caught in the middle."

"Have you been aware of the relationship between your brother Barry and Ms. Marcel?" Chief Ligurio asked.

Colby shrugged and raised his eyebrows. "What relationship?"

Rascal grunted. "Answer the question."

Colby grinned and Wynona was amazed at how calm he appeared. She could feel his anxiety thrumming against her barrier, but thanks to Mrs. Strongclaw's suggestion, it wasn't truly affecting Wynona, she was merely aware of its presence. Colby settled deeper into his chair. "Old man Barry has had me running between him and his lady love for weeks." Colby smirked. "It's amazing how easy it's been to keep ya'll in the dark, you know?"

"Colby," Alpha Strongclaw snapped.

Colby winced at the reprimand in the tone, but his smile was back almost immediately. "Just callin' it like it is," he joked. "Barry needed an inside man." Colby chuckled. "Guess I'm a sucker for true love."

"What have you been doing to help them?" Chief Ligurio asked.

Colby pursed his lips. "Just the usual...playing guard for them when they meet behind the guest cabin, or distracting Mama when she gets a little too curious."

Wynona stilled. The note. He hadn't mentioned the note.

Either it wasn't about Opal, or there's something he's hiding, Violet muttered. *I'll bet a good bite on his fanny would make him talk.*

Hush, Wynona sent to her familiar, glancing at Rascal to make sure he hadn't heard the conversation. His stoic face said her barrier was doing well. *No fanny biting. Besides, I thought you liked him.*

He's got snark, I'll give him that, but lying is a whole other matter.

"Do you know if they had any designs to get rid of Bermin? Was the bodyguard interfering with their meetings?" Chief Ligurio continued.

Colby shook his head. "Nope. I'm just the muscles, not a fortune teller." He grinned at Wynona. "You could probably handle that though. You never did tell us how many powers you have." He winced again and shot a look at his father. "I didn't say anything wrong."

"Where were you during the murder?" Chief Ligurio asked.

Colby shook his head. "Don't know. I ate dinner, same as everyone else. Only time I saw him was when Dad and I had to kick them out."

"Does he usually accompany Opaline when she...visits?" Alpha Strongclaw asked. He ignored Chief Ligurio's dark look.

Colby shook his head. "Not that I know of. I was led to believe I was the only one who knew they were meeting at all." Those broad shoulders shrugged again. "But who knows? It wasn't like I was digging into all their little secrets."

"Don't go far," Chief Ligurio muttered, glancing down at his phone as he wrote in a few notes.

"You really think I might've killed Bermin?" Colby asked with a laugh. "That'd be asking for a death sentence. The whole Marcel pack would be down our throats and I'm not looking for a war.

Earl Grey with a Hint of Murder

Besides, why would I hurt the guy? He might be an idiot, but I've got no beef with him."

"Doesn't matter," Alpha Strongclaw stated. "Do as he says."

Colby rolled his eyes and stood, walking away as if he hadn't a care in the world, but Wynona could feel differently. What she couldn't tell was whether he was afraid because he was hiding something, or because he simply was anxious about being in an interrogation. Colby was fun and carefree, making it difficult to imagine him as a cold blooded killer.

You have a hard time imagining anyone as a cold blooded killer, Violet grumbled.

Maybe that's because I like to believe the best of creatures.

And maybe you just think everyone's as nice as you, the mouse shot back. *Face it, Wy. We've all got a little killer in us when necessary. Even you.*

A flashback of a time when Wynona had slipped into a dark place and her protective instincts for Rascal had taken over came to mind, and Wynona shivered. She knew Violet was right, but it wasn't a pleasant thought.

So we keep him on the list?

Violet's nose twitched. *I don't see how we can put him off...yet. But I don't think he had a good motive. The only thing I can see was if he was protecting Barry, or if he and Beefy got in a fight over Sartel.*

But Sartel wasn't here.

We didn't think Beefy was either.

Wynona sighed and nodded.

Rascal's hand landed on her lower back. "You okay?" he whispered.

Wynona nodded again. "Fine. Just trying to work it all out in my head. The murder itself just doesn't seem to make sense."

Rascal nodded. "I know. We have to be missing something."

"Agreed."

"Mrs. Strongclaw...please come in," Chief Ligurio said, his voice slightly more polite than it had been with Colby. "Have a seat."

Wynona put her focus back on the interrogating. They had lots of creatures to talk to and none of their clues were making sense. Not to mention, she would need to track down Colby at some point and find out why he lied, or at least, what he was hiding. That note meant something. Whether it had to do with the case was questionable, but it sat heavily in Wynona's mind and she knew she wouldn't be able to let it go until she had satisfied her curiosity.

And I get my bite in.

Wynona shook her head again. *No biting, Violet. I mean it.*

Violet grumbled and curled into a ball on Wynona's shoulder. *Party pooper.*

Holding back another sigh, Wynona focused. Right now she needed a useful clue and Violet's tendency toward violence wasn't going to help.

Chapter Twelve

Wynona rubbed her temples. "I'm really starting to hate this side gig," she muttered.

Just heal it, Violet grumbled sarcastically. *Only the most powerful witch in the world would constantly forget that she has the power to never hurt again.*

Wynona sighed and dropped her arms, glaring at Violet. "Have you eaten lately? You're getting grumpy."

Violet muttered again and turned her back.

Sighing, Wynona did as her familiar suggested and sent a small burst of magic to her migraine. Leaning back in her chair, Wynona stared at the window where the sun was just coming up. They'd spent all day yesterday talking to family and other pack members, but nothing had been revealed.

The Strongclaws knew nothing, though Wynona had yet to pin Colby down. Alpha Marcel had been completely belligerent and refused to answer much of anything, while Boyer was pale and looked like he was about to pass out. The neighboring shifter had had very little to say, though his attitude had been much different than his father's.

The evening had ended very late and Wynona was wiped out, but her mind wouldn't stop moving and sleep had been only a passing fancy.

Determined not to disturb her husband, she had quietly slipped from their room and come out into the small sitting room with a cup of hot tea. It wasn't her usual custom brew, but it was definitely better than nothing.

She took another sip, watching the light begin to shift over the forest, and tried to find serenity. There had to be something they were missing. Every case ended up that way. Some tiny clue, some overlooked piece, that always, *always,* led them in the right direction. And considering right now, they didn't have a direction at all, Wynona was desperate to see that piece.

You're thinking too hard, Violet offered.

Wynona nodded, her eyes still on the window. "I know, but I can't seem to get my brain under control. I can ease the pain, but I can't control my thoughts."

That'd be a handy trick, Violet quipped, climbing up the chair leg and settling in Wynona's thigh.

"I don't think I'd like it," Wynona whispered, absently petting her familiar. "I already have the ability to force someone's obedience and that's enough of a responsibility."

Figures a creature who wouldn't use it would get it.

A small smile tugged at Wynona's lips. Violet's snarky, violent side was interesting and kept Wynona on her toes, but deep down, she knew that the mouse wouldn't truly hurt someone just to hurt them.

Shows what you know, Violet sent back, obviously having understood Wynona's thoughts.

Wynona laughed softly, taking another drink, only to discover it was the last of the cup. She sighed and set it down.

What does it say?

Wynona paused. Should she look? Her readings in the tea leaves almost always left her with more questions than answers.

Earl Grey with a Hint of Murder

It can't hurt, Violet said, standing up on her hind legs with her whiskers twitching, as if she could read the leaves herself.

"I don't want to wake Rascal," Wynona said.

Violet rolled her eyes. *Coward.*

Wynona huffed. "Fine. But you're dealing with the cranky wolf then."

Easy peasy. Bring it.

Another smile spread across Wynona's face and she picked up Violet, leaving a small kiss on her soft head. "Thanks."

Violet wiggled, aiming for Wynona's shoulder, her favorite place to settle. Curling her tail around Wynona's neck, she settled in, skin on skin, to better help Wynona channel her magic.

"You ready?" Wynona asked.

Oh, the cliches I could answer that with. Violet sighed dramatically. *But only one will do...I was born ready.*

Shaking her head, Wynona closed her eyes and held a hand over her mug. Immediately, a charge went through the air and Wynona felt her hair begin to lift. She kept her concentration, having been through this process several times. While Wynona enjoyed staying in the background, her magic enjoyed a little drama.

Careful to keep the flow consistent and controlled, Wynona heard the wind begin to shift small objects in the room and soon some of the furniture was moving slightly. The cup rose from her hand and Wynona knew if she opened her eyes, it would be spinning in the air, but instead, she focused on control and kept her hand outstretched to catch the cup when it was done.

Sweat beaded on her forehead at the waterfall of magic that wanted to erupt, but Wynona knew she was stronger than she'd ever been. Hours upon hours of practice and discovering new powers through her investigations with the police department had given her the ability to be in charge of her magic, which often felt like a living, breathing entity. Unfortunately, it was one that wanted freedom and that was the one thing Wynona couldn't give it.

Just a little bit more, she thought through her tight jaw. The last couple of moments felt like hours, but finally the wind died down and the furniture stopped moving and Wynona was able to relax. She breathed out a long breath and slumped in her seat just as the mug fell into her hand.

"Please tell me that was worth it," Rascal said in a low, gravelly tone before yawning and stretching his arms in the air.

Wynona gave him a sheepish smile. "It was Violet's idea."

Way to throw me under the bus! Violet retorted.

"I told you I would," Wynona responded easily.

Violet snorted. *Read the leaves, Witch Woman. At least that'll give me something to work with.*

Wynona turned the mug and stared at the patterns in the bottom.

"Well?" Rascal asked, his back turned to her as he rummaged through the small fridge.

It looks like a bunch of animals, Violet offered.

Wynona nodded and pointed with her free hand. "That's the Falcon. It means..." She hesitated, but really...there was no point in holding back. "It means a persistent enemy."

Rascal snorted. "That could be anything."

Wynona pointed to the next one. "That's the Hare, which tells us there's a long journey ahead."

Is that last one a lion?

"Very good, Vi. Yes, a lion means greatness through powerful friends." Wynona sighed and set the cup to the side, brushing her chaotic hair out of her face. The wind from a tea reading always made it unruly. "I don't know what I'm supposed to take from that."

Rascal walked over and kissed her forehead before heading to the table with a bowl of cereal. "Take what you want from that, but you make your own destiny."

Wynona nodded, her mind running with the prophecies. A persistent enemy...was it one that was still going to show up? Or one that had already been in her life? One could claim Death, himself, was her enemy, since he seemed to follow her everywhere she went.

"I can hear you thinking," Rascal said through a mouthful.

Earl Grey with a Hint of Murder

"Sorry," Wynona said. She turned to him. "I just...Granny used to actually understand and tea reading helped her. There's got to be things in my readings that are useful." She tucked some hair behind her ear. "I just wish I had someone to help teach me a bit more."

"Careful what you wish for," Rascal said, his tone having dropped.

Wynona frowned as she watched him slowly rise from the table, one side of his lip curling. "What do you mean?" He didn't answer, but his eyes never left their front door and in a few moments, Wynona heard multiple voices heading their way. "You've got to be kidding," she muttered, jumping to her feet and running to the bedroom to grab a sweater. She hadn't exactly planned to meet company in her nightgown, but knowing who was coming meant there wouldn't be time for a full change.

"Call off the hounds," Uncle Arune said wryly as he walked through the front door without knocking.

Rascal growled and stepped forward. "What are you doing here?" he snapped.

Uncle Arune's eyes darted to Wynona, who stood in the bedroom doorway, arms folded over her chest, before coming back to Rascal. "I don't want to hurt anyone. Call them off and we'll chat."

"Better do it," Celia said, pushing past her uncle and coming inside as if she owned the place.

Arune rolled his eyes, but stepped aside and allowed Rayn to walk in. Her smile would normally cause Wynona to smile back, but right now the group was anything but welcome.

"Just how many creatures did you bring?" Rascal demanded.

Prim flounced in, followed by a very serious Daemon. He gave Wynona an apologetic look while Prim ran across the room to hug her best friend.

"We didn't want to let them come on their own," Daemon explained. "And Chief didn't ask me to accompany him yesterday."

"So how did you manage to get here today?" Rascal pointed out.

"He's taking some vacation leave," Prim supplied, leaning against the wall next to Wynona. "We all are."

Growls and snarls from outside the cabin grew so loud Wynona could barely hear and she covered her ears. "What's going on out there?" she shouted at Rascal.

"It would seem your uncle is using a spell to hold them at bay and they don't like it," Rascal sneered. "Packs are territorial and the land has been breached...without permission, I might add...and your uncle didn't seem to feel the need to check in with my father before coming straight to our little cabin."

Wynona rubbed her tired eyes. "Uncle Arune...you can't just march in here like you're in charge."

"Believe it or not, I actually do have a reason for coming," he argued. "But time is of the essence and I see no reason to have to ask permission to talk to my own niece."

"Drop the spell," Rascal demanded.

"Call them off," Arune shot back. "If I drop the spell, I'll just have to use something else to keep them from hurting me and mine and somehow I doubt you would enjoy that."

"You promised," Wynona said softly.

"I promised not to attack, I didn't promise not to defend. In fact, I made that very clear," Arune said bluntly.

Wynona closed her eyes, seeking strength and calm in the chaos of noises surrounding her supposedly-honeymoon cabin. Her life was beginning to look worse than the Cursed Circus.

Next time we leave, we're heading straight to the human world, Rascal sent her. *They'll never find us there.*

I wouldn't be too sure, Wynona muttered mentally. Deciding she was done with the male stand-off happening right in front of her, she reached into the air, grabbed the magic she could feel and twisted it until the spell Arune had been using snapped.

Her uncle's head snapped back as if he'd been punched, but when he turned to her, it was with eagerness and pride in his eyes.

Ho, ho, Violet cackled. *Let's have a little fun.*

Earl Grey with a Hint of Murder

Realizing that the wolves were now scrambling up the front porch steps, a purple bubble went up on every entrance to the cabin, door and window alike, stopping them all in their tracks.

Huffing, Wynona used her magic to push her family and guests to one side of the room and walked to the front door. "Alpha Strongclaw?" she called out, unsure which wolf was her father-in-law.

He transformed immediately, his face nearly purple with rage. "Let us in," he demanded, causing every wolf to shift at the weight of his command.

Wynona bowed her head slightly, trying to let him know she acknowledged his authority, but she held her ground. "I want to apologize," she said softly, knowing he could easily hear her. "They shouldn't have come onto the property like that." She turned, showing the angry alpha the group. "This is my sister, Celia."

Celia gave a happy little wave, obviously not the least bit upset that Wynona had her pinned to one side of the room.

"My best friend, Primrose Meadows and another officer, Daemon Skymaw. He works with Rascal and is a personal friend of ours."

Daemon nodded while Prim bounced on her toes.

"And last, we have my Uncle Arune and his soulmate Dr. Rayn." Wynona turned back to the alpha. "I'm asking for a personal favor that you allow them on your land," she continued. "I know their arrival wasn't proper and my uncle seems to have no manners whatsoever when it comes to dealing with any type of social situation."

Violet cackled so hard she choked, while Prim giggled behind her hands. Arune, for his part, looked bored.

"But he felt the visit was important and that time was of the essence."

"Does his arrival have anything to do with my son?" Alpha Strongclaw asked.

Wynona shrugged. "I don't know. And I won't know until we can all sit down and talk. But I can't do that if their lives are being threatened," she ignored Arune's scoff, "by your entire pack."

Alpha Strongclaw eyed the group once more. "I'm willing to grant permission, but they have to meet some demands in return."

"Of course," Wynona responded.

"If they threaten or hurt any member of my pack in any way," Alpha Strongclaw stated, "my agreement to allow them visitation rights, is off. I won't stop my pack and family from tearing them to shreds if necessary."

"Understood," Wynona responded. "And one-hundred-percent agreed to." Wynona felt the hairs on the back of her neck rise and she spun, pinning Arune with a glare, knowing that he wanted to argue.

After a moment he held his hands in the air and sighed. "I already said, I'll defend, but I won't attack."

Wynona turned back to the alpha.

His slow nod gave her the courage she needed to let down the barrier between them.

Alpha Strongclaw turned and sent the group away, waiting until even the last reluctant wolf had disappeared, before spinning and walking inside the cabin.

The little two-person dwelling was becoming extremely crowded as he closed the door behind him and stood guard. "I won't be able to hold my wife off forever," he warned Wynona.

Wynona gave him a wry smile. "I'm surprised you held her off at all."

He grunted and looked back at the group. "So...Arune...tell me why you've come."

Arune narrowed his eyes and set his jaw.

"Anything you have to say to me can be said in front of him," Wynona warned her uncle. "After all...Alpha Strongclaw is my family too." She was positive Arune muttered something like "pity" under his breath, but Wynona ignored it.

His nostrils flared and his pale cheeks were slightly colored when he turned to Wynona. "While I don't know everything that has happened out here since you left, I needed to warn you...that your father is behind it all."

Chapter Thirteen

Rascal scoffed. "Her father? President Le Doux had nothing to do with killing a girl's bodyguard."

Arune scowled. "You have no idea what that warlock is capable of," he snapped.

Wynona walked to the dining table and sat down. "Why don't we all relax for a second. I don't have enough food to feed everyone, but–" Her words cut off with a knock on the door.

Alpha Strongclaw huffed. "Woman never listens," he grumbled before turning around and opening the door.

Mrs. Strongclaw stood in the doorway with a veritable army of shifters behind her, each holding a tray of steaming food.

How in the world did she do that? Wynona asked Rascal.

He gave her a smug grin. *I don't know and I don't care. I'm starved.*

Well, I do, Violet argued. *That was amazing and I need to know how. Imagine the parties I could have...*

Wynona shook her head and stood up. "Thank you, Mrs...Mom," she corrected, coming up behind Alpha Strongclaw. "It was really generous of you to bring that." Wynona took the tray from the closest pack member and brought it inside.

Prim and Rayn followed suit, helping bring the food in while the Strongclaws all glared at each other, more than likely having an internal conversation that Wynona didn't want to hear.

"Thank you," Wynona said to a young woman who set down a tray in the kitchen. The dining table was small and had quickly been filled. Now they were maneuvering food around the small kitchen and Wynona hoped they wouldn't have to start putting food on the bed or the floor. Surely there was a way to fit it all.

The girl nodded and Wynona realized it was the same young woman who had been with Boyer and Bermin. The one Colby had flirted with.

"You were with Boyer," Wynona said. "You're from the Marcel pack."

The young woman looked startled, then nodded, her face pale.

"I think I heard it, but could you remind me of your name?"

She chewed her lip and looked around, but everyone else was still occupied. "Sartel," she finally replied.

"That's right. You're friends with Opal? Boyer made it sound like you two were close?" Wynona asked.

Sartel nodded. "We're best friends."

Wynona smiled, trying to help calm the nervous young woman. "What brings you here? I thought Alpha Marcel didn't want his pack spending time here."

Sartel shrugged. "We used to come a lot before Alpha Marcel got upset about Baryn. We've all been close since we were pups."

Wynona nodded. "It must be hard to have them both gone," she said. "I'm sorry."

Sartel's eyes filled with tears. "I wish I knew if they were okay. No one can pick up their trail and that worries me."

"Understandable." Wynona gave the young woman's arm a quick squeeze and rub and bit her cheek to keep from offering deeper assurance. Barry and Opal needed to stay hidden or this would all go downhill. "But don't worry. We'll get it all sorted soon."

Sartel nodded and wiped at her face.

"Sartel," Mrs. Strongclaw scolded, coming up behind them. "Child, you need to get home. You know your alpha isn't going to be happy you're here."

Sartel nodded and darted away, ducking past the alpha and out the door without talking to anyone else.

Mrs. Strongclaw watched her go with a shaking head. "That girl. She's been sneaking over here to spend time with the boys for years." Making a face, Mrs. Strongclaw turned to Wynona. "Colby flirts mercilessly with her, but I'm not sure she thinks of him that way." Mrs. Strongclaw tsked her tongue. "I just hope nobody gets their heart broken. Alpha Marcel won't care how they feel about each other, if it came down to it."

Wynona made agreeing noises, then decided it was time to call everything to order. She clapped her hands, adding a little magic to make it loud enough to gain everyone's attention. "Why don't we all grab plates and we can sit and eat while discussing what's going on?"

Murmurs of the crowd's agreement met her ears and Wynona stepped back, guiding traffic as each creature filled a plate and found a seat. While the food trays had found homes on tables and counters, there certainly wasn't enough room for every creature to have a chair and several individuals ended up leaning against the wall or sitting on the floor.

Wynona's hostess side hated it, but she pushed the emotions aside. It wasn't like there was anything she could do. It was what it was and they were all adults, they could deal with it.

She cleared her throat. "Uncle Arune, perhaps you could share your thoughts a little more thoroughly with us? I have to admit that I'm of the same mind as Rascal. I don't see how anything that's happened here could possibly have anything to do with my father."

Arune set his plate in his lap and stuck his chin in the air. "The very first thing you need to know is that everything, *absolutely everything*, has to do with your father."

"We aren't under his jurisdiction out here," Alpha Strongclaw said forcefully.

Arune shook his head. "While I'd like to tell you that you're safe, you're not. Anything that escapes his notice is because he wanted to ignore it. That warlock's reach is deeper than you can imagine and nothing happens without his fingerprint on it."

Rascal growled. "I'd like to see you prove that. How does this have to do with him? My brother and his girlfriend have been meeting behind their parents' backs and somehow her bodyguard was killed. Please explain to me how President Le Doux is involved."

"I don't know."

Rascal raised an eyebrow. "That's it? I don't know?"

Arune scowled back and Wynona felt the tension of the room rise again. "Despite my many powers, I'm not all-seeing," he snapped. "But when I heard there'd been a murder, I knew I had to warn you."

Wynona was extremely grateful that Arune had yet to mention the visitors she had sent him. Hopefully, he would understand the need for secrecy if she sent two creatures to hide at her house.

He might not know, Violet offered. *He's been staying with Rayn.*

"Hmmm..." Wynona murmured, turning her attention back to her uncle's speech.

"Somewhere, in a dark corner where light no longer shines and no sane creature would ever venture, lies a connection to your father. And he likes it that way. He likes having power over life and death and as soon as he can get Wynona out of the way or bring her to his side, he plans to rule all of the paranormal world like the lunatic he is," Arune finished with a flourish. He had a flair for the dramatic, Wynona had to give him that.

Shouts and growls erupted and Wynona clapped again, this time the sound like thunder. It had been an automatic reaction, but the results were spectacular. The cabin shook and the voices stopped, all eyes turning to her.

Earl Grey with a Hint of Murder

"I don't know whether Uncle Arune is right or not," Wynona said, purposefully keeping her voice soft, hoping no one would be able to hear the tightness of it. "But we need to be willing to hear him out. He's spent decades cursed by a witch that possibly helped my father kill my grandfather, in the very bid for power that Arune is talking about." Wynona slowly set her plate at the table and stood from her seat. "We're all adults and despite the differences of our creatures, we have much more in common than we're unique. In fact, I would say that some of the strongest creatures in our world, who would most definitely be opposed to my father becoming the next emperor, are right in this room and if you could simply stop acting like children, maybe...just maybe...our combined forces and minds will be enough to not only figure out this murder, but find a way to keep my father from power."

The silence was deafening and after a moment, Wynona finally realized exactly what she had said. Her eyes immediately went to Rascal and the anguish in his expression was almost her undoing.

I didn't mean it that way, she hurried to send him. *I just wanted everyone to stop fighting.*

His eyes closed and he hung his head. *Whether you meant it or not,* he sent back, *we both know that the odds of you escaping from his shadow are slim to none.* Rascal's eyes were filled with moisture when he opened them again. *I just got you,* he whispered hoarsely. *I'm not ready to start a war at the risk of your life. Maybe that makes me a coward, but I'm just not ready, Wy. But how do we escape it? We can't even have a proper honeymoon without a death getting in the way. If your father really is behind these things, then he's been working for an awfully long time to keep you from the path your uncle wants you to be on.*

Wynona ran over, throwing her arms around his neck and breaking into tears. Rascal's large arms came around her, nearly squeezing Wynona's breath from her lungs, but she didn't want him to ease up. She'd been feeling for a while everything he had just put into words. The harder she tried to get away from him, the closer her father seemed to get.

"As touching as this scene is," Celia interrupted, "I think we need to take Wynona's little peace speech into consideration."

Wynona leaned back from Rascal just enough to look at her sister as she sniffed and wiped at her face. "What?" she asked, completely shocked at the words Celia had just said.

Celia rolled her eyes. "Believe it or not, I don't want the old man making the rules either and if you finally managed to wake up enough to realize that you're going to have to lead the charge for his take down, then hallelujah and amen to that. Because it might be the first competent thing I've ever heard you say."

Wynona shook her head and leaned into Rascal's chest again. Leave it to Celia to fill her praise with underhanded remarks.

Are we sure Arune wasn't her actual caregiver? They seem to have an awful lot in common, Rascal pointed out.

Pretty sure, Wynona answered. *Sarcasm and rudeness must run in the family.*

He kissed the top of her head just as another knock came at the door.

"What now?" Alpha Strongclaw barked, yanking open the door to an unimpressed vampire.

Chief Ligurio's red eyes went through the room, landing just a bit longer on Celia, before taking in everyone else. "I missed the memo."

"Come in, Chief," Rascal called out. "The meeting is impromptu, but your presence is welcome." Rascal made a point of looking around. "If you can find room, that is."

"There's a few inches next to my chair," Celia called out cheekily, swinging one leg over the other and looking a little too pleased with herself.

Wynona knew that vampires didn't actually blush, but if they could...that's exactly what Chief Ligurio would be doing right now. As it was, his hand came up to his neck, but he forcefully shoved it back down before clearing his throat and walking across the room to the spot Celia had indicated.

Wynona had to bite the inside of her cheek to keep from smiling. Those two were still crazy about each other, even if they weren't ready to admit it out loud. Pride was awfully good at keeping people apart.

Chief Ligurio cleared his throat a second time, gaining the attention of the room. "While I'm interested to hear what was going on in here, I have the lab reports." He handed Rascal a manila folder.

Rascal took it and began pulling out papers, then thumbing through them. Before Wynona could get very far in reading them, his head jerked up toward his boss. "Are they sure?"

Chief Ligurio nodded. "Yes."

"Despite the many talents that Wynona was referring to earlier," Arune drawled, "mind reading seems to elude everyone in this group. Care to share?"

Rascal was quiet as he flipped through the papers one more time. "Bermin," Rascal looked at Arune, "the dead bodyguard…was killed from deep scratches on his neck."

"We knew that," Alpha Strongclaw said, folding his arms over his chest.

"But there were signs of other injuries," Rascal continued.

"What?" Mrs. Strongclaw shouted.

Wynona's head jerked. She'd actually forgotten that Mrs. Strongclaw had stayed after bringing the food. The chatty woman had been exceptionally quiet.

Rascal took in a long breath. "There was muscle bruising under his jaw and on his abdomen."

"I didn't see any of that," Alpha Strongclaw said, stepping forward.

Rascal shook his head, handing Wynona the papers. "They were partially healed," Rascal pointed out. "His wolf healing was helping with those."

The room grew quiet.

"There were tiny scratches on his hands that must have been larger as well," Rascal said, pushing a hand through his hair. "Because they found smears of his blood on his jeans, consistent with someone wiping their hands."

"So what exactly does all this mean?" Prim asked, her hand tightly clasped in Daemon's.

Daemon looked down at her, then back up at Wynona and Rascal. "It would appear he was in a fight before the final blow landed," Daemon said in a low tone.

Rascal nodded.

"Is there any way to tell if it was all with the same person?" Wynona asked as she read the results. "Can we tell how much earlier the first fight happened?"

"Wolf healing makes that nearly impossible," Chief Ligurio pointed out, his hand resting on the back of Celia's chair. It was the closest Wynona had ever seen them stand without threatening each other.

"But they couldn't have been very far apart," Mrs. Strongclaw said hoarsely. Her eyes were wide and frightened. "Bruising heals very quickly and scratches on his hands would only last an hour or two. If they weren't quite gone, then the two fights couldn't have been far from each other."

Rascal closed his eyes. "Depending on the depth of the initial bruising and scratches, they could have been as close as ten or fifteen minutes from each other."

Wynona frowned. "But Barry was at the dinner table. He couldn't have been involved in the first fight."

"Where was he before dinner?" Chief Ligurio asked. His eyes went around the room when no one answered.

Alpha Strongclaw finally shook his head, admitting he didn't know.

Wynona's stomach churned. Barry had to be innocent. He *had* to be. The mild mannered wolf wouldn't have killed another shifter, especially in cold blood. But how could she prove it? She quickly glanced at the papers again. "Chief?"

"Yes?"

Wynona's eyes skimmed the page. "The report says they found four wolf hairs on his clothes? All blonde, apparently."

Chief Ligurio's brows pulled together.

Wynona looked up. "Why didn't they test it?"

"I..." He hesitated and frowned. "I don't know."

Wynona held out the papers. "It says they found fur but didn't send for a DNA test. I think we need to do that."

Chief Ligurio grabbed the stack and stared at the paragraph before he cursed under his breath.

"They probably assumed it was Bermin's," Rascal grumbled. "Azirad's getting sloppy."

"Or his new hire is as useless as he is loud," Chief Ligurio snapped. He pulled out his cell phone and walked toward the front door. "As soon as I have this fixed, we'll talk about whatever this group thought they were doing without me."

The front door slammed and the room stayed quiet for a few seconds.

"And now?" Rascal pressed. "Still think the president's involved?"

Arune's eyes flared for just a moment. "Look deep enough," he warned, "and you'll find his boney fingers everywhere. Nothing happened just now that has caused me to adjust my convictions."

Chapter Fourteen

Wynona sent another jolt of magic to her head, easing the returning migraine while the crowd slowly dispersed from her cabin. Mrs. Strongclaw still hadn't said much, but she was currently showing Arune, Rayne and Celia to guest cabins that they could stay in while the investigation was ongoing. To Wynona's surprise, Chief Ligurio had asked for one as well, claiming that he wanted to personally be involved in this case and would appoint another to handle the precinct until he came back. Daemon and Prim were going to go back to the city and keep track of things from there.

Rascal snorted. "Too bad I'm the one supposed to do that while he's gone," he muttered.

"Who'll do it then?" Wynona asked, wiggling her fingers to wash the dishes that were piled in her sink.

"My mom will be back for those, you know," Rascal said as he stretched out on the couch, folding one ankle over the other.

"I know, but at least I can send them back to the main house clean." Wynona paused. "Are she and your father going to be okay?"

Rascal snorted. "They're fine. A little marital spat never hurt anyone."

Wynona made a face. She wasn't so sure about that, but she was glad the Strongclaws wouldn't let one situation break them apart. Another question was sitting on the edge of her tongue, but she was slightly afraid to bring it up. There was so much unknown between them and their marriage was so new. Would it be wrong to talk about the heavy topics? Should she wait until things had settled? Or maybe when the investigation was over? Would some of it even matter at that point?

"I can hear you thinking," Rascal said wryly, cracking open one eye. He grinned and held out his hand. "Come here."

Hesitantly, Wynona walked over and took his hand, sitting down on the edge of the couch when he tugged on her fingers.

"Wy...if you think I'm gonna run away with my tail between my legs just because you've got some stupid, major fight coming up with the fate of the entire paranormal civilization resting on your shoulders...you don't know me very well."

Wynona shook her head. "I wasn't even thinking clearly when I said it," she argued.

"Maybe not," Rascal said, turning onto his side and propping his head up on his elbow. "But I think we both knew the admission was eventually coming. We can't run forever." Rascal's voice dropped. "I meant what I said about not being ready but...sometimes the only way to outrun a storm is to run at it."

Wynona's vision grew wavy with tears. "I don't want to be president," she said thickly. "I don't want to fight my dad. He's not much of a parent, but I don't want to fight. It's going to get ugly, we both know it is, and someone or something is going to get hurt. Possibly even killed." Wynona's breathing was growing out of control and her tears began to spill down her cheeks.

Rascal groaned and reached up, wiping at the moisture. "You're killing me, sweetheart," he whispered. "Don't cry. You're not alone. Or did you not listen to yourself today? You've managed to gather around you the exact group of creatures who have every resource you will ever need in taking down your father. You have the police, the vampires, the wolves, witches, dragons and even a black hole and random fairy on your side. How could he possibly win?"

"He already beat Arune and Rayn once," Wynona argued. "And Granny! How can we hope to compete with that?"

"Ah...but you're forgetting one thing." Rascal gave her a significant look. "They didn't have you."

Wynona huffed and wiped at her face.

"You forget that your powers are the key to taking him down. You can't do it alone and none of us would ask you to, but your powers were so great that your own grandmother cursed you in order to keep you from your father's clutches. If your parents had control of you, they'd never lose. They *need* you. Arune and Rayn both said as much. Your father hasn't made his move yet because he knows you can oppose him and he's not confident enough in his win to step out publicly." Rascal grinned devilishly. "Just imagine being so powerful that the second most powerful being in the paranormal world is too scared of you to act out. That's pretty amazing."

Wynona shook her head. "I can't risk all your lives," she said, standing and walking away before he could stop her. "If I take this on, I'll lose someone I love and I don't think I can handle that."

Rascal didn't respond and the topic was dropped, but Wynona knew it hadn't truly gone away. She'd have to address it fully sooner or later, but right now she was absolutely going to use the murder investigation as a means of procrastination.

No judging, Violet said as she scuttled into the kitchen. *But we both know you're not dumb enough to let him win.*

Wynona began humming to herself. If her mind was full of music, she wouldn't be able to hear her familiar's snarky thoughts.

Nice try, but I won't press...for now.

"We need to figure out our next step," Rascal said with a yawn.

Wynona turned to look at him and folded her arms over her

chest. "You're awfully calm for someone whose family has been accused of murder."

Rascal sighed and sat up. "I'm ready to tear down the compound, if I thought it would clear my brother's name. But we both know that wouldn't help." He stood and stretched. "Instead, I'm going to figure out what to do next and we'll take it from there. One step at a time is all I've got," he said with a shrug.

How boringly mature of you, Violet muttered.

Rascal smirked and Wynona shook her head while she wiped her hands on a dishtowel. "Actually, I know exactly what we should do next."

"You do?"

Wynona nodded. "We need to talk to Colby."

Rascal opened the front door and they walked out into the sunshine. "Why Colby?"

Wynona gave Rascal a look. "Because he lied in his interview."

That calm that Rascal had been emitting evaporated. "What do you mean, *lied*?"

Wynona held up her hand. "Hold on and we'll talk to him together."

Rascal picked up the pace. "We need to make it quick. Chief was still planning to come back after he reams whoever was responsible for the oversight at the lab."

Wynona followed as quickly as she could. She wasn't the shortest of women, but Rascal could outpace her any day.

He grinned over his shoulder. "I'll bet you could use magic to keep up, you know."

She rolled her eyes at him. "Not everything is fixable with magic."

"Maybe not." He opened the back door of the main house. "But most things are."

Wynona stepped inside the mudroom and waited for Rascal to lead the way. "Where are we going?" she whispered as they made their way upstairs.

"His room," Rascal stated. "With Dad running around trying to fix things, odds are Colb is laying low and refusing to do any work."

Violet snorted. *Sounds like my kind of shifter.*

Rascal choked on a laugh and pushed open a door without knocking.

"Hey!" Colby shouted, jumping up from his gaming chair. Bright lights and flashes were crossing a screen and Wynona tried to figure out what was going on, but she was so out of touch with the video game world that nothing she was seeing made sense to her. "What're you doing?" Colby cried, turning off the television and slumping back into his seat. He huffed. "You have your own cabin, big guy."

Rascal walked over and picked his brother up by the collar of his shirt. "Why did you lie?" he demanded, giving Colby a small shake.

Colby immediately began to growl and Wynona could see his skin rippling, which was always a dangerous sign. "Put. Me. Down." His eyes flashed a very familiar gold color.

"Rascal," Wynona said carefully. "I don't think—"

Rascal gave Colby a shake. "What did you do? How could you set up Barry like this?"

"WHAT ARE YOU TALKING ABOUT?" Colby bellowed back.

Wynona winced, she had to take care of this.

I don't think Colby really wants Rascal to put him down. Doesn't he realize what those words mean in the human world?

Wynona ignored the snarky banter of her familiar and snapped her fingers, bringing both men to a halt. "Rascal," Wynona said in a low tone. "This isn't how we do this. I know solving the case is important, but we were already worried about being too close and this is too much." With a shift of her hand, Wynona separated the men, then released them, but held both within a bubble.

Rascal growled at his brother and paced the small confines of his space. "How could you do that to your brother?" he demanded.

"I don't know what you're talking about!" Colby shouted back, pounding his fists against his shield.

Earl Grey with a Hint of Murder

"Stop it!" Wynona hissed. "Rascal. I mean it! Get yourself under control. This isn't like you at all!"

Rascal squeezed his eyes shut and put his fists to his temple. "I can't...I feel..."

Wynona paused and let herself tune into what was going on. Thinning her emotional shield just a touch, she focused on Rascal and gasped. She had no words for what was going on, but she could feel a fight going on inside. Anger and violence were warring his controlled, rational side and it was unlike anything Wynona had ever seen before.

What in the paranormal world? Violet asked, her nose twitching.

"Have you ever seen anything like it?" Wynona asked.

Violet shook her head. *No...except, sort of...*

Wynona jumped back when Rascal burst into a wolf and snarled at the barrier, tearing at it with his teeth.

"What's happening to him?" Colby asked, his tone changing from angry to fearful.

Wynona shook her head. She could feel Rascal's power against her shield and it shocked her how strong it was. His golden eyes were trained on Colby and she realized he hadn't looked at her once. Taking a chance, she stepped in front of the angry wolf, creating a visual barrier between Rascal and Colby.

The snarling immediately stopped, but Rascal's sides were heaving.

Wy...you know what you need to do, Violet said.

Wynona blinked several times and kept shifting as Rascal moved to be able to see Colby again. He wasn't in his human mind at all. At the moment, he was all wolf, but still wasn't willing to growl at Wynona. Something in his wild side seemed to recognize that she was important to him. But the chaos in his brain was hurting Wynona to listen to.

Wy...

Wynona's vision grew blurry, but she nodded and waved her hand toward Rascal. "Sleep," she whispered.

The growling stopped and Rascal swayed on his paws before eventually slumping into a heap and starting to snore.

"What the heck just happened?" Colby asked breathlessly.

Wynona turned to look at her brother in law. "I was actually hoping you could tell me," she said hoarsely, trying hard not to cry. Something wasn't right, but she had no idea where to even begin to figure it out.

"He's becoming an alpha."

Both Wynona and Colby jerked toward Alpha Strongclaw's deep voice. "Dad," Colby breathed. "Did you see that?"

Alpha Strongclaw looked at Wynona and raised his eyebrows. "Was anyone hurt?"

She shook her head, causing tears to spill over.

"Why don't you release Colby, and we can talk while Rascal sleeps." Alpha Strongclaw sighed and started back down the hall. "You can meet me in my office."

Wynona looked at Colby. "Do I just leave him here?"

Colby scratched the back of his head and shrugged. "I guess so? I'm not sure what Dad meant when he said Rascal's becoming an alpha. I've never seen anyone go wild like that."

"I've heard of shifters going wild," Wynona said, turning back to look at Rascal. "But I thought it only happened when they spent too long in their animal."

"Hey, sis. Let me out, huh?"

"Sorry." Wynona let go of Colby's shield, but double checked that Rascal's was back in place. His mind was quiet now that he was asleep, but with as much power as was pulsing through him, she wasn't sure how long he would stay that way, especially if she put her focus on other things.

"Whew." Colby stepped up to her side and threw an arm around her shoulders. "Come on. Dad'll have answers and Rascal can sleep it off."

Wynona nodded, but her tears continued to fall. She let Colby lead her, her eyes too full of liquid to see straight.

Earl Grey with a Hint of Murder

It'll be fine, Violet assured her. *I'll stay here and keep an eye on things. But I expect a full report, you hear me?*

Thank you, Wynona sent back. She needed to talk to Alpha Strongclaw to find out what was going on, but leaving Rascal felt terrible. Violet's kind gesture was much appreciated.

You can thank me with a cookie later.

Done, Wynona promised. She sniffed, wiped at her face and straightened her shoulders. Time to get this figured out. There were simply too many things going on at once and she needed to solve at least one of them before her life completely fell apart.

Chapter Fifteen

Alpha Strongclaw was sitting behind his desk, looking ten years older than he had the day before when Wynona had first met him. There were dark circles under his eyes and his skin looked paler, giving him the haunted look of the weary.

"Have a seat," he murmured, waving toward the unoccupied chairs.

Wynona sat in one, with Colby in the other.

Sighing heavily, Alpha Strongclaw leaned back, eyeing the two of them. "While I have questions for you, son, I'm sure Wynona would like an explanation for her husband's behavior." He tilted his chin down and raised his eyebrows.

Wynona nodded, though hesitantly. "I've never seen him get like that before. I mean...he's always been protective, but this was more than that. It's like his wolf had completely taken over."

Alpha Strongclaw nodded and pinched the bridge of his nose. "We call it 'becoming'. All alphas go through it as they come into their leadership powers, if you will." He looked up at Wynona. "Rascal has always had alpha tendencies, so this isn't a surprise." He

Earl Grey with a Hint of Murder

leaned back, his eyes glancing to Colby. "What *is* a surprise is what brought them out and how strong they are."

Wynona frowned. "What do you mean?"

"Usually a becoming happens when a wolf is preparing to start leading." Alpha Strongclaw's bright golden eyes pinned Wynona in place, looking much stronger than they had only moments before. "Since I have no intention of stepping down, I can only guess that something about your relationship with Rascal or the case started to bring the powers forward." Alpha Strongclaw grunted. "And the strength of them is usually enough to make a wolf moody, not to completely take away his common sense."

"Can we stop it?" Wynona asked.

Alpha Strongclaw shook his head. "He's going to have to go through it. There's really nothing we can do about it except wait him out. You'll find there are times when he's extremely calm, almost too calm, and there will be times when he's like a teapot ready to explode." The alpha slowly shook his head. "I wish I could tell you more, but I've never seen it happen quite like this, so it's uncharted territory for all of us."

Wynona tucked her hair behind her ear. "And just what are these alpha powers he's developing?"

Alpha Strongclaw clasped his hands on the top of the desk. "The power of his voice, for one," Alpha Strongclaw explained. "I'm sure you've noticed that I have the ability to order those in my pack into a certain level of obedience."

Wynona nodded.

"Every alpha's level of obedience varies." One side of Alpha Strongclaw's lips lifted up. "I'm guessing Rascal's will be exceptionally strong." The smile fell. "Although, without a pack, I'm not sure how well it will work for him."

"Anything else?" Wynona pressed.

"Calmness in times of trouble. The ability to communicate with his wolves or pack. Extra physical strength and his other senses will be heightened. His vision, smell and hearing will all become more than other wolves'."

Wynona twisted her fingers together. "I can feel power pulsing through him," she said softly. "I don't know how long my spell will hold him under."

"Let it sit for now," the alpha said calmly. He turned to his other son. "Sit, Colbium. I think it's time you told us why you lied to the chief."

Colby huffed and sat down. "I don't know what you're talking about," he argued. "Just like with Rascal."

Alpha Strongclaw looked at Wynona and gave her the floor. "The note," Wynona said, then cleared her throat. "What note did you pass to Barry at the table yesterday?"

Colby's eyes widened. "Between Rascal's new powers and yours, I can tell this family is headed in the wrong direction."

"Colbium," Alpha Strongclaw snapped.

Colby grunted and shifted in his seat. "It's not my fault that the stronger creatures get, the less fun they like to have." He rolled his eyes at his father's glower. "Fine. I already told you that I had been helping Barry and Opal meet up at times. They needed an inside wolf and I was happy to play the role."

"What did the note say?" Wynona asked.

Colby turned his head to look at Wynona. "If your sibling asked you to help them spend time with their mate, wouldn't you do it?"

Alpha Strongclaw growled low. "Enough, Colbium," he snapped.

Wynona put up her hand to show the alpha she wasn't upset at the question. "It's alright," she assured her father-in-law. Twisting in her seat, she faced Colby. "While I don't have a good relationship with my family, my sister *has* asked for my help. And I gave her what I could." Wynona tilted her head to the side. "I'm not condemning you, Colby. I'm not here to say what you did was right or wrong. But I am trying to help find the creature that killed Bermin, and I'm trying to clear your brother's name in the process. That note could have had repercussions, whether you realize it or not. I've helped with enough cases to know that even small, insignificant occurrences cause ripples in a pond." She raised her eyebrows. "Is the note so personal? I'd be surprised if they were passing love letters the old fashioned way."

Colby snorted and looked down at his lap, his fingers clenching and unclenching against his knees. "No, it wasn't a love note. At least not as far as I know." He huffed. "Usually they're times and places to meet, and I assumed this one was no different."

Wynona finally realized why Colby was so defensive. "You didn't read it this time, did you?"

Colby's nostrils flared and he shook his head.

"And you're worried it contained information that can either condemn Barry or exonerate him." Wynona leaned back in her chair, turning to the Alpha. "So we have no way of knowing what was in the note." Well...she did...but she couldn't say so. Maybe if she and Rascal could sneak away for a few minutes, Wynona could ask Barry personally, but the less they interacted with the couple, the better the chances were that they'd stay safe in their hiding spot.

Alpha Strongclaw took a deep breath, his thick chest heaving. "Not unless we track down my wayward son."

Colby threw up his hands. "We all know that Barry couldn't have done this," he persisted. "Why can't we just leave them be? Alpha Marcel is a bully and a jerk and Opal's better off without him. Let them live their lives." Colby's hands fell again. "It's the only one they're going to get."

Alpha Strongclaw looked down at the desk, seeming to study the grain of the wood before lifting his eyes to his second eldest. "I wish I could," he said in a low tone. "But we both know that Bermin's killer needs to be found and that Barry and Opal need to go about this the honorable way. Running away from a murder scene is against everything we stand for."

Colby growled and stood up. "It's against everything *you* stand for. Some of us just want to be able to make our own choices." He slammed the door on his way out and Wynona turned a sympathetic gaze to the alpha.

"Sorry," she said. "I didn't mean to cause a big fight."

Alpha Strongclaw ran a hand over his head. "It comes up every week or so anyway. This isn't anything new." He gave her a wan smile. "Rascal used to be like this too, you know. Headstrong and fearing responsibility."

Wynona laughed. "Really? He's very driven at the station."

Alpha Strongclaw shrugged. "Which is why we let him go. He didn't want to be alpha here, and he left to find his own path."

Wynona nodded knowingly. "And you let him, knowing it would teach him the exact principles you were trying to teach all along." She smiled and leaned back, crossing one leg over the other. "Sneaky, Alpha Strongclaw. Very sneaky." Her smile grew. "I might have to steal it years from now when I have my own children I'm working on."

He smirked at her. "Those days can come much faster than you think, daughter."

The door burst open and Wynona jumped in her seat. Rascal's haggard appearance made bile rise in her throat and Wynona swallowed hard.

"The fur wasn't Bermin's."

Wynona blinked several times, clearing her thoughts as well as her vision. "I'm sorry...what?"

Rascal ran his hands through his hair, calming down the crazy strands. "I got a text from the chief. The fur wasn't Bermin's and we're all meeting back at the cabin. Dad, he'd like you to call all the wolves you can think of who were in the area, so they can be tested."

Alpha Strongclaw nodded and closed his eyes for a moment, apparently sending a mental message to those he deemed necessary.

"I knew it," Wynona grumbled. She grabbed a jacket and threw it on before slipping on her boots. "I don't know why they didn't test it in the first place."

"Yeah, well...that redcap has been doing this job longer than I've been alive, so I'm guessing it wasn't him who dropped the ball." Rascal stepped aside, letting them through the office door.

Wynona picked up Violet from Rascal's hand and led the way. She was starting to be able to find her way around the house now that she'd been through it so many times. The sunshine was bright and made her squint, but it was the man at her side that was making her nervous.

Do I talk to him about it? Wynona asked.

Violet's nose twitched. *Later. He's pretty embarrassed at the moment. Leave it for the two of you.*

Wynona nodded, but Alpha Strongclaw broke the silence.

"Son...if you'd like some help–"

"I'm fine Dad."

Alpha Strongclaw pinched his lips together. "Chief Ligurio said there was someone new in the office?"

Rascal snorted and took Wynona's hand as they began to walk. "Not anymore, there's not."

Wynona made a face. "I wasn't trying to get anyone fired."

"I know." Rascal walked a little faster. "But if someone's not doing their job, they're not going to be kept on the payroll."

They reached the cabin much too soon for Wynona's liking, but still, she was curious to see whose fur it was.

Any guesses? Rascal asked.

Not Barry's.

Rascal gave her the side eye, but didn't respond.

Wynona ignored his skepticism. She knew that Rascal wanted his brother to be innocent but was just too afraid to hope. That was alright...Wynona would have faith for the two of them.

The cabin was filled with creatures by the time Rascal and Wynona walked in and they had to squeeze through the crowd in order to reach a clear spot along the wall. Mrs. Strongclaw took Wynona's hand as soon as she saw her and gave Wynona a weak smile.

"I'm glad you're here," she whispered.

Wynona squeezed back. "We'll get this figured out," she assured Mrs. Strongclaw.

"It sounds like solving this murder is only the beginning of your troubles," Mrs. Strongclaw offered. "I just wanted you to know that we'll be here when you need us."

Wynona didn't have a response for that. While she was grateful for the sentiment, Wynona wasn't ready to dive into her family troubles. One can of worms at a time was enough for her.

"Thank you for coming!" Alpha Strongclaw boomed. "We've had a development in the case and if you've been called here, it's because you were somewhere near the main house during the time of the murder."

Murmurs began to move through the crowd, but the alpha cleared his throat, silencing them.

"In order to identify a piece of evidence, we need a single hair from each of your wolves." The crowd's chatter picked back up. "We will be forming a single line and Mr. Azirad, who works with the Hex Haven Police Department, will be taking a sample from each of you. Thank you for your cooperation."

Rascal patted Wynona's back. "Just wait here and I'll be back."

Wynona grabbed his arm. "But I can vouch for you the whole time."

Rascal shrugged. "Sometimes we have to set an example, whether we want to or not."

With those words of wisdom hanging over her head, Wynona let him go, realizing that Rascal was right. If she were in Rascal's place, she'd also get in line. Because it was the right thing to do. And eventually, there would be no way to deny that taking down her father would also be the right thing to do.

But not right this second, Wynona reassured herself.

No, Violet added. *Not right this second, but it's coming faster than we think and Arune is right. We need to start preparing soon.*

Wynona pinched her lips, then nodded. She needed time to finish this case, and a few days with Rascal, but then they'd start talking about her father. And this time…she'd be willing to listen.

Hours went by and Wynona had finally taken a seat in the

corner. Her eyes were heavy and she wanted nothing more than to gain back the sleep she had lost the night before, but she didn't dare give into the sensation until after all the test results were back.

The line of wolves was gone, but Azirad and his workers were still going through each individual sample. The process was tedious and slow and nobody was in a good mood as each result came back negative.

"None of them match," Azirad growled, throwing down his pen and snatching his glasses from his face. He massaged the bridge of his nose. "There has to be someone else here."

"We could gather the whole compound," Alpha Strongclaw said. "But I believe it would be a wasted effort. I gathered every wolf who was within a hundred feet of the house that night. The fight had to have happened somewhere else."

Chief Ligurio scowled and put his hands on his hips. "Who else would he have fought with? Could it have been back at his home? Before he came that night?"

"Why would he have fought at home?" Wynona asked. "Or could it have been a play fight? Like you were with Colby, Rascal?"

Rascal shrugged. "It's possible. The only way to know is if we test them as well."

Alpha Strongclaw rubbed his hands down his face. "We're asking for trouble going over there."

"We don't have a choice," Mrs. Strongclaw snapped. "If the fight happened with one of them, we need to know."

Alpha Strongclaw looked older and more tired as he stared at his wife. "I know," he admitted. "But that doesn't make it any easier."

Mrs. Strongclaw's jaw tightened, but she didn't argue.

Wynona braced herself. She knew Rascal would go along, which meant she would as well, and the alpha was right. It wouldn't be easy. Alpha Marcel was already difficult to speak to. Accusing one of his own of being involved would definitely take things over the top.

Chapter Sixteen

"Well, we're not gaining ground by waiting here," Celia snapped.

Wynona jerked. She hadn't even realized her sister was in the room.

She ported Azirad, Rascal said with a chuckle.

Wynona gave him a sheepish shrug. *I got too caught up in the goings on, I guess.*

Remind me later to tell you how the porting went.

Violet snickered. *If she doesn't remember, I will. This sounds like my kind of story.*

"Strongclaw!" Chief Ligurio shouted. "Let's go."

Wynona couldn't help but laugh slightly when half the room looked at the chief, but Rascal nodded, indicating he knew it was him being talked to.

"Are you coming?" he asked Wynona.

"Of course." She took his hand and they all headed outside.

"Wynona, you take Wolfy Boy and your in-laws," Celia directed. "I've got Short Stuff and the two big guys. Dragon lady and her lover can fly."

Earl Grey with a Hint of Murder

"What?" Wynona shook her head, trying to interpret who her sister was referring to.

Dr. Rayn snorted, steam coming out of her nostrils, and she began to walk to a different part of the lawn. "We'll see you there." Within the blink of an eye, a large dragon stood in the space and Arune climbed up just as huge, red wings took them upward.

You've got Rascal, Alpha and Mrs. Strongclaw. She's going to take Azirad, Daemon and the chief. Violet cackled. *If I didn't hate her so much, your sister and I would get along well. Her descriptions are spot on.*

Wyona shot her familiar a look, then nodded at Celia, who was impatiently waiting for Wynona to catch up.

"I haven't done a group this size," Wynona admitted to her family. "So I apologize in advance if it's a little rough."

Violet gave a beleaguered sigh. *I'll try not to lose my lunch.*

"It'll be fine," Rascal told her.

"I don't know where we're going," Wynona realized. "Celia... have you ever been to the Marcel compound?"

Celia shrugged. "Nope. But it can't be that hard to find."

"I..."

Celia rolled her eyes. "Just follow me." With her entourage holding her hands and arms, Celia disappeared.

Wynona's eyes widened and she began to panic. "What!"

"Wy..." Rascal soothed. "Close your eyes and follow the magic. It should be fine."

Swallowing down her protests, Wynona did as directed and pushed her fear into the corner. If Celia thought it was easy, surely Wynona could figure it out. Sending magic out around her, Wynona allowed her mental vision to change.

She'd only done something like this once before and she was starting to understand why Violet said they were going to need to practice before they took on Wynona's father. There was so much she didn't know.

There!

Wynona paused her perusal and realized that there was a silver thread dangling in the air. Recognizing it as the same color as Celia's magic, Wynona tightened her hold on the creatures with her and concentrated on sending them along the same line.

For just a moment, it felt as if her body was being squeezed through a garden hose, but the sensation was over so quickly that Wynona had almost forgotten it by the time they all stumbled to their feet.

Breathing heavily, she let go of her charges and put her hands on her knees, catching her breath and sucking in pine scented air.

"You did good," Rascal told her, rubbing her back. "Thank you."

"I have to admit," Celia said as she sauntered in their direction, "I wasn't sure you could do it."

Wynona stood, straightening her spine ever so slightly. "So you were just going to leave us back there?" she asked with a little snip in her tone.

Celia raised an eyebrow and smirked. "If you're going to start a revolution, you're going to have to start calling some shots, dear sister. Get used to it." Spinning on her high heeled boot, Celia walked away.

"I hate that she's right," Wynona whispered under her breath.

Me too, Violet chirped. *But don't worry. You can still kick her backside in magical strength. You just need to wait for the right moment to remind her who's boss.*

"What are you doing on our land?" An angry woman stormed out of a large house, her golden blond hair billowing behind her. Her eyes were dark and glowing and Wynona knew immediately this was Alpha Marcel's wife. Opal was the spitting image of her mother.

Alpha Strongclaw walked to the porch, his hands in the air. "We have some evidence from Bermin's murder," he assured her. "And we need to speak to your husband."

Chief Ligurio came up beside the alpha. "I'm Chief Ligurio, Hex Haven Police Department. This is official business, Mrs. Marcel. Please bring the alpha here."

Her chin went up. "He's not here."

"When can we expect him?" Chief Ligurio asked, his tone tight.

"He's in town at the office," Boyer said, coming up behind his mother. He narrowed his eyes. "What do you need, Alpha Strongclaw?"

"We found a piece of fur on Bermin," Alpha Strongclaw explained. "It doesn't match my wolves. We're trying to find who it belongs to."

Boyer's face paled and he swallowed hard.

"I'm afraid you'll have to come back," Mrs. Marcel told them. "You can't do anything without my husband's permission."

"Mom..."

Mrs. Marcel shook her head at her son. "But you won't be finding anything here anyway. None of our own would be involved in Bermin's death."

"Mom..." Boyer insisted.

"Hush," she told him.

"Mrs. Marcel," Chief Ligurio argued, stepping up closer. "I don't think you understand. This is official business and you will either give us leave to talk to your wolves or we will do it without your permission. If you obstruct our investigation in any way, I'll be forced to arrest you for such."

Rascal left Wynona's side and stood beside his chief, followed quickly by Daemon. The three of them were an imposing force, but Wynona's eyes were stuck on Boyer, who was beginning to sweat.

Mrs. Marcel began to growl and Wynona stepped forward without a second thought.

"Quiet."

The noise immediately stopped and Mrs. Marcel's eyes widened impossibly large, latching onto Wynona.

Wynona stepped in front of the men and kept her focus on the son. "Boyer," she said softly. "What do you need to tell us?"

Boyer looked at his mother, then at Wynona, his breathing growing too quick and the hairs on his head starting to stand up.

"Boyer?" Wynona urged.

"You...shouldn't push my mom," he began.

"I know," Wynona assured him. "That's why I stopped her before she could start a fight. But you have something to tell us, don't you?"

Boyer nodded, his mouth trembling. "I...you don't need to test our wolves."

"Why is that?" Wynona asked when he didn't speak any more.

"Because...because I'm the one you're looking for."

Wynona nodded. "I thought as much." She turned around. "Chief?"

Chief Ligurio held out his hand and motioned with his fingers. "Come on, Mr. Marcel. Let's take this downtown."

Mrs. Marcel jumped in front of her son, her eyes glaring, but her mouth was still shut.

Wynona let the wolf loose.

"You can't have him," Mrs. Marcel immediately snarled. "He's just a boy and has done nothing wrong."

"How old are you, Mr. Marcel?" Chief Ligurio asked.

Boyer swallowed. "Twenty."

Chief Ligurio nodded. "He's a legal adult, Mrs. Marcel. Please move out of the way."

The woman continued to scream, but she didn't shift, for which Wynona was very grateful. All they needed was a wild she-wolf after them as they took Boyer downtown.

"Celia," Chief Ligurio said, his hand on Boyer's shoulder. "Let's do this quickly, please."

Celia was unusually subdued as she walked up and held out her arms so the creatures she was transporting could hold on. When they disappeared, Mrs. Marcel fell to her knees, wailing, and Wynona felt a surge of guilt.

"Don't," Rascal warned her. "We have no idea what's going on here. Fur on a pair of pants only means they were near each other, which we technically already knew. This could be nothing, so don't you go feeling bad for following a lead."

Earl Grey with a Hint of Murder

Wynona nodded, but her stomach still churned. "Let's go," she said, waiting until her own charges were touching her before porting to the precinct.

The noise of the traffic startled Wynona when they landed on the sidewalk and a startled pedestrian almost ran into Alpha Strongclaw's back, but they all made it inside safe and sound to see Chief Ligurio walking Boyer down the hall.

"Strongclaw!" Chief Ligurio shouted without looking back.

"On it, Chief." Rascal picked up the pace and wove his way through the front room to follow his boss.

Wynona caught Amaris's eye. The vampire was still wary around Wynona, but things had been on the mend. "Amaris, I need a place to put all these people while we wait for Chief Ligurio."

Amaris's red eyes darted around the group, then widened even further when the door opened and Arune and Rayn walked in.

"Sorry!" Rayn said cheerfully. "I got a little lost flying over the city. It's been awhile since I've seen it from above."

Arune gave her an indulgent look, then straightened his shoulders. "What's going on?"

"Chief Ligurio and Rascal have Boyer headed to an interrogation room," Wynona responded. "Amaris," Wynona indicated the front desk vampire, "was going to help me find a place for you all to wait."

The whole group looked at Amaris, who fumbled with some papers on her desk. "I think in this case, we can safely send you to the chief's office," she finally stammered.

Wynona nodded. "I think that works great. Thanks." Waving a hand in encouragement, Wynona led the way and guided them to the right place. She might still have trouble with the Strongclaw home, but Wynona knew the police station like the back of her hand.

Violet scrambled down her side. *I'm going to check in,* she said.

Wynona was torn. She wanted to hear how things were going with Boyer, but she also didn't feel right leaving the group by themselves. There were several in the group who could easily wreak havoc, if not kept under control.

Stay, Rascal sent her way. *I'll let you know how things go.*

Wynona made a face. He was right, but she hated not being in the room. It was never as good second hand.

"You could just listen in, you know," Arune said wryly.

Wynona frowned. "What?"

"Your soulmate connection," he stated. "Keep it open and you can just listen in to the whole conversation."

Wynona tilted her head as she thought it over. "It's that easy?"

Arune smirked and tapped his temple.

"Huh." Deciding she had nothing to lose, Wynona closed her eyes and leaned back against the door. She reached for Rascal in her mind. *Hey, Arune says if we leave the link open, I can just listen in.*

Rascal didn't respond verbally, but she felt him open their connection wider and Wynona jerked back as the sounds of the room landed in her mental ears.

"Why don't you tell me what happened before you got to the Strongclaw compound," Chief Ligurio said, his voice sounding much more frustrated than he had before they'd arrived at the precinct.

There was a long pause and Wynona wondered if she'd lost her connection when Boyer spoke up.

"I...I think I should speak to a lawyer."

Crud, Violet muttered. *The dude is clamming up.*

Wynona sighed. "Looks like this might take longer than we thought." She listened in for another thirty minutes before Rascal and Chief Ligurio gave up and came to the office.

Rascal gave Wynona a tired smile when they walked in and he came to stand by her.

"I'm actually a little surprised at how well he's holding up," she whispered. "He seemed to be scared at his house."

Rascal nodded. "Yeah...he's sweating like he ran a marathon. He's definitely hiding something."

Wynona let her head fall back against the wall. "He's so young."

Rascal nodded.

"I just..."

Earl Grey with a Hint of Murder

"Wy…" Rascal groaned. "One of these days you're going to have to figure out that age, demeanor, job…none of it matters. Creatures kill creatures. That's just all there is to it."

Wynona pursed her lips. "I don't know."

"You don't think Barry did it. You don't think Colby did it, or my father for that matter, don't think I haven't noticed that you haven't even investigated that possibility."

Wynona shrugged.

"And now you don't think that our only other lead didn't do it."

She nodded.

"Someone killed Bermin," Rascal stated.

"I know, but I just don't think it was him."

Rascal snorted and shook his head. "Come on. Let's go home for a bit while we wait for the whole lawyer situation to settle itself down." He took her hand and they headed out to the front of the station.

"What about everyone else?" Wynona asked.

"They're adults. They can handle themselves." He took them to the side of the building. "Wanna just port us home? We can check on you-know-who and get a little rest."

Wynona nodded. Double checking on Violet, who was in Rascal's pocket, she grabbed Rascal's hand and took them back to their small cabin.

Wynona smiled and took a deep breath of heavy, forest scented air. She loved her little meadow. It was full of magic and pine. Just perfect for someone wanting a little privacy and beauty all at the same time.

The curtains at the front of the home twitched and Wynona gave a little wave to reassure her hidden guests they were safe.

"Come on," Rascal said gruffly. "I'm starved."

Wynona had just taken his hand when a pop of magic landed behind her. She spun, her purple shield coming up automatically.

Chief Ligurio tore his hand out of Celia's, making a tight fist as if embarrassed to be found holding onto the witch.

Celia rolled her eyes.

"W-what are you doing here?" Wynona asked, fear immediately thrumming through her. She hoped that Barry and Opal were watching, because this was a disaster waiting to happen.

Celia tossed her hair over her shoulder. "Chiefy here wasn't happy you two ran off." She smirked. "So we tracked you down. Apparently, a meeting is in order."

Wynona glanced at Rascal, who was shifting his weight.

"Let's go, Strongclaw," Chief Ligurio said, heading for the house. "I want to talk about what you picked up with Marcel."

Celia followed after the men and Wynona ran ahead of them, throwing open the front door. "Oh, look!" she shouted, her eyes racing around the empty space. "My house. Just as I left it." *Please hide somewhere...please hide somewhere and be quiet.*

Rascal was holding back laughter as he walked past her toward the kitchen area and Chief Ligurio was giving Wynona an odd look as he followed.

Celia stopped at her sister's shoulder. "Who was hiding here?" she whispered conspiratorially.

Wynona shook her head. "No one," she stammered.

Celia tsked her tongue. "You're a terrible liar." She grinned. "The question is...did Rascal know?" With a raised eyebrow and devilish grin, Celia pushed past her sister and went farther into the house.

With a sigh of relief and a quick plea that they stay hidden, Wynona closed the front door only to open it again when there was a knock. After seeing who had arrived, Wynona sighed and held it the rest of the way. "Come on in," she greeted. Apparently, *everyone* wanted in on the meeting since the whole group from the office had arrived. Uncle Arune must have condescended to using his porting powers with the entire group.

So much for a nap, Wynona grumbled.

Popularity has its price, Violet said gleefully. *If you'd just be as rude as I am, you wouldn't have this problem.*

Wynona closed her eyes and shook her head. *Yeah...I'll get right on that.*

Chapter Seventeen

Kill me now, Rascal grumbled as he sat on the couch with his eyes closed and head back.

Don't tempt me, Violet shot back. She grumbled and nestled deeper into Wynona's hair.

Much as she wanted to scold them, Wynona couldn't bring herself to do it. The crowd at her house was driving her crazy as well. Arune was acting as superior as ever, Chief Ligurio and Celia wouldn't stop fighting and flirting with each other, the Strongclaws were standing in the corner looking like they wanted to be anywhere but there and Rayn was whistling in the kitchen as she baked up something that smelled suspiciously like charcoal.

"All we need is—" Wynona cut off as someone knocked at the door.

Nooo! Violet cried. *Tell them to go away! I can't take any more!*

Wynona sighed and stood up, walking across the house to the front door. "Prim," she said with a forced smile. Wynona loved her fairy friend, but this was like adding fuel to a forest fire. Prim never sat back and let things lie.

Prim bounced on her toes, squeezing Daemon's hand. "We have news."

Wynona stepped back and smiled at Daemon. "Come on in." She shut the door. "It's a little crowded, as you can hear."

Prim shrugged. "No biggie. We need to talk to everyone anyway."

"Okay." Wynona stopped at the entrance to her sitting room and waved an arm. "Have at it."

Prim grinned and looked up at Daemon. He rolled his eyes, but smiled. With a wiggle of her fingers, Prim caught the attention of a plant in Wynona's corner and started having it slither through the room.

Violet perked up from her place on the coffee table and went to the edge, watching it move around the room and shift in between everyone's feet. The mouse snickered.

"Prim," Wynona warned.

"Oh, I'm not hurting anyone," Prim said with a wink. ""But I *am* going to get their attention." With a grip of her fist, the vine gave a jerk on almost everyone's leg.

Chief Ligurio was knocked off balance and fell into Celia's lap. Mrs. Strongclaw grabbed her husband's arm and scowled. Rascal's leg was tugged on, but he merely gave Prim a look from his place on the couch, not the least bit impressed. Arune, however, growled and snapped his fingers, and the vine withered.

"Hey!" Prim shouted.

Arune's eyes flashed. "If you think your childish pranks are funny, then I think we should have a chat, young lady."

"Oh, leave her alone," Rayn scolded, coming in with a tray and something sort of resembling cake on it. "We could all use a little lightening up in here. There's been too much talk of murder and destruction." She held up the tray with a wide smile. "Charred banana bread! My specialty! Who'd like some?"

Wynona shrank back a little. It might be fine for a dragon to eat charred food, but Wynona's stomach was already protesting and she hadn't even had a bite yet.

Earl Grey with a Hint of Murder

Chief Ligurio stood up, his jaw tight and looking like he would gladly strangle Prim if given half a chance. "You wanted our attention?" he said in a low tone, causing Daemon to step closer to Prim. "You have it."

Prim put her chin in the air. She might be tiny, but she didn't let anyone push her around. "If you all didn't argue so much when you got together, perhaps I wouldn't have had to use drastic measures."

Chief Ligurio growled low and Celia chuckled darkly. "That's a bit like the cauldron calling the kettle black, isn't it, Tiny?"

Prim stepped forward, but Daemon stopped her. "Boyer's ready to talk," he said in his usual serious tone.

The whole room stilled.

"His lawyer arrived?" Chief Ligurio asked.

Daemon nodded. "And they're ready to discuss things."

Chief Ligurio looked at Rascal. "Think we'll get any answers?"

"More than we have now." Rascal groaned as he stood up and stretched his back. *I'm getting too old for this.*

Wynona gave him a look. *Not yet please. We've only been married a week! I get at least fifty years before you get to start saying that.*

He grinned at her and came over to take her hand. "I guess it's time to head back?"

"Son?"

Rascal looked back at his dad.

"I think we should go back to the house." Alpha Strongclaw turned to Wynona. "Do you mind dropping us off first?"

"Of course not," Wynona assured them. She looked at Celia. "Are we splitting the same way as usual? Is everyone going?"

"Prim and I will drive back," Daemon said. "I'll need my vehicle later."

Wynona nodded.

Chief Ligurio straightened his shirt. "I'll go with Ms. Le Doux."

Celia smirked and polished her fingernails on her shirt. "Of course you will," she cooed.

Chief Ligurio's stoic face didn't budge.

Those two are going to be better than reality television, Violet said with a laugh.

"Arune?" Wynona continued, ignoring her mouse.

"Rayn and I have multiple ways of being there," he said. "But...I wonder if we're needed?" He turned to the chief. "If we're not allowed in the interrogation room, then perhaps I'm better off here, where I can do some research." His speech slowed down on the last word and Wynona caught his meaning.

Should I?

Rascal grunted. "Your call," he told her, his eyes stuck on Arune.

"I don't trust him," Celia stated with a toss of her hair.

Arune turned to Wynona. "Your jaded sister is one thing," he said. "But you, Wynona. You know me." He gave her a wry smile. "Probably better than anyone outside of Rayn and Saffron." Arune put a hand to his heart. "I have sworn to protect you and you know where I stand on saving our world. Rather than have me stand around doing nothing, why not put my expertise to work?"

Wynona was torn. Like Celia, she wasn't sure how much she trusted the warlock, but his argument made sense. Wynona was only one creature. She couldn't research her father and ways to defeat him at the same time she was solving a murder. But putting something as powerful as her grandmother's grimoire into his hands could have dangerous...fatal...consequences.

Do it, Violet said, though her tone was unusually soft. *I trust him. I know he's an arrogant jerk most of the time, but his affinity with animals has let me get to know him very well.*

Wynona looked at her familiar. *Is that why you two were so close when he was still a brownie?*

Violet nodded and chitted. *I could feel that he wasn't really a creature the way I was, but we still had a connection. His methods aren't always ethical, but his motives are good.*

Wynona squished her lips to the side and stared at her uncle. She let her magic rise, tingling her fingertips, and tried to feel his emotions. She didn't have much to go on, but she liked Rayn and she trusted Violet.

"Okay," Wynona finally said. "Celia. We'll meet you at the station as soon as I take the Strongclaws home and get Uncle Arune settled."

Celia let out a soft snarl, grabbed Chief Ligurio's hand and disappeared.

Wynona held in a sigh. It seemed she would never be able to please everyone in her life.

"See ya later!" Prim danced out the door, Daemon right behind her.

Wynona held out her arm to her in-laws. "Uncle Arune, I'll be right back."

He rocked back on his heels, looking a little too pleased with himself. "I'll be waiting."

Wynona gave her husband a glance, then ported back to the compound.

"Thank you," Mrs. Strongclaw said, shaking her head a bit from the trip. "That's a quick way to travel."

Wynona smiled. "Sorry it's a bit bumpy still. I'm still learning."

Alpha Strongclaw's large, warm hand landed on her shoulder and he gave her a squeeze. "We're grateful for you." His chin tilted down and he raised his eyebrows. "For *all* you're doing," he stated.

Wynona felt heat creep up her neck. "I'm grateful for the chance to help," she responded.

Mrs. Strongclaw stepped forward and wrapped Wynona in a tight hug. "We couldn't do this without you. I know that you coming into Rascal's life isn't a coincidence." She stepped back, holding Wynona's arms, her eyes full of tears. "You're going to save both our sons," she whispered thickly. "And I've never been more grateful...or more proud."

Something stirred inside Wynona's chest and it took her a minute to realize that it was a sense of pride. She'd never had a parent figure speak to her like this before. For too many years, she'd been called worthless and put down and even after breaking free of her parents, Wynona had done little but put out fires with those around her.

Rascal loved her, Violet and Prim did as well, but never once had a parent loved her, let alone been proud of her.

This is why children go to such lengths to get their parents' attention.

Rascal's chuckle came through loud and clear. *I've known you were amazing all along,* he assured her. *It's nice to see you're starting to believe in yourself.*

Wynona smiled at Mrs. Strongclaw. "Thank you," she responded. "I'll do my best."

With one last arm squeeze, Mrs. Strongclaw stepped back and her husband put his arm around her.

"Be patient with Rascal," Alpha Strongclaw advised. "Things might not be easy on him for a while."

Wynona nodded and made a mental note to have a conversation with him eventually. He'd brushed off any attempt to discuss her putting him to sleep, but if he was manifesting powers, they'd have to figure it out sooner or later. Wynona knew from personal experience that waiting too long meant that something always went haywire at just the wrong time.

Giving a small burst of magic, she landed back at the house. "Hold on, Arune," she said, walking back to her bedroom. Magically unlocking her closet, Wynona picked up her granny's grimoire and shut up the rest. She definitely wasn't ready to give any of the black magic ones to Arune. Their darkness really needed to be destroyed, but that was a problem for another day.

Her steps were slow, but Wynona brought the book to her uncle and held it out. She had to force her fingers to release it when he reached out, though his touch was reverent.

"Awww...Saffron," Arune cooed, his long fingers brushing the front of the book. "It's almost as good as having you here."

The words caused Wynona to relax. It was easy sometimes to

forget that Granny was Arune's sister. Hopefully that connection was enough that he wouldn't abuse her memory or magic.

Rascal stepped up next to her. "We need to go," he reminded her.

"Right." Wynona bent down, waiting for Violet to scurry across the floor and climb up. After setting the mouse on her shoulder, Wynona took Rascal's hand and ported out before she could think better of it.

"I'm going to have the Vespa out for a joyride soon," she muttered as they arrived at the station. "It hasn't been used in too long."

"Why drive when you can port?" Rascal teased. "Riding a scooter seems a little blase, don't you think?"

Wynona gave him a look, but she couldn't stop herself from smiling. "The day I'm too good for the scooter is a day I hope I never see."

It is a pretty amazing ride, Violet agreed. *Nothing quite like riding up front with the wind in your fur.*

"I'll take your word for it," Wynona said as they stepped inside.

"Interrogation room four," Amaris told Rascal.

He nodded and they walked down the hall, Wynona's stomach flipping with each step. She hated that they were here and that they were investigating someone like Boyer. He was so young. Only twenty and yet they were now presented with the very real possibility that he might have had something to do with Bermin's death.

Wynona shook her head. *No...I really don't think he could have done this.*

Violet sighed. *You don't think anyone could have done this. Wake up and smell the magic, Wy. Creatures kill. They make stupid mistakes. Not to mention, we don't actually know he killed Bodyguard Guy. Only that Boyer said the fur had to be his. It could mean anything.*

"I guess we'll find out," Wynona responded. She waited while Rascal knocked, then let them into the right room.

Boyer was leaning in the corner, while a man in a suit sat across the table from Chief Ligurio, and Wynona was sure it was the family lawyer. The open briefcase was a dead giveaway. Now the question would be how much the creature would interfere with the interrogation. Some of them became quite troublesome at times.

"Have a seat," Chief Ligurio said to Boyer.

The young man nodded and sat down, looking as if the weight of the world was on his shoulders. His eyes had dark circles under them and his hair was a mess, as if he'd run his fingers through it one too many times.

Wynona could feel his distress and guilt, but she still couldn't convince herself that he was a killer. There simply had to be another explanation.

Wynona sat against the back wall, Rascal at her side. It had become their usual place in an interrogation and gave Wynona a clear view of the room, allowing her the opportunity to read emotions, whether through magic or simply observation. If she needed to ask a question, she'd move up, but right now she wanted to observe.

"For the record, you're confirming that you're twenty, is that correct?" Chief Ligurio asked.

Boyer nodded jerkily.

"And you don't want your parents present?"

"No."

Chief Ligurio eyed the quiet lawyer and leaned back in his seat. "Okay then. Why don't you tell us what happened?"

Boyer's wide eyes went around the room, landing on Daemon, who guarded the door, to Rascal and Wynona in the back. Wynona knew the young man wouldn't be able to shift, if he decided to make a break for it. Daemon was not only larger, but his black hole abilities would keep the shifter from becoming his wolf.

Apparently deciding there was no getting out of it, Boyer took a deep breath. "I...got in a fight with Bermin earlier in the day."

"About?" Chief Ligurio asked.

"My sister."

Chief Ligurio nodded. "Would you please explain exactly what happened?"

Boyer pushed a hand through his hair, causing it to stand up on end. "I knew that she'd been going over to meet Barry. I mean... Opal's never been very good about obeying Dad, so it wasn't hard to guess that she would go behind his back when he got upset about them."

Chief Ligurio began typing things into his computer. "So you wanted Bermin to stop her?"

Boyer shook his head. "No. I..." He groaned, throwing back his head. "I don't know what I want." Boyer leaned forward, his eyes pleading. "My dad's a good alpha, but he's...hard. He doesn't see how his old ideas are hurting us."

"Was he hurting your sister?" Chief Ligurio continued.

"Not exactly. He just wouldn't listen to her." Boyer made a face and leaned back again. "I don't know why she had to marry an alpha. I mean...I..." He swallowed and his eyes dropped.

Wanting Opal to marry an alpha told Boyer he wasn't good enough...didn't it? Wynona asked Rascal.

He gave her a subtle nod.

Once again, her heart went out to the young man. He seemed so torn between his ideals. Wanting to please his father, wanting to be enough, but wanting to help his sister as well. It had to be a difficult line to walk.

"I wanted to talk to Bermin about looking the other way," Boyer said, studying his hands. "I knew he'd eventually catch on. Dad was starting to become suspicious and that meant Bermin was going to be given new rules." Boyer glanced up. "Opal was about to lose any moment of freedom she had and I knew it would break her."

"So you what? Explained the situation and tried to convince him to give her space?" Chief Ligurio asked. "Forcefully?"

"No!" Boyer shouted, then groaned. "Yes...I don't know. I just..." He slumped in his seat. "He got angry that Opal was going behind his back and was worried my dad was going to do something about it. You know...take it out on him."

Wynona clamped her hands together. She had the almost uncontrollable urge to go hug the young man and comfort him. The strain of his emotions was beating at her barrier, letting her get a glimpse of what he must go through most days as he tried to figure out who to be.

"I told Bermin my dad didn't know, but Bermin didn't believe me. He wanted to confront Opal and I wouldn't let him." Boyer's face crumpled. "And that's when we fought. I hit him in the stomach and got a few punches to his face, but he was able to hold me off and his hits were harder." Clenching his fists until his knuckles were white, Boyer continued. "I finally broke into my wolf. Bermin was so much bigger than me that I didn't think I could fight him any other way and I...I wanted to protect my sister."

"What happened next?"

The softness in Chief Ligurio's tone caught Wynona off guard. While the vampire wasn't cruel for the sake of being cruel, he also wasn't one to be soft about anything.

"Bermin didn't turn," Boyer choked out. "I think he knew that my dad would have a fit if we got into a wolf fight. But at one point, I had him pinned and was so...angry! I was snapping at his face and he was using his hands to hold my mouth off."

That explains the cuts and bruising, Rascal said with a sigh.

Wynona nodded, her eyes riveted to Boyer. The sinking feeling in her gut was growing stronger, but she simply couldn't bring herself to believe he was a murderer. He was too young for this!

"Did you kill him?" Chief Ligurio finally asked point blank.

A wail broke out of Boyer's mouth and he doubled over. "I...don't know..." he sobbed.

Wynona went to stand, but Rascal stopped her. It was breaking her heart to watch this.

"I don't know what happened after we fought. I knew he was bleeding, but I don't know how bad. I could hardly see straight, I was so angry and my wolf had almost completely taken over."

Wynona let her weight fall back to the chair.

Boyer sat crying in his chair, his words indistinguishable.

The lawyer reached over and awkwardly patted the young man's shoulder. "I think that's enough," he stated. "He's told you what he knows. Bermin was alive the last time Boyer saw him and other than a few normal fight injuries, we have no reason to believe that Boyer had anything to do with Bermin's death."

Chief Ligurio tapped his fingers against the table, taking a long moment to consider. "I'm not quite ready to let him go," the vampire finally announced. "I won't formally charge him for now, but unless you've made bail, I plan to keep him here while I check on some new leads."

The lawyer sighed and pulled out his phone, immediately typing something.

The chief gave a signal and Boyer was taken away, shuffling down the hall, still sniffling.

The lawyer looked at Chief Ligurio. "I'll be in touch," he said before slipping out the door.

"That was much less helpful than I'd like it to be," Chief Ligurio snapped.

Wynona nodded, but her eyes were stuck on the door. She had that tickling sensation in the back of her brain again...the one that told her she was missing something.

Why can't I gain a magical power to help me realize what I'm not seeing?

The whole world would be after that one, Violet said wryly. *Give it a minute, maybe it'll come to you.*

"We can only hope," Wynona whispered. "Too much is depending on it."

Chapter Eighteen

"So now what?" Wynona asked, clasping her hands in her lap. "I don't really feel like we learned that much, other than the fact that Boyer is stuck between a rock and a hard place."

Chief Ligurio leaned back, his face up toward the ceiling. "There's got to be more to this," he muttered. "A creature can't simply die without any evidence at all."

"Do you think there's any chance that Boyer's fist fight killed Bermin?" Wynona asked.

Rascal shook his head. "Probably not, but it's not impossible." Rascal scrunched up his nose. "He did say his wolf was running rampant, so he could have scratched Bermin's neck without truly realizing it, but we're not completely incoherent when we're in our wolf form. Even when the wolf is stronger, we can still see what's going on."

"So if he scratched him, Boyer should know," Chief Ligurio stated.

Rascal nodded. "He should. Unless someone else was controlling him and Boyer has no memory of it."

"Is that possible?" Chief Ligurio sat up and twisted in his seat. "Could there have been a spell involved?"

Both men looked at Wynona. "While I'm sure it's possible," Wynona said carefully, going through the scenario in her head, "I don't think it's probable. There was so little magic on the wounds that I don't believe there could have been a spell involved."

"Would there be residue on the wounds?" Rascal pressed. "Wouldn't the spell have been on Boyer?"

"Skymaw?" Chief Ligurio snapped.

Daemon stiffened. "Sir?"

"I want you to go and get a good look at Mr. Marcel." The chief pressed his lips together. "And the home. You can tell them that you're looking for evidence, but I want to know about magic. See if there's anything unusual."

"On it." Daemon turned and left the room, the door shutting softly behind him.

"As for the rest of us," Chief Ligurio said, "I think we should go talk to Arune and Rayn. They might know of magic that could cause the type of memory loss Boyer might be suffering from."

Wynona nodded and held out her arms.

Chief Ligurio shook his head. "Celia's in my office. I'll have her take me."

Wynona couldn't have stopped her smile to save her life. "I see."

The chief cleared his throat. "Don't make assumptions, Mrs. Strongclaw." He headed toward the door. "They're usually wrong."

Wynona waited until Chief Ligurio had left the room before breaking out into laughter. "I'm sorry," she told Rascal through her giggles. "But it's so obvious, even if he doesn't want it to be."

Rascal grumbled. "I'm not exactly looking forward to my boss being my brother-in-law."

Wynona paused. "I hadn't thought of that." She frowned in consideration and tilted her head. "It might be a bit awkward."

Rascal snorted. "Come on. Back to the house we go."

Wynona took his head and sent them home. The house was quiet as they walked in and Wynona headed straight for the kitchen.

"Back so soon?" Arune asked, his head never rising from the grimoire.

Wynona paused. "Where's Rayn?"

"She ran back to the house for a few supplies." Arune finally lifted his head and leaned back in his seat. "Apparently, your house isn't equipped with her usual style of snacks."

Wynona shuddered. "I don't think I want to know."

Her uncle's smile was nothing short of mercenary.

"I'm surprised Celia and Chief aren't here yet," Rascal muttered.

Violet snickered.

"Don't even think it," Wynona warned her familiar, though Wynona couldn't stop the thoughts running rampant through her own mind either. A pounding at the door caused her to jump and Wynona made a face. "Why don't they just come in?" she muttered, walking back toward the door.

Rascal growled behind her. "Shield up, Wy. That isn't Chief or Celia."

Wynona stopped and took a second to use her senses and she knew immediately what Rascal was talking about. The magic at her front door wasn't familiar...and it definitely wasn't friendly.

"You heard him," Arune said, his voice coming closer as he walked up behind her. "Shield up."

Wynona sent a jolt of magic through the house. She didn't want the shield to be as obvious as usual and she hoped it blended in with the walls enough to keep whoever was here from asking too many questions.

"Well done," Arune said in a low tone. "Getting better every time."

Wynona raised her eyebrows at Rascal, who walked ahead of her. "Wait," she said as he reached for the door.

Rascal paused.

"Better let me," she said. "I don't want to shock you again."

Earl Grey with a Hint of Murder

Rascal made a face. "Fine. But I'm staying right here."

"I wouldn't expect you to do otherwise."

The pounding resumed. "Open up!" the voice shouted.

Wynona opened the door before they could try to break it down again. "May I help you?" she asked.

The man at her door glowered and lowered his hand. His suit was immaculately cut and his hair pristinely styled. The three creatures behind him, though different in species, were all dressed the same, even the woman on the end. Her short stature and green skin told Wynona she was a goblin, but the serious look on the creature's face matched her colleagues.

"We're here in an official capacity," the first man stated.

"Officer Locus," the man said with a smirk. He flipped open a wallet to show a badge. "I'm here to tell you that you're being removed from the case involving the murder of one..." He flipped through his phone. "Bermin Devdan." The phone went back inside his suit coat. "Effective immediately."

Before Wynona could reply, she felt a strong jolt to her shield and it caused her to jump. "Um...what department are you from?" she asked, pressing for time so she could figure out what had just happened.

"The Federal Bureau of Paranormal Investigations," Officer Locus said.

"There's no such bureau," Rascal argued, stepping up next to Wynona.

There's not?

Rascal subtly shook his head, never turning from the visitors.

Officer Locus's smirk grew. "I realize that you're probably feeling a little possessive over a case involving your own brother, but it's no longer your concern."

"It is if I say it is," Chief Ligurio said, walking around the corner of the house. "This is my jurisdiction and my case. You have no power here."

"Not anymore, it's not," Officer Locus said easily. He showed his badge again. "As Chief Investigation Officer for the Federal Bureau of Paranormal Affairs, this case is now mine." He leaned forward, his eyes flashing a deep green. "Now stand aside, Chief Ligurio, or I'll have you removed."

"Not until I have official notice," Chief Ligurio ground out.

Wynona put her hand on Rascal's arm as his growling grew louder.

The new arrival barely gave Rascal a glance, but he pulled out a piece of paper from his inner suit coat pocket and handed it to Chief Ligurio.

Chief Ligurio studied the paper and crumpled it in his fist before dropping it to the ground. "This means nothing."

Officer Locus's eyes darkened and he stood toe to toe with Chief Ligurio. "Are you refusing to follow an order, Chief Ligurio?"

Wynona's fingers twitched.

Easy, Rascal warned her. *Let Chief handle it.*

I was just going to cover him with the shield, Wynona replied.

It'll be seen as an act of aggression, Violet muttered. *Let Chief Vampy stand on his own two feet.*

Wynona squeezed her hands into fists to stop the desire to take care of her friend. She knew he was a strong vampire, which was why he'd been chief for so long, but she hated not being able to help.

"If there'd been an order, I would happily oblige," Chief Ligurio stated baldly. "But a document with nothing more than a fancy header on it isn't enough. Bring me real orders, and I'll provide you with what you're looking for."

The three other officers shifted and their leader held up his hand, bringing them to instant stillness. "While I'm perfectly capable of fighting my own battles, Chief Ligurio," Officer Locus began, "I'm going to enjoy rubbing that smug nose of yours into the ground when the president hears of your insubordination."

"I'll look forward to it," Chief Ligurio said with a sharp, toothy grin. "Oh, and do pick up your paper before you leave. Littering is a punishable offense, as I'm sure you know."

Earl Grey with a Hint of Murder

No one from Wynona's party moved as Officer Locus snapped his fingers, causing one of the other creatures to jump over and pick up the crumpled paper, stuffing it in their pocket before they all clambered back in the black SUV's they arrived in.

"Officer Locus!" Uncle Arune called out, halting the processional.

The large man turned and raised an eyebrow.

"I just wondered..." Arune stepped into the doorway. "You're aware that Ms. Le Doux had been helping, yes? Surely her family status gives her some jurisdiction over this case as well?"

The man snarled and his eyes flashed toward Wynona, before glaring daggers at Arune again.

"If Ms. Le Doux has an issue with our work, then she'll need to take it up with her father," Officer Locus retorted. "We don't answer to her and won't be using her help."

Arune nodded humbly and backed away. "That man wasn't an officer," Arune said as soon as the SUV's were out of sight.

Wynona let down her shield and they stepped outside. "How do you know?"

Rascal huffed. "I told you the bureau they said they were from didn't exist," he pointed out.

"I know," Wynona mused. "But somehow I don't think even you know every secret society my father keeps under his belt." She turned to Arune. "So again, I'll ask, how do you know?"

"Because he didn't realize what Ms. Le Doux Arune was asking about," Celia pointed out as she came around the side of the house. The corners of her mouth were pulled down. "They assumed *you* were Ms. Le Doux. Meaning they don't realize you're married and they don't know that I've been helping." She turned to Arune. "You think *he* sent them, don't you?"

Arune chuckled and folded his arms over his chest.

"But why?" Chief Ligurio demanded. "Why come out here and try to scare us off? We're no closer to solving this case than we have been since the beginning." He turned to Wynona. "And by the way, your shield is better than I gave it credit for." He rubbed his forehead. "Dang near impenetrable."

Wynona frowned. "I'm so sorry. It must have been you two porting that hit it!"

Celia grunted. "You could say that."

"Are you alright?"

Violet snickered. *Wish I'd seen that. I wonder if they landed on their faces in the dirt.*

Celia glared at the mouse. "I won't miss this time," she warned.

Try it, sister, Violet challenged. *I'm ready for you this time.*

Wynona snapped her fingers. "Enough!" She looked pointedly at her uncle. "What does this mean? If those guys were fake and we think my father sent them, what does it mean for us going forward?"

Arune raised an eyebrow. "What indeed? I do believe we just caught my nephew making his first powerplay in this investigation... which tells me...he just might have something to lose."

"But what?" Chief Ligurio demanded.

Arune shook his head, his face revealing his frustration. "I wish I could say."

Celia let out a growl. "It's just like him to send Edge out to play house rather than showing up himself."

Wynona's eyes widened. "You *knew* him?" she screeched.

Celia scoffed. "Of course, I did! He's one of dad's thugs."

"That might have been helpful," Arune snapped. "I realized they weren't real officers, but if you knew who they were, why didn't you just say so?"

Celia threw up her hands. "I'm sorry. Do you want me to interrupt you or not? It seems like if I speak my mind, I'm in trouble for speaking. If I don't say anything, I'm in trouble for that too! Just make up your mind!"

"I would think a woman of your age would know when to do both!" Arune shouted back, losing his usual composure. "Or do you not realize that we're dealing with creatures' lives?"

Celia stepped forward, her upper lip curled. "I'm not the one who went up against a creature he couldn't hope to beat and spent fifty years in a curse."

Wynona's head began to thrum. Celia's magic was dripping off her fingertips and Arune wasn't far behind. His pale face had turned red and Wynona could feel his magic aching to be released.

"Maybe we need to calm down," Chief Ligurio said, his voice unsure. "We're all on the same side, after all."

"You would defend her." Arune snorted. "Open your eyes, *Chief*. The president is playing us for the fool and you're too wrapped up in how pretty the package is to realize it's likely to bite."

Chief Ligurio leaned forward. "You're going too far. Back down or I'll have you arrested."

"On what charge?" Arune argued back. "Hurting your feelings?" He shook his head. "This whole situation spells disaster. We need to go after your father now." Arune spun as he spoke, looking directly at Wynona.

She could barely hear anyone at this point, as the heavy weight of the magic began to cloud her brain. Her eyes hurt to keep open and Wynona narrowed them, putting her hand over her forehead. "I..." She swallowed hard, the bile in her stomach starting to rise.

"Strongclaw?"

Wynona looked over to see Rascal bent at the waist, holding his stomach and groaning.

You're latching onto his emotions! Violet screamed. *Get out, Wy! Get out of his head!*

"No..." Wynona breathed, realizing that Rascal was about to have another one of his alpha 'becoming' episodes. She squeezed her eyes shut and tried to break their bond, but it wouldn't budge.

Chopping at it with a mental ax was like hitting concrete with a metal bat. The damage was minimal, but the twang against herself was enough to double her migraine. Wynona fell to her knees, feeling completely out of control.

"Strongclaw!" Chief Ligurio shouted. "Pull yourself together! Fight it!"

"Wynona?"

A cool hand landed on Wynona's forehead and she jerked away from it.

"Stop," Celia shouted. "Make it stop!"

"I can't," Arune shot back. "They're too connected. His episode is killing her."

"Wynona!" Celia grabbed Wynona's shoulders and shook her. "Cut it off! You have to get yourself back!"

"I…" Wynona put a fist against her temple. "I…can't…Ahhh!" she screamed as one last jolt of pressure burst through her hair, taking away her sight and ability to think. The world spun and Wynona barely kept from throwing up. She felt a squeezing sensation, similar to being ported, and fell over with a heavy thud right before the world went black.

Chapter Nineteen

Gasping for air, Wynona's back and shoulders heaved as she worked to catch her breath. Her hands were being poked by twigs and leaves, and purple was bouncing along her skin like strands of live electricity. Her hair had fallen to the side of her face and the black color looked almost beautiful with the magic dancing in and out.

Slowly, she stood on shaky knees, looking around in order to figure out where she'd landed. Apparently, the feeling of porting hadn't been in her mind and now she was lost. There was a heavy hum in the air that seemed familiar, but Wynona couldn't quite place it. The natural magic wasn't hurting her, but nor was it welcoming her with open arms.

Slowly spinning, she paused, noting something just beyond the tree line. With a jolt, Wynona realized it was her cabin, telling her that she hadn't gone very far. She gasped, then spun again, frantically looking around. She'd somehow landed *inside* the Grove of Secrets. How she'd landed there accidentally, she could only guess, but now she needed to know if she would be able to make it back out alive. Wynona's mind began racing and her thoughts grew chaotic and random. Taking a deep breath of heavy, moist air, she forced her breathing to calm down. In...two, three, out...two, three. Over and over, she counted her breathing, manually releasing muscles and slowing her lungs' rapid pace.

It took several minutes for the fear to release from her body, but finally Wynona was able to hold onto calm long enough to control her thoughts.

"Okay," she whispered out loud to herself. "I'm not really sure why I came here, but now I need a game plan." She turned around once more. "I can see the cottage. Let's start there."

Very little was known about the forest, except that it held heavy magic and the creatures who came inside, never came back out. She had learned through her investigation with Dr. Rayn, however, that there were pockets within the forest that held no magic and could be lived in, if a creature knew how to work the system a bit.

Right now, however, Wynona could feel the weight of the forest's magic on her like a heavy blanket and she knew she was not in one of those pockets. She'd felt the magic before just from walking close to the forest's edge, but this time, it was different...stronger and more tangible.

Slowly, she began to walk, her eyes focused between the trees and on her house. An odd stillness surrounded her as she walked, stumbling several times since she refused to look down at her feet. No birds chirped, no animals scuttled into holes...yet it felt as if dozens of eyes were fixated on her and a shiver ran down Wynona's spine as she recalled all the yellow eyes she'd seen when walking to and from Rayn's house.

None of the creatures had breached the magic line, but right now Wynona was in their territory. Her legs sped up of their own accord as fear tried to tighten its hold on her chest again, but Wynona clenched her fists and worked on her breathing.

Something was wrong though. She hesitated, then sped up again. No matter how she walked, the vision of her house never seemed to grow any closer. "Please," Wynona whispered, breaking into a run. Two minutes later, she stopped, breathing heavily.

The house stayed the same distance.

The magic of the forest wasn't allowing her to gain any ground.

A howl caused her to jerk and Wynona put a hand on her racing heart. There would be no calming it down this time. The organ pounded against her chest and her back became soaked with sweat. Wynona's fingers twitched and she fought the urge to bring up her purple shield for protection.

In magic this heavy and wild, Wynona had no idea how her powers would react in the environment and for now, that thought was enough to hold her bubble at bay. She squatted slightly when movement sounded in the trees around her. It echoed around the trunks, making it difficult to pinpoint where exactly it was coming from.

Slowly, she spun in a circle, her eyes desperately trying to find the means of her terror. A sudden yearning for all that she'd never accomplished in life hit her chest and stole what little breath was left. If she died here, she'd never have more time with Rascal. At this point she didn't even know if Rascal was alright or if his emerging powers had left him in his wolf form or if one of the other creatures at her house had hurt him.

Other unfinished business tugged at her. She'd never get to know Arune and truly understand what happened to her family. She'd never fix her relationship with Celia or hold Violet again. Prim would never get to throw the wedding reception of the century and most of all...Wynona would never have a chance to raise a child in the exact opposite way that her parents had.

The idea of being a mother had never moved from its spot at the back of Wynona's brain as far in the future until just this moment when she realized with a fierce intensity that she wanted to give life and love in a way she'd never experienced. She wanted to raise a child she and Rascal had created together and teach the creature to be kind, to look at others as equals and to give back to their community in a way that their society desperately needed.

A vision of a petite girl with wild, dark curls and bright golden eyes burst into Wynona's mind like a shot of lightning and she nearly sobbed at the ache she felt to hold and protect the little one.

Movement to her right had Wynona spinning and purple flaring from her fingertips without her permission. She wasn't ready to die. She didn't know what had brought her to the forest, or how to get out, but Wynona couldn't go down without a fight. Not yet. There was still too much to accomplish and it started by staying alive.

"And eventually taking down my dad," Wynona whispered as a promise to herself. The little girl in her vision wouldn't be born into a world with President Le Doux at the helm. Not while Wynona had the power to change it.

"Wynona?"

Wynona stiffened and she narrowed her eyes as she stared into the trees. "Who's there?"

Voices began to grow louder and the shuffling grew into pounding footsteps. "Wynona!" Barry shouted as he burst through the tree line, Opal attached to his hand. "I..." Barry smiled wide and shook his head. "I can't believe you're here! We were just talking about you!" Letting go of Opal, he ran over and engulfed Wynona in a hug that squeezed her until she couldn't breathe.

"Barry," Wynona wheezed. She coughed a little as he let her go. "What in the world are you doing here?" Wynona looked from Barry to Opal, and back again. "Oh my word...is this where you ran to when everyone showed up at the house?"

Opal slowly walked up, eyeing Wynona carefully as she joined Barry and took his hand once more.

Barry's smile didn't budge. "It wasn't like there were a lot of options," he said with a shrug.

Wynona's eyes widened. "Are you insane?" she screeched.

Barry shrugged again and Opal cuddled in. "We're still together, so not too much, I suppose."

"Why not continue down the meadow? You didn't have to come

inside the Grove." Wynona was completely stumped. They had to know how dangerous it was to be here.

"It was also the only place we could think of where they wouldn't be able to track us down." His cheeks turned pink and he shrugged, looking much more like the quiet, shy brother Wynona had been introduced to. "It's hard to hide from wolves," he said. "Especially when you are one. One strong command from my dad and I'd be scrambling to obey." Barry looked around, tilting his head back to take in the view of the trees. "But in here, the magic keeps us from being pulled back." He rubbed the back of his neck.

"I'm guessing, however, that you've also realized it also keeps you from leaving," Wynona said wryly. Her fear was thankfully gone at this point, though she couldn't deny that the thought of dying had taught her some harsh truths that she would need to consider later. For some reason, knowing she wasn't alone, even if there were still dangers lurking, made everything look much brighter.

Barry scrunched his nose and looked at Opal, who gave him a wan smile in return. "Yeah," he said, coming back to Wynona. "We shifted a couple of times and have tried running from one end to the other, but we haven't been able to reach an edge. We can see the tree line sometimes, but can't ever get there."

Wynona nodded and spun, pointing. "Just like I can see my house but can't get there."

Barry's eyebrows went up. "That must be frustrating."

Wynona huffed a laugh. "I suppose you could say that." She studied the couple again. "Since we're not going anywhere for a few minutes, why don't we have a seat and you can tell me exactly what's been going on. Everyone is worried sick about you two, Boyer is the prime suspect at the moment, though I don't really believe he's guilty," Wynona continued quickly when Opal gasped. "And a federal bureau is trying to take over the investigation." Wynona decided that telling them the truth about her father's hand in all of this wasn't necessary. If Alpha Strongclaw wanted to share, that was fine, but otherwise, the fewer people that knew there were fake officers running around, the better.

Barry's eyes widened and he stepped back. "Um...we had no idea that us running away together would cause so much trouble. All we want is to be together, nothing else!"

"I don't think it has anything to do with you running away," Wynona explained. "It's about murder." She raised her eyebrows. "And while I believe in your innocence, I'm hoping you have more information for me than you shared back at the cabin. There have to be some answers you haven't given us."

Barry made a face and looked away. "Not as many as you probably want," he said softly.

Opal tugged on his hand and shook her head. "We don't know her," she argued, giving Wynona a look.

Barry smiled and tucked a piece of hair behind her cheek. "We can trust Wynona," he assured his girlfriend. "She's Rascal's soulmate and she's helped solve murders in the past." He glanced at Wynona, then down at Opal. "She won't turn us in."

Opal didn't look as convinced, but she stopped glaring.

Barry gave Wynona an apologetic grin. "Opal's learned to be mistrusting."

"And you?" Wynona asked, sensing there was something he wasn't saying.

Barry's smile grew. "I inherited just a touch of my mother's empathy. I can usually get a vague sense of a person's intentions." He tilted his head, consideringly. "And yours are as pure as they come, though I can tell you didn't inform us of everything that's been happening while we've been gone. I'm sure you have your reasons though."

Wynona blinked several times and looked away. On one hand, she felt slightly violated that he could tell so much about her. On the other hand, having him trust her so implicitly was amazing, especially after a lifetime of creatures distrusting her because of her last name.

"We didn't do it," Opal blurted out. "Kill Bermin." Her large, blue eyes filled with tears. "We told you he was dead when we found him."

"I believe you," Wynona assured the frightened wolf. "But go over it again. There has to be something we've missed."

Barry nodded his agreement. "I left the dinner table to sneak off with Opal, but when I went in the sitting room to help her through the window, Bermin's body was already there."

Wynona frowned. "So Opal can't corroborate your testimony?"

Barry sighed and pushed a hand through his hair, causing it to stand up in a perfect imitation of his brother's. "I suppose not. I helped her in and we were discussing the body when everyone found us."

Wynona sucked in a long breath and put her hands on her hips. "And you didn't hear anything? No fight? No arguing? The dining room was loud, but you were walking through the house. His death couldn't have happened much before you got there."

Barry nodded. "I know, but I didn't hear it. I was completely shocked when I walked in that room."

Wynona grunted in frustration.

"So where does that leave us?" Barry asked.

"Do you know why Bermin was there? He'd already been escorted out. How did he get back in?"

Barry pinched his lips and looked at Opal. She stared at him without speaking, then finally shrugged.

"I don't know," Opal admitted, turning to Wynona. "My only guess is that somehow he'd discovered I had left and was coming to stop me."

"So he what...snuck into the house after being kicked out?" Wynona asked. "I'm still so surprised that no one heard anything or smelled anything."

Barry made another face. "The smell thing is my fault. I left the window open on purpose and I walked around with socks and stuff from Opal, in my pocket all the time so that her smell was everywhere. It helps hide her when she comes over."

"Did anyone know about your running away?"

The couple looked at each other again before shaking their heads. "Colby, I'm sure, picked up on a few things," Barry said. "He passed notes for us all the time and stood as lookout when we needed it. But other than him...no."

"I don't have any close friends," Opal admitted sadly. "Boyer is younger than I am and is so desperate to catch our father's attention that we've never truly seen eye to eye. I've actually been under heavy lock and key since Dad found out we were in love."

Barry rubbed Opal's back.

"But I've figured out the right excuses to use to get away from Bermin." She sniffed. "Or I *had* figured them out. I'm positive that if my father finds us, he'll drag me back and I'll never see Barry again."

"I think you're probably right," Wynona muttered, her mind churning through the facts she had. Still...the feeling remained that she was missing a vital piece. Why was Bermin there? What had brought him back inside? And how had he died without anyone in the Strongclaw family knowing about it?

Wynona rubbed her forehead. "You know, for two seemingly intelligent adults, you two have really caused a huge ordeal for your families."

Opal turned away, but not before Wynona could see more tears in her eyes.

"Have you ever wanted something more than life?" Barry asked quietly. "And yet those who are supposed to be looking out for your best interests are doing nothing but standing in your way? Keeping you from the very source of your happiness? And all because they're in charge and you're not?"

Wynona immediately felt guilty. Hadn't she spent her whole life being treated exactly like that? Like her opinion didn't matter? In her case, it was because she was cursed. In Barry and Opal's case, it was because they loved the wrong person.

Her determination to change the world she lived in grew stronger and Wynona straightened her spine. "Okay, first things first. I need to get out of here."

"Don't you mean we?"

Wynona shook her head. "No. You two have obviously figured out how to stay alive in here, and while I think it's a bit crazy, you're right when you say it's the best place to hide." Wynona pushed her lips to the side. "But I need to get back so I can help solve Bermin's murder and clear the way for you two to go live your lives." She huffed. "The main question is...how?"

"But you can't just leave us here!" Opal shouted. "What if we never make it out?"

"Well, in that unlikely event," Wynona said, trying to infuse her voice with confidence, "at least you'll have each other." She smiled to soften the blow. "But, if I can get myself out, I believe that when the coast is clear, I can help you as well." Her eyebrows shot up. "There are pockets of the woods that have no magic. Have you run into any?"

"Ooooh..." Opal said slowly, looking up at Barry. "There have been a couple of meadows that we can't walk into. I'll bet that's what's going on there."

"Shoot," Wynona muttered. The woods apparently weren't going to let her use a magicless trail...unless... "Can I build my own?" she murmured to herself.

"Excuse me...what?" Opal demanded.

"I need you both to stand back," Wynona responded, backing away from the couple. "I'm going to try something and I don't want to risk you two getting hurt if it goes wrong."

Opal immediately scuttled backward and Barry went with her, though much more slowly. His eyes were fixated on Wynona, a fascinated look on his face.

Closing her eyes, Wynona spread her arms and hands, bringing her magic to her fingertips. Immediately, she felt the forest react and the pressure of magic grew stronger. It didn't want her to show her power.

I'm not here to harm you, Wynona assured the land. *I just want to find my way home.* Pushing against the weight, Wynona managed to expand her magic into a protective bubble just barely larger than herself. She wasn't sure how long she was going to have to hold onto the spell, so she didn't waste energy by making it larger.

"Here goes nothing." Wynona began to walk toward her house, but after five minutes, she realized she still wasn't gaining ground. Stopping, she looked at her feet and jerked. The ground was no longer green and lush. Instead she was walking on dirt and dead leaves.

She walked sideways, then forward again, watching the ground with every step. No matter where she went, the ground looked dead as long as it was within her bubble, but once it was outside the shield, it went back to being green.

"Now what?" Barry called out.

An idea was forming in Wynona's mind and Wynona blinked until her magic vision was working. Masses of blue, green and brown magic were swirling through the air, touching everything in sight... except the ground just below her feet. "Now we try a little more magic," she responded, facing her house again. Gathering her energy and strength, Wynona thrust her arms forward without waiting to give the forest warning, throwing her magic straight to the edge of the forest and building a tunnel of purple.

At first, the magic shot out easily, but the forest didn't stay caught off guard for long and Wynona felt it respond within only a few moments. It screamed in anger at the section of land she was confiscating and pounded on her shield, wanting it back.

"In just a moment," she said through gritted teeth, bending her knees and straining with every muscle in her body. She had to be getting close to the edge of the forest, it simply couldn't be that much farther, but her strength was waning and the pressure of the forest was suffocating.

From her first experiment, however, Wynona knew she needed to open the magicless tunnel the whole way, or she'd still end up walking in circles again.

Earl Grey with a Hint of Murder

"Come on...almost...there..." She reassured herself, hoping desperately that it was true. After what seemed like an eternity, Wynona gasped and fell forward, landing hard on her knees. Her tunnel held and Wynona immediately stopped her forward momentum, having finally broken through the tree line.

She climbed onto shaky legs and brushed herself off. Glancing over her shoulder, Wynona said, "I need to hurry. I can't hold the forest off for long, but as soon as it's safe, I'll come back for you. Don't move too far from this spot."

Barry's face was pale and Opal looked like she was going to pass out, but both nodded.

Wishing she'd worn sneakers rather than cute flats, Wynona took off running. She kept the tunnel open only a few feet behind her, trying to save her energy as much as she could as she ran. And this time, it was working. Her house was getting closer, but with the forest demanding her to stop, even a few feet felt like miles as Wynona made her way over the dead landscape.

"WY!"

Her eyes widened and she latched onto a dark figure at the entrance to her tunnel. "Stay back!" she gasped, waving her hand. "Don't come in!"

A loud growl ripped down the tunnel and Wynona put on more speed. She could feel him now and his anxiousness was about to rip him apart.

The forest doubled down and Wynona stumbled, almost landing back on her knees, but she lifted her feet higher and ran on. *All... most...there...*

She broke through the treeline and crashed into Rascal's waiting arms. Both of them landed hard on the ground and Wynona felt a sharp snap of pain as her magic rebounded and the tunnel closed.

She'd done it. She'd landed in the Grove of Secrets and escaped and was now back to the safety of Rascal's arms.

She clung to his neck, crying and shaking and feeling proud of her accomplishments all at the same time.

Abigail Lynn Thornton

Rascal's arms were bound around her like steel and Wynona knew he wouldn't let her move even if she wanted to. Eventually, she would have to tell him what happened and they would have to put what clues she had back into place, but for just a few minutes, she was going to hold the creature she loved most in the world and send a *thank you* to the universe for giving her a second chance.

Chapter Twenty

"How did you know where to find me?" Wynona asked, her voice slightly muffled against Rascal's neck.

"I'll always find you," he murmured back, his hold tightening.

Wynona leaned back just enough to look at his face. She brushed her fingers through his hair. "I know that, but still...how did you know?"

Rascal shook his head, his eyes glowing. "I'm not really sure. As soon as you disappeared, I shifted and took off running. I wasn't even thinking of *where*. I just went and I ran along the forest's edge for a couple of miles before coming back and landing at this point." Sighing, he cupped her cheek and ran his thumb along her wet cheekbone. "Something told me not to leave and then a few minutes ago I felt a major shift in the magic at the trees." His eyebrows went up. "The rest you know." He frowned. "How did you end up in the forest?" He sat up, pushing Wynona back a little. "And for that matter, how did you get out? No one ever comes out of the forest. I didn't think you had any of those weird pockets so close to the house."

Wynona glanced over her shoulder, half afraid she would find an angry forest spirit bearing down on her. Luckily, nothing looked out of the ordinary, but she knew getting Barry and Opal back out would be twice as difficult now that the forest knew how to react to her magicless tunnel.

"I..." Wynona wiped at her cheeks and turned back to Rascal. "I guess I kind of created my own pocket."

His eyes widened.

"I'm not really sure how I ended up there in the first place, but that's where I landed when I came out of the port," Wynona explained. She went on to tell him about being able to see the house, but not able to get any closer, and how the magic kept her from leaving. "And then I ran into Barry and Opal."

"WHAT!" Rascal leapt to his feet, his eyes going straight to the forest.

Wynona scrambled up, holding up her hands. "Hold on!" she called out, reaching for him. "You need to let me finish."

Rascal's eyes were glowing so brightly, Wynona could barely look straight at him. "You're telling me that my brother and his girlfriend are inside the Grove?" he asked, his jaw clenched and his teeth slightly elongated. "That's where they went when everyone surprised us at the house?"

"Yes," Wynona said calmly. "But I need you to let me finish before you try to go inside and ruin everything we're doing."

"Could you not get them out with you?" he demanded. "Are they okay? Something had to be wrong if they didn't come with you!"

"Rascal!" Wynona shouted. She cupped his face and forced him to look at her. "Seriously. Listen."

His heaving chest calmed down just a little and Rascal blinked several times, but finally he nodded. "I'm listening."

"Good. Now stay that way." She smiled when his lip twitched. "They're fine. They ran into the forest when the house became flooded with people. It was the only place they could think of where no one would track them."

Rascal's face fell and he pulled back. "They're stuck, aren't they?

Earl Grey with a Hint of Murder

I could see how difficult it was for you to bring yourself out. You can't bring them too."

While his duty-driven officer side had been angry and wanted justice even if it meant turning in his own brother, Rascal, the shifter, just wanted Barry to be alright. And on that note, Wynona knew he'd blow up again when she told him what she'd done.

Back up just slightly, she braced herself. "I left them there on purpose."

Rascal's ears began to turn red. "What?" he asked, his voice tightly controlled. His breathing was picking up again and Wynona held up her hand, asking for calm. The last thing she needed right now was another one of his shifting episodes. They were going to have to discuss those sooner, rather than later, at the frequency for which they'd been happening.

"They've obviously figured out how to survive in there...at least for now...and there's nowhere safer for them at the moment. When the investigation is over and we've found the real killer, I'll get them the same way I got myself," Wynona reassured her husband.

Rascal closed his eyes and muttered a couple of choice words before sighing and looking at Wynona again. "While I understand why you did it, I can't say I like it." He pushed a hand through his hair. "But...on the other hand, having them somewhere out of the way, and especially out of police hands, is a good idea." His head dropped back with a groan. "I can't believe I'm breaking the law this way."

Yeah, well...Chief Vampy broke it first, so...

"Violet!" Wynona bent down and picked up her familiar, who was racing across the yard.

Ditch me like that again and I'm living with Arune permanently.

Wynona cuddled the mouse close. "It wasn't on purpose," Wynona assured her friend. "I was picking up Rascal's emotions and I couldn't control them." She leaned back to look at the tiny face. "If you'd stuck around you would have gotten to see what the Grove of Secrets looked like from the inside."

Rascal paced away from them and Wynona realized he was upset about what she'd just said. "Shoot," she muttered.

Violet sneered. *Hey...over here,* Violet demanded. *First of all...I was scared you were going to blow a gasket...literally. Second, you always have all the fun without me! How in Hades did you end up there?*

"Long story," Rascal answered for Wynona. He'd apparently decided, yet again, that he wasn't going to talk about the alpha situation. His eyes lingered on the forest and Wynona wondered if Barry and Opal could see all of them standing in the yard. "We need to get back to the house and call in the crew. I don't think we need to mention my brother, but we do need to create a plan of action in moving forward." Rascal took Wynona's hand and they began walking. "After you disappeared, the whole crew went crazy and I left before I heard what they all were planning."

Wynona patted her back pocket. "I don't know where my phone is."

Rascal wiggled it in the air and handed it back. "It landed on the ground after you ported. And somehow I had just enough brain left in me to grab it before shifting." He grinned. "You're welcome."

Wynona laughed lightly. "Thanks." She kissed his cheek and then sped up her walking. "Call the chief. I want this case over with so we can focus on other things."

Rascal stopped moving and their combined fingers pulled her to a stop as well. "Why do I get the feeling I'm not going to like these 'other things'?" he asked in a low tone.

"You're not," Wynona admitted.

His eyebrows went up.

Wynona sighed softly. "I had a realization while I was inside," she explained. "There were a few moments when I was sure I wouldn't make it out alive and I realized that I wasn't ready to die. There are too many things I want to experience, so I knew I had to fight." Wynona took a slow breath. She loved Rascal with everything in her, but she wasn't quite ready to share all her visions with him...

especially since they hadn't spoken about having a family at all. "And I don't mean just fighting to get out of the forest," she explained. "I realized that in order to live the life I want for myself and...those I love..." Those dark curls were starting to become a permanent fixture in Wynona's mind. "I'm going to have to fight something much bigger than the Grove of Secrets."

Ahhhh, yeah! Violet screamed, dancing around Wynona's head and shoulders. *Revolution time, baby! Who do I get to bite first?*

Wynona shook her head. The topic was much too serious for laughing, even at Violet's bloodthirsty antics. "One of the things I want most," Wynona continued, stepping closer to Rascal, "is a life with you." She paused. "And I realized that I'll never get it if I leave my father in charge, because he'll always be lurking around the corner and whatever he's planning right now is not going to allow any of us to live the lives we want."

Wynona had a few more things to say, but Rascal's kiss cut her off from finishing her thoughts.

Puh-lease, Violet whined. *Save it for later, huh? Why do creatures always kiss when their lives are in danger? It's revolting. Fight first. Suck face later.*

Wynona did laugh this time and pulled back, though she couldn't quite keep her eyes from Rascal's. "I think because when we're in danger we realize what matters most," she whispered as a reply to her familiar.

Violet snorted, but didn't give an audible reply.

"However, in this case...it's murder first," Rascal said with a teasing grin.

Wynona nodded and laughed. "Murder first."

Now we're talking, Violet added. *Call Vampy and I'll get Arune. There's a killer on the loose and I want first crack at 'em.*

It took nearly an hour to gather everyone back at the house and Wynona was feeling much more calm by the time they all arrived.

They could do this. They could figure out who killed Bermin, why there was a fake bureau knocking at her door, and they could eventually set themselves up to be able to take down President Le Doux. Her time in the forest had taught her that there was a lot to stand up for and Wynona wanted to make good on those emotions.

Yes, things were hard. Of course they were. Nothing good ever came easy, but hard also didn't mean she was on the wrong path. It was all uphill right now, but eventually...the fight she was gearing up for would turn into the type of freedom that most creatures only dreamed of. And most importantly, that freedom wasn't just for her... it was for everyone, and that made it all the sweeter.

Wynona carried the tray of tea and cookies to the coffee table, handing out cups as the crowd settled in. "Are we all here?" she asked, looking around while the cup in her hands warmed her cool fingers.

"As much as we're going to be," Arune answered, crossing one ankle over the other. "Rayn sends her apologies, but she has urgent business to take care of." He tapped his temple. "She'll be with us as she can."

Wynona nodded. "And Prim?"

"She had a wedding," Daemon offered. He made a face. "I hope the bride still gets what she wants because Prim wasn't happy we were all meeting without her."

Rascal chuckled. "Ah...sweet irony," he muttered.

Wynona sent him a look. "Okay, thank you everyone for coming. First of all...I want to apologize to those who were here, how I disappeared. I understand I worried some of you and I had little control over anything at the time, so I'm sorry."

"I don't want apologies," Arune said with a narrowed eye. "I want explanations. Where did you go?" He glanced at Rascal. "And what's happening with the wolf?"

Rascal's lip started to curl. *Don't,* Wynona warned him. *We have to do better if we're going to get through this.*

Rascal huffed, but cooled off his anger. "While I'm sorry for my out of control shifting, it's not something that's pertinent to the case."

He tilted his chin up stubbornly. "Wynona and I will work through it as we can, but we need this case off our plates first."

"Agreed," Wynona said, backing him up. "I'm more aware of the situation now and will be more prepared if Rascal ever has an episode again." She straightened her shoulders and pinned Arune with a hard stare. "We all know I pick up on others' emotions and when those closest to me are constantly in a state of arguing, it gets difficult to stay on top of it all."

Arune sipped his tea, not looking the least bit repentant.

"That's it?" Celia snapped. "That's all we're going to get?" She glared at Rascal. "You could have killed her and you won't even tell us what's going on? What happens the next time you go crazy? We're supposed to just stand around like it's all normal while you burn my sister's brain to ash?"

"Celia, stop," Wynona began, but Rascal jumped to his feet.

"You want an explanation?" he demanded, leaning into her space.

"Rascal!"

He shook Wynona's hand off.

"Fine," he spat. "Somehow, someway, the fates have decided to actually bring me up to snuff to be part of your sister's life," Rascal sneered. "Do you know what that means?"

Celia glared and Chief Ligurio stepped up closer to her chair, as if to break up an impending fight.

"Well? Do you?" Rascal said through a tightly clenched jaw.

Celia raised an eyebrow, but Wynona felt her sister's nervousness and pulses of power were beginning to come off of Rascal in waves. She stepped back involuntarily, realizing that she had never felt anything so strongly from him before.

Rascal stood and swung around, facing the crowd. "It means that even though I'm considered rogue and have no true pack...I'm being turned into an alpha."

Wynona felt as if her heart was going to beat out of her chest. Rascal's strength was immobilizing. The more he talked, the stronger he became and his entire being seemed to grow. She knew if she turned on her magic vision that she would see something completely different than every other shifter she'd ever encountered.

"And not just any alpha," Rascal continued, his voice dropping low and heavy. "An alpha to help rule." His bright golden eyes turned to Wynona. "An alpha to stand beside the witch who has been prophesied to take back the paranormal world and take down the villain who's posing as its leader." Rascal smiled, but it was far from kind. "Would you like a demonstration?"

Wynona felt the power stirring around him and she felt a sliver of fear.

His eyes darted to her. *I won't hurt anyone,* he assured her. *But it's time they knew.*

Wynona smiled. She knew Rascal, and she believed him...but this was a new part of him that she'd never seen before and the unknown had her nervous. His words, sounding dark and prophetic, were also worrying her. She had been gung-ho to take on her father after coming out of the forest, but now it was changing...again.

Twisting his fingers into a hard fist, Rascal straightened. "Turn around!" he ordered.

Every body in the room shifted and Wynona's eyes widened as she felt the pressure of his command on her own mind. She immediately put up a shield, metal like Mrs. Strongclaw taught her, and was able to keep from moving in a circle, but a few of the other creatures in the room weren't so lucky.

"Enough!" Arune shouted, though his pale face was paler than normal. He had kept from moving, but it was obviously costing him, if his clenched hands on the chair arms were any indication.

Rascal twisted his neck and shifted his shoulders. Sweat was cascading down his temples and he released his hand, letting it fall to his side as if too heavy to keep holding up.

"How did you do that?" Chief Ligurio asked, his nostrils flaring with each word. It was clear he was also unhappy about the predicament and was having trouble holding in his temper.

Earl Grey with a Hint of Murder

Celia plopped back in her seat, looking shocked and exhausted.

Daemon stood, stoically as ever, though there was a wariness in his eyes that Wynona had never seen before. His unfailing loyalty had just reached a questioning point.

Arune cleared his throat as Rascal stumbled to the couch and sat down heavily. "Wynona, before we dig into Rascal, tell us what happened to you." He held up a hand when there were shouts of protest. "I'm asking for a moment," Arune shouted over the voices. "I believe it will be clear after." He raised his eyebrows at Wynona.

Wynona glanced at Rascal. She hadn't planned to tell everyone about Barry and Opal, but now she wondered if the whole truth needed to be in the right hands.

Rascal's eyes were closed and he looked like he was fighting the flu. Using that amount of power had completely wiped him out. She moved in his direction, but he opened his eyes and stopped her. "Tell them," he whispered hoarsely.

Violet scrambled off the coffee table, leaving a half eaten cookie, and climbed up Rascal, nuzzling into his neck. *I've got him*, she assured Wynona.

Taking in a fortifying breath, Wynona began. The more she talked, the more she told, until she felt as exhausted as Rascal looked. Breathing heavily, she threw her hands in the air. "So...now what?"

Multiple sets of eyes blinked back at her, but Arune tilted his head to the side, considering her. "It seems to me," he began softly, "that your powers are growing." He glanced at Rascal. "Even merging in some ways."

"And what does that do for us?" Celia asked.

Arune didn't turn away from Wynona. "It means we have some training to do, first of all," he murmured. His eyes narrowed even further. "And it means that the paranormal world is preparing for war."

Chapter Twenty-One

The room was quiet for several very long heartbeats as Arune's words sunk in. There were too many people in the room for it to stay that way, however.

"You think the paranormal world is preparing for war?" Chief Ligurio asked, genuine curiosity in his voice. "As if the world at large were a living entity?"

Arune pinched the bridge of his nose. "Not exactly," he muttered. "But magic...is."

Wynona frowned. "Magic is living? I've...never thought of it that way."

Arune stood and stretched his back a little. "The simplest way to explain is that the world must stay in balance," he said. "Right now, it's swinging out of balance and magic is preparing to fix it." He tilted his chin down. "You and, it appears, Rascal have been chosen to take the lead."

Wynona rubbed her forehead. "That makes no sense! How can we be *chosen* by magic itself?"

Arune held his hands out. "Don't you remember your little speech at the cabin only yesterday? Somehow, despite having no leadership experience, and no magic until you were an adult, you've managed to gather to you a large group of paranormals, who are all, in one way or another, extraordinary at their craft." Arune pointed to Daemon. "A black hole. Rare in its own right, but Officer Skymaw has shown depths that we didn't even know were possible. And his little fairy friend." Arune snorted. "Her ability with plants is also rare. She might not have wings, but she was given an extra dose of magic and it can only be to your advantage."

Arune next went to Celia. "Your sister. Her reputation leaves much to be desired as a whole, but her skills in wind are unmatched, even by your father."

Celia scowled and folded her arms over her chest.

Arune next went to Chief Ligurio. "While I don't know of any extraordinary powers of our dear police chief, the fact that he *is* the police chief might be enough. If the stories that I heard through the grapevine were correct, he already withstood the wrath of your father once. Between him and Celia, we have insider information that no other rebellion party has ever had before."

Chief Ligurio's eyebrows shot up before he narrowed his gaze, staring Arune down.

Arune pointed to himself. "Rayn and I bring knowledge and great powers in our own right. A dragon is nothing to sniff at and my powers are more than likely just behind your father's in strength, especially since I've lost the last fifty years." Arune sniffed as if admitting that made him feel weak. "I wasn't enough back then and with no training, I'm more than likely not enough now, but I add a sizable amount of wisdom and ability."

Next he turned to Rascal. "Now we have your husband. And not just any husband. A soulmate." Arune's eyes flared. "That bond connects you in ways that even the shifters don't understand and your powers are beginning to merge. You feel him more than any other creature. Your growing powers are bringing out his own. And now he's becoming an alpha of a group of creatures that aren't even supposed to be in a pack." Arune slowly shook his head. "How can you not see how every piece of your life in the last two years has brought you to this day? How it's preparing you to take on a man who's been lurking in the shadows for too long." Arune threw a hand toward the back of the house. "Even the forest now knows you!" he said, his voice growing louder. "I don't know how that will help us, but creatures don't simply pop in and out of the Grove of Secrets without there being consequences," he insisted. "The Earth is starting to know who you are, Wynona. You are what we've been waiting for."

Wynona's fists clenched and unclenched. She had already committed herself to taking down her father, but hearing Arune spell it out in such a dramatic style made Wynona want to rethink her plans.

"Don't run from it," Arune said in a low, persuasive tone. "Embrace it, my dear niece. It is what you were born to do and you will not find peace nor joy in this life until you walk your path."

Wynona blinked, tears causing her vision to grow blurry. Her lips trembled and her knees shook, but Wynona kept herself upright. She might not like everything Arune was saying, but there was no denying the truth hanging in the air. It was almost tangible and Wynona knew she was not alone in the feeling.

Determination, fear, anger, grit and a sense of strength were floating around Wynona like a breeze, caressing, soothing and yet strong enough to hold her in her spot.

Slowly, she turned her head, facing every creature there, head on. It was an odd group, as Arune had pointed out. There were stark differences in each one, and they often butted heads, but Wynona would never be able to put into words why she had kept them around all this time.

Each creature that came into her life has stayed. They didn't have to. Most of them probably didn't even like each other, but they had stayed with Wynona. Arune's insistence was beginning to show her *why*.

The fact that you didn't mention how awesome I am either shows us that you're full of rotten troll parts, or that I'm simply too amazing to have to be mentioned, Violet said with more than a little snip in her tone. *And it better be the latter, or you better be finding a way to get back in my good graces.*

Arune chuckled and Wynona smiled while she wiped at her wet cheeks. "My little one," Arune cooed, walking over and picking up the purple mouse. "None of this would ever have started if you hadn't found her first."

Violet sniffed and smoothed her fur. *That's what I thought, brownie boy. Now don't blow it.*

"Someday I want to hear what the rodent has to say," Celia said with a smirk. "I have a feeling it's funny...sometimes."

Violet ignored the witch and Wynona took a deep breath. "Thank you," she said to Arune. "I appreciate your confidence. I don't know how much I can actually do, but I can tell you that I'm willing to try."

Arune nodded, his long fingers still stroking Violet's fur.

"However, before we can get to that, I still feel strongly that we need to—"

Someone pounded on the door, interrupting Wynona's acceptance speech.

"It's them again," Rascal said, his voice sounding stronger. He staggered to his feet. "I can smell them."

"Them?" Wynona spun and her eyes widened before turning to Chief Ligurio. "Why do they keep coming here?" she whispered.

"Just another mistake, telling us they're fake," Arune said in a low tone. He shook his head. "We can't let them stick around, or take over the case." He turned to the chief. "How do we get rid of them without hurting your job?"

Chief Ligurio stared into space for a moment while the visitors pounded on the door again. "Let me try something," he said.

"Deverell," Celia said, causing Wynona to do a double take. Her sister actually sounded concerned.

"Stay," he told her, then softened his tone. "I'll be fine. But I don't want them to know you're here. You've stayed under the radar so far, let's keep it that way." He sent a look to every other creature there and they nodded in turn.

Straightening his spin, Chief Ligurio left the room and went to the door.

"Don't, Wy," Rascal warned, hurrying to catch up with Wynona as she followed the chief.

"It's my house," she whispered over her shoulder. "I should be at the door."

"Gentlemen!" Chief Ligurio said loudly as he pulled open the door. "What a surprise."

Wynona came into view of the doorway behind the vampire, Rascal right at her shoulder. A quiet scuttling sound let Wynona know that Violet was joining the crowd.

"What brings you by?" Chief Ligurio asked cheerfully.

Officer Locus scowled and removed dark glasses.

Hasn't he ever heard of cliches before? Violet muttered.

"We've been ordered to find Baryn Strongclaw and Opaline Marcel," Officer Locus said, an unmistakable threat in his tone. "We're here to search the house." He leaned in. "Not only will we not take 'no' for an answer, but any more interference on your part will result in your arrest, Chief Ligurio."

Chief Ligurio put his hands up. "You caught me off guard last time and I realize I might have acted hastily." He stepped back. "Come in!" His voice was loud and Wynona realized he was warning everyone else. "You're welcome to search the premises and if you'll provide the proper documentation this time, I'll even be happy to let you join my own investigation."

Officer Locus hesitated and Wynona didn't blame him. This was so far out of Chief Ligurio's normal personality it was almost comical. She wasn't quite sure where the chief was going with it, but she trusted him and decided it was best to go along.

"As this is *my* home," she pointed out. "I need to see a warrant."

Earl Grey with a Hint of Murder

Officer Locus's wariness faded and he jerked a piece of paper out of his suit coat, handing it to her.

Wynona glanced at it, trying to act the part of semi-detective. "Rascal?" she asked, holding out the paper to him.

Rascal raised an eyebrow at her, then glanced at the paper and nodded, but still scowled at the visitors. "It looks legit," he admitted sullenly.

Nicely done, Violet said with a laugh. *You guys' acting skills are top notch.*

It took great restraint to keep from rolling her eyes, but Wynona managed it. She just hoped that her stall gave everyone enough time to slip out the back window. The pressure of a port would have been felt by the whole household, and Wynona hoped the rest of her visitors knew that.

"Let us in, Ms Le Doux," Officer Locus demanded. "You can't hide them forever."

Wynona pulled her door open wider. "The Chief of the Hex Haven police department is here," she snapped. "Just where do you think I'd be hiding two shifters?"

Officer Locus stuffed the paper back in his coat. "Where isn't the problem." He sneered as he stomped by her. "It's why and when we find out the answers to both of those, we'll be dragging you back to the office."

So that's the end game, Violet chittered. *Dad's looking for a way to bring you in...lawfully. That way you won't fight your way out of it.*

He's betting that you'll protect family, Rascal added. *Even if it's just my family.*

He's right, Wynona said with a smirk, folding her arms over her chest. *I am protecting them. And so is everybody else.*

"What's in this closet?" a voice bellowed.

Wynona's eyes went wide. The closet with the grimoires was locked...for good reason. It would take a great deal of power to open it, but Wynona needed to protect those books at all cost. In the wrong hands, they were more than just dangerous. They were fatal.

"Coming," Wynona choked out. She looked at Rascal for help, but he shrugged, not having the ability to do anything to help her.

"Have you checked the kitchen?" Chief Ligurio called out, walking quickly in the opposite direction of the bedroom. "I'm sure there are some cupboards you missed."

"Now, Ms. Le Doux," Officer Locus said from his place just outside her bedroom door. He smiled coldly. "A locked closet is certainly a little suspicious, don't you think? Why would a witch need to keep her closet locked?"

Wynona put her chin up, her mind scrambling to find a way to keep the grimoires hidden. "Why wouldn't I?" she asked in return. "I brew custom teas. If anyone and everyone had access to my tea workshop, there's no telling what would happen to business."

Officer Locus's face fell slightly and Violet snickered. "Open it," he snapped.

Taking a deep breath and working up the courage to use her magic, Wynona brought it to her fingertips. If he felt her using it, it would ruin everything. Grasping the handle of the door, Wynona sent the magic into the wood, the same way she had with the shield the first time they had come.

She pictured her workshop in her mind's eyes and did her best to portray it in exact detail as a mirage in the doorway.

"I said *now!*" Officer Locus shouted.

Rascal growled and the two men began to face off.

Just do it, Violet said hurriedly. *Wolfy isn't going to stay calm much longer, not when they're threatening you.*

"Officer Locus?" Wynona asked, calling his attention to her. She yanked open the door and immediately was hit with the smell of herbs and flowers.

What in hades is that? Violet asked.

Wynona couldn't believe how realistic the room looked. The black magic was being held behind the mirage and unless someone tried to step in, her picture was near on perfect. But the smell? She had no idea how she was creating something so realistic. Spelling the scent of the room hadn't even occurred to her.

Officer Locus stared at the room, then grunted in disgust. Muttering under his breath, he didn't even bother coming to the entrance, simply stormed down the hall, shoving past Rascal.

Rascal allowed himself to be knocked into the wall, making it slightly more dramatic than it had to be.

You need an Academy Award for that one, Violet said wryly.

Rascal winked at Wynona, gave her a discreet thumbs up about the room, then put his angry face back on and stormed after the officer.

"How'd I do that?" Wynona whispered to Violet. She closed the door, then looked at her hand as if it held the answers she was looking for.

A tapping on her bedroom window brought Wynona's head up and her hair blew in a breeze that shouldn't have existed. Wynona blinked and pulled her hair out of her face.

I don't think you did, Violet snickered.

Celia smirked and polished her fingernails against her chest before shooting a finger gun at Wynona and disappearing from view.

"Life just keeps getting weirder and weirder," Wynona muttered breathlessly.

I, for one, think that was one nifty trick, Violet said. *Almost makes me like sissy poo.*

Wynona gave a soft laugh, then began to walk toward the doorway. It was time to get the officers out of the house. Her sister's little breeze had been beyond clever and gave Wynona hope that Arune's words were truly as prophetic as they had sounded. But they needed their dad's minions out of their hair first, then Wynona had some thinking to do.

Some ideas had been whirling since meeting with Opal and Barry and with a little time, Wynona thought she just might be able to put the pieces together...or at least come close.

There were still a few questions to be answered, but at least she now had a direction. Maybe. Hopefully.

You have no idea, do you? Violet grumbled.

I have an idea, Wynona corrected. *I just don't know if it's a good one or not.*

Well, it can't be worse than the fact that Vampy Man just took off with the officers, offering to help them search the Strongclaw compound.

"He what?" Wynona ran the rest of the way, finding Rascal at the door. "He left with them?" she asked breathlessly.

Rascal nodded and slowly shut the door. "He's going to keep them off the right trail so we can take care of things here." Rascal put his hands on his hips. "I'm shocked Chief didn't shred me for letting you hide my brother, but I think your dad's interference has him changing some of his priorities."

Wynona nodded and sighed. "I know. Everything's all mixed up right now."

"Then let's put first things first," Arune said, coming back into the house from the back door. He sat down in his favorite armchair. "Starting with putting a murderer behind bars." He pinned Wynona with a stare. "Then preparing you for your father."

Chapter Twenty-Two

The truck bumped along the dirt road, leaving a trail of dust as Wynona, Rascal and Violet rode to the station.

"You really think speaking to Boyer is going to help?" Rascal asked. "I thought we'd set him aside as a suspect."

Wynona pursed her lips, staring through the windshield. "I don't know," she admitted. "But I've got a couple ideas in my head and I'm hoping he'll have a few answers for me."

"I'm not sure how much his lawyer will allow him to answer," Rascal muttered, resting his head against his hand. "Everything gets more complicated when there's a lawyer involved."

Wynona nodded. "I know, but right now all I have are bits and pieces and I'm trying to put them together." She turned to Rascal. "I still don't think Boyer did it. We don't have any real evidence he did and I'm not trying to change that, simply find out a few more pieces of the puzzle."

Rascal gave her the side eye. "You think you know who the culprit is?" he asked, his voice rising in surprise.

Wynona ticked her head back and forth. "No...yes...maybe..." She blew out a raspberry. "I just have some thoughts and I feel like they could possibly lead back to the same person."

The cab was quiet except for Violet's light snoring.

Rascal gave her another side eye. "You're really not going to tell me?" he asked, his voice rising in surprise.

Wynona made a face. "I'm still unsure enough that I don't want to cast aspersions on someone."

Rascal grunted. "That's how police work works, you know. We talk about our ideas."

Wynona sighed. "I know, but...I'm still not ready to share."

His jaw set and Wynona felt bad, but she was concerned about Rascal's emotions. He just didn't seem stable yet and she wasn't ready to hurt him with her idea. His temper had been off the charts and his powers were constantly throbbing around him. She had no idea what would set him off and wanted to avoid it as much as possible.

Several minutes later, they pulled into the police station, several cars pulling in behind them. "It feels weird to take so long to get here," she teased, hoping to lighten the mood. "We've been porting around for this entire case and I have to admit, it certainly made things easier."

Rascal grunted again, shrugging his shoulders. "It probably also sucked out a bunch of your energy. Driving is fine." He climbed out of the truck and walked around to her side.

Wynona waited for him, hating the distance between them. Maybe she should confide her ideas? But what if she was wrong? She simply didn't have enough information to know anything for sure and if Wynona's crazy brain caused Rascal to think differently on someone he loved, then Wynona would feel far worse than she did now.

He'll be fine, Violet said with a stretch and a yawn. *He's not quite himself yet. Give it time.*

How much time? Wynona asked as Rascal opened her door. *I hate that we're supposed to be on our honeymoon and instead we're bickering with each other.*

Yeah, well, imagine if he'd started his alpha thingy while you were sunning on a beach somewhere, huh? At least this way you know what's going on. Someday this'll all be a distant memory.

Wynona sighed mentally and walked inside. It didn't pass her notice that Rascal didn't take her hand like he usually did and she ached all the more. She had a sudden urge to confront her father and just get this whole thing over with.

That would be the epitome of stupidity. Violet grunted. *But it might be fun to watch.*

Wynona frowned. *I'm just tired of it all...and yet, in some ways, we haven't even started.*

Violet's tail rubbed across Wynona's neck. *I know. But seriously... it'll all work out. Just give him time. This isn't easy for him either.*

"Has the chief come in?" Rascal asked Amaris as she sat typing away at the front desk.

Amaris nodded. "He's with some guests in his office."

Wynona pinched her lips between her teeth. *Guests* was an interesting way to describe the fake federal bureau.

Rascal nodded curtly and headed for the hallway beyond the desk. Wynona scrambled to catch up.

Should we get the chief before we talk to Boyer? Wynona sent to her husband.

Rascal shrugged. *We'll leave him be. He's got bigger spells to cast right now.*

Wynona nodded.

Looking back over his shoulder, Rascal called out. "Skymaw. Bring Marcel to number three."

Wynona turned to see that their entourage had followed, as expected. Uncle Arune was walking with Celia and Daemon, but Daemon cut off, presumably to follow Rascal's orders.

Rascal opened the door to interrogation room number three and

Wynona, followed by their guests, followed inside. She took her usual spot at the back of the room, but Rascal shook his head.

"I think you need to sit up here," he said, indicating one of the two chairs at the table.

"I..." Wynona hesitated, then stood and followed his suggestion. "You're right, sorry."

Rascal didn't respond, but stood at the back of her chair, standing at attention while they waited for Daemon to arrive with Boyer.

It was another ten minutes before the shifter was escorted into the room. His face was pale and his shoulders slumped, with a hag's thread entwined across his wrists.

Does he really need that? Wynona asked, looking up at Rascal.

Rascal glanced her way. *Standard procedure, you know that.*

Wynona sighed quietly. "Hello, Boyer," she said in a soft tone. "How are you?"

He glared at her. "Are you seriously asking me that?"

Boy's got bite, Violet said with a snicker.

"Sit down." Rascal's tone was authoritative and Boyer obeyed quickly.

Wynona wondered if the shifter had recognized the alpha power in Rascal's voice, but when young Boyer didn't say anything, Wynona let it be. "I have a few questions for you," she said, leaning forward onto the table. She clasped her hands and tried to smile, but Boyer wasn't about to smile back.

His eyes narrowed. "Do I need my lawyer for this? Aren't you supposed to wait to talk to me until he's here?"

Wynona nodded. "We can do that, but all I have are some questions. You're welcome to answer them, or if you feel it necessary, we'll wait and call your lawyer." Wynona held her breath. She really didn't want this chat to be hindered by a lawyer, but she also couldn't force Boyer to let go of his rights. It would strictly have to be up to him.

Boyer shook his head and looked at the wall. "I guess you can ask." He scowled. "Who are you again? You were at the Strongclaws while I was there and yesterday when that chief guy was talking to me.."

Rascal stepped up closer. "This is my wife, Mrs. Strongclaw. She's an independent consultant for the department and we've asked her to lend her expertise to the investigation."

Boyer glared at Rascal. "Of course you would," he said with more than a little bite in his tone. "I'm surprised they let you on this case at all...considering your brother should be in this chair instead of me."

Wynona immediately put a hand on Rascal's leg to keep him from stepping forward. She didn't need to look at his face to see that it would be sneering at the impertinent young man. "Boyer," Wynona said, drawing his attention to her. "I want to talk about your fight with Bermin."

Boyer paled and his bravado seemed to deflate. "I didn't kill him," he said hoarsely.

Wynona nodded. "I'm not accusing you of that, but I do want to talk about the fight itself." She tilted her head. "You said you were fighting to stop him from tracking Opal down, correct?"

Boyer hesitated, his eyes darting up to Rascal, then back to Wynona. "Yes."

"But Bermin was afraid that if *you* knew Opal was sneaking out, Alpha Marcel wouldn't be far behind and then Bermin would get in trouble for it."

She hadn't truly asked it as a question, but Boyer nodded anyway.

"Can you explain to me why you were the one bursting into the Strongclaws' house, if it was Bermin's idea to track down your sister? Bermin wasn't the one leading the charge...you were."

Boyer's eyes narrowed and he grew much more suspicious. "I didn't kill him," Boyer repeated.

"I'm just asking a question, Boyer," Wynona said soothingly.

Boyer huffed and shifted in his seat. His hag's thread didn't allow him to cross his arms, so he laid back lazily in the chair, putting on an act of nonchalance. Wynona could feel the anxiety rippling off the boy, letting her know nothing about his position was real. "I couldn't let Bermin go alone," Boyer finally said with a sniff. "If he'd busted down the Strongclaws' door, my dad would've had pups and then skinned us all alive."

"So you...what?" Wynona tried to clarify. "You decided to use Bermin's anger as a way to get inside?"

Boyer shrugged, looking down at his lap. "She was missing," he said, his tone softer now. "No matter what Bermin thought, we needed to find her."

"And you trusted that Bermin could protect you," Wynona finished.

Boyer glanced up under his dark lashes. They were enough to make any girl jealous. The young man's looks probably made him popular, but his dad's rejection must create a barrier very few young shifters would want to cross. "It's not illegal," Boyer defended.

"No, it's not," Wynona said. "But you were pretty indignant at the Strongclaws'. I'm starting to wonder about your fight with Bermin. Did you pick it on purpose? Were you baiting him so that you had an excuse? Or was it something much more last minute *after* you fought?"

Boyer jerked forward. "You said you weren't accusing me of anything, Mrs. Strongclaw," he spat.

Wynona held her hands up and edged sideways as she heard Rascal's growling. "I'm asking questions, it's what I do."

She heard some shuffling noises behind her and Wynona realized she had an audience. She'd forgotten that Arune and Celia were in the room. She wondered what they were picking up on that she wasn't. There might be much to talk about once Boyer was sent back to his cell.

Boyer growled. "You're not asking questions, you're trying to get me to trip up! To admit to something I didn't do!" He pounded his chest. "I didn't kill him! Isn't that enough for you?"

"Not when I'm still trying to figure out who did," Wynona responded coolly. She wasn't ready to share what she really thought. But sometimes, bringing a suspect to the brink of their emotional capabilities brought out information that meant all the difference in the world. Wynona hated to do it, but she needed this case solved.

The door burst open. "What's going on in here?" Officer Locus demanded, his large frame taking up the doorway.

"I told you that this wasn't your domain," Chief Ligurio argued from down the hall. "When an interrogation is in progress, you have no right—"

Wynona's eyes widened when she heard the sound of flesh hitting flesh and Chief Ligurio's words cut off. She jumped to her feet.

"This case is ours," Officer Locus snarled.

"Not until I have a signed affidavit from the president himself," Rascal argued, stepping in front of Wynona in a protective stance.

Arune arrived at Rascal's side, lazily playing with a ball of magic in his hand, letting it dance from finger to finger. Daemon stood quietly next to the door, but Wynona could see his fists clench and unclench as he prepared to step in.

Celia stayed in the shadows and Wynona stepped up next to Arune to keep the thugs from knowing her sister was there. "Please leave," Wynona demanded.

"Your father won't like this," Officer Locus warned, his eyes flashing in anger.

Wynona stepped forward, letting her magic dance along her skin. Sparkles and bits of fire were visible in her peripheral vision and she could feel her hair starting to lift with the display. When Officer Locus's eyes widened, she knew she was accomplishing the intimidation she had set out for. "You can tell him that I, absolutely, one hundred percent...do not care." She spun, throwing her glowing hair over her shoulder. "Come back with the affidavit, Officer Locus. Or don't come back at all."

The room shook with the slam of the door and Wynona held herself rigid for a few moments before letting her magic and shoulders fall.

Wowzers. Violet laughed. *That was some display.*

Celia held out some of her hair, studying it. "I think I'm actually singed." She grinned at Wynona. "But man...I'm glad I wasn't on the receiving end of that display."

Wynona gave her sister a tired smile, then slumped into Rascal's waiting arms. "Someone needs to check on Chief Ligurio. I could swear I heard them hit him."

Celia started toward the door, but Daemon stopped her. "Better let me," he said, giving her a respectful nod.

Celia hesitated, then agreed and Daemon opened the door, but he didn't get very far before more shouting interrupted them.

Wynona followed Rascal and Arune to the door.

"WHERE'S MY SON!"

Ah, crud, Violet grumbled. *I didn't think things could actually get worse.*

"Sir, you'll have to wait!" Amaris shouted, following the large silhouette of Alpha Marcel as he marched down the hall.

When his green eyes landed on Rascal, they narrowed and his stride became all the more determined. "Let him go," Alpha Marcel demanded, stepping toe to toe with Rascal.

"Daemon," Wynona whispered, causing Alpha Marcel's ears to twitch. She could see his skin rippling and knew they were about to have a major fight on their hands.

Daemon's eyes started to grow black and Wynona felt the magic being sucked from the space.

"I can't do that, Marcel," Rascal stated bluntly. "You know that."

Alpha Marcel didn't back down, even as his wolf disappeared. "You don't understand," he growled. "Let Boyer go. He's innocent."

"And what proof do you have?" Rascal argued.

Alpha Marcel's nostrils flared and his face flushed. "My proof is that I did it. I'm the one who killed Bermin."

Chapter Twenty-Three

You've got to be kidding me, Violet drawled.

"Excuse me?" Rascal asked. "Are you aware of what you're saying, Alpha Marcel?"

The shifter put his haughtiest expression on and looked Rascal in the eye. "I. Killed. Bermin."

Wynona tilted her head and put her concentration into feeling the emotions of the hallway without getting overwhelmed.

A loud bellow echoed through the precinct and officers began pouring from every doorway.

Rascal backed up, the hair on his arms standing up. Wynona noticed it and turned wide eyes to Daemon. His black ones looked at her and he gave her a strained nod. Swallowing hard, Wynona realized that Rascal's alpha powers were beginning to match hers...and Daemon could no longer hold them back.

"Let it go," Wynona told the black hole.

His head jerked her direction. "You can't be serious."

"She'll protect us," Arune reassured Daemon, his eyes on the traffic jam of bodies in the space. "Let it go before you get hurt."

Daemon's lip curled, but he nodded and stepped back, shutting down his magical barrier.

Alpha Marcel's hair began to match Rascal's and spells began zinging over their heads.

"Watch it!" Wynona shouted, immediately sending a purple shield over her party. She stood on tiptoe, trying to get a feel for what was going on down the hall.

"How many of those things can you do?" Rascal shouted, ducking as another spell hit the shield, though it didn't penetrate.

"What are you asking?" Wynona snapped. Sweat was beading at her hairline as she held off all the attacks. She wasn't sure where they were coming from and had no idea if they were intended for her and her friends, but something was going on in the front of the station and it was completely out of control.

"Can you put a singular shield over every creature here?" Rascal asked. "To keep them from hurting each other until we can figure this out?"

Wynona jerked. "A single one over each person?"

He nodded and looked over his shoulder. "It's the only way I can think of to stop it all."

Give it a try, Violet said, wrapping her tail around Wynona's neck. *We're here to help.*

Arune put his hand on her shoulder. "Use my magic if you need to."

Another hand landed on her other shoulder. "I'm here too," Celia whispered, though she stayed ducked down as if to keep her face hidden.

Gratitude surged through Wynona and she knew she couldn't waste any more time. The fight at the front of the station was actually getting worse, rather than better. She blinked, turning on her magic vision. "Help me, Daemon," she ordered.

Daemon's eyes went black. "What can I do?"

"You're taller," Wynona responded. "Let me know if I miss anyone." Using her physical sight, Wynona began flicking fingers at the creatures closest to her. A bubble went over Alpha Marcel first and he came to a screeching halt. She winced when his fist banged against the wall, but Wynona moved on, ignoring his tantrums.

One by one, she worked her way down the hall, enclosing every bit of magic she could find within its own cage.

"There're a couple creatures without magic," Daemon pointed out.

"Try closing your eyes," Arune offered. "Look for life force instead of magic."

Huffing with frustration, Wynona did as she was told and squeezed her eyes closed. *Life force,* she reminded herself. *Look for the life force.*

You've done it before, Violet assured her. *Only this time, they won't be connected to you like Rascal and I were.*

A lightbulb went off in Wynona's mind and she understood what Violet was referring to. Reaching her consciousness outside of herself, she found her mental eyes overwhelmed with the display of colors and lines in the hall.

"Narrow them down, one by one," Arune whispered directly into her ear. "Contain each one separately, as much as you can, and then we should be able to get a handle on this commotion."

The process was painfully slow, or at least it felt that way to Wynona. Slowly, she separated colors and put a cage over each one. Howls, screams and shouts rang through her walls of the building with each created shield. Every creature was angry and confused at her interference, but Rascal and Arune had been right. The more forces she contained, the more the chaos died down.

"Almost there," Wynona said through gritted teeth. A warm hand landed on her lower back and Wynona almost sighed in relief at Rascal's touch. His warmth heated her cold, clammy skin and sent strength straight to her core, adding a much needed bit of energy to her work.

"All done?" Arune asked.

Wynona tilted her head to the side, still keeping her eyes closed.

"No...there's a large...tangle at the front and they're moving around so much that I can't..." She jerked back when one of them collapsed to the floor, its color rapidly growing fainter. "I think they're killing someone," Wynona whispered.

Rascal growled and his hand came off her back.

Wynona felt the loss of his touch immediately and her knees began to buckle.

Wolfy! Violet shouted and Rascal's arms wrapped all the way around her. "I've got to get up there," Rascal said, shifting Wynona in his arms.

"I can go," Daemon said, his eyes focused down the hall.

"Can you let him out?" Arune asked.

"Incoming!" Daemon shouted, moving forward as far as the shield would let him.

"What?" Wynona's eyes were wide open at this point, but she was still struggling to hold her head up. Keeping all the shields intact was draining more than she was prepared for, even with Rascal's help.

"Wynona," Daemon warned. "Let me out. NOW!" he bellowed.

Before Wynona could react, one of her connections snapped, slapping her mentally and nearly causing her to black out. The purple shields visible shimmered.

Daemon's shoulders began to heave and a great pressure built in Wynona's brain.

"You're going to kill her!" Rascal shouted at his officer. "Stand down!"

Daemon turned, his eyes having turned the deepest of blacks, swirling like they had back at the house only days before. "They're getting away," he said in a tone that sounded far away and only distantly like Daemon's normal low, smooth tone.

"Stand down!" Rascal shouted again.

Wynona's head lolled on Rascal's shoulder and his growling grew worse.

Earl Grey with a Hint of Murder

Don't you dare close those eyes, Wy. Fight it! Stay with us! We need you to help keep this from turning into a massacre!

A burst of magic in her chest had Wynona sucking in a lungful of air and she blinked rapidly, realizing that Celia was sending her extra help. *Thank you,* Wynona sent to her sister. Determination took over and though her legs shook, she stood up, keeping one hand on Rascal's shoulder to steady herself. Putting a hand to her forehead, she gritted her teeth and forced her splitting head into focus. "Go, Daemon." She grunted. "Go now."

The shield was flickering and he eyed her before slipping out into the hallway. The snap was smaller this time, but still painful, and Wynona cried out with the impact of it.

"Let them drop, Wy," Rascal demanded. "Let them drop."

Wynona shook her head. "No. We need to keep them from killing anyone else."

"We need to go upfront," Arune said, his words slow. He turned from where he'd been watching Daemon walk away. "If you haven't noticed yet, Alpha Marcel is gone."

"What!" Rascal shouted. "Just ours, Wy. Take ours down. Not the others." He pulled one of her arms over his shoulders. "Come on."

"RASCAL!"

Arune's arm went around Wynona's waist. "Go," he urged Rascal. "Wynona, do as he says. Take our shield down. Celia, stay with me and help us walk to the front while Rascal goes to see what's happened."

Celia grunted, but came up on Wynona's other side, taking the arm that Rascal was letting go of.

Wynona took a deep breath, focused her magic and let their shield drop. She tensed, waiting for more spells to hit them, but the area was quiet of magic, other than the hum of her cages.

Rascal bolted, weaving through the caged bodies and ignoring the shouts of outrage.

"The shield," Wynona panted as they slowly followed her husband's footsteps. "That had to be the snap."

Arune nodded. "I didn't see who came up behind him, but somehow another creature broke through and took Alpha Marcel with them."

"He went willingly?" Celia asked with a grunt. "Really?"

"No. He was being carried over someone's shoulder," Arune clarified. "All I could see was his back bouncing among the bodies." He took a deep breath. "Our dear black hole might have had a better viewpoint."

"WY!" Rascal shouted, coming back into view of the hallway. "We need you," he pleaded. Rascal's breathing was ragged. "He's dying."

"Who?" Celia demanded, but Wynona didn't care who. If Rascal cared, she cared and she forced her legs into compliance. Stumbling forward, she let go of Arune and Celia, using the wall and the shield still up around officers and station visitors to make her way around the corner. "NO!" she cried, falling to her knees and crawling the rest of the way. "Chief," Wynona whispered, putting a hand to his cold face.

A scream of anguish rang through the room and Celia nearly knocked Wynona over as she clambered to be close to the vampire.

"What happened?" Wynona asked, climbing over Chief Ligurio's legs to get on the other side. There was no way she was asking Celia to step away. Wynona wouldn't have left if it was Rascal.

"I don't know," Rascal said, his voice high pitched and his eyes wild. His hands tugged at his hair.

Daemon stood next to him, still and quiet, but just as confused. "He was bleeding out when I got out front," Daemon responded. "I don't know who did it or how it happened."

"The life force," Wynona muttered to herself. "The one I saw fading."

Bingo, Violet said, speaking up for the first time in several minutes. *And it doesn't really matter what happened. Focus on how you can fix it.*

Wynona's hands shook. "Can I?" she asked her familiar.

Only one way to find out.

Wynona reached out and rested her trembling fingers against his sternum, taking a deep breath to cleanse her thoughts and focus her abilities once more. It took longer than she was comfortable with to find his life line and what she saw nearly tore her out of her trance.

Lines of red were bleeding out of his back at an astonishing rate and Wynona knew there was a large wound there. One too deep for his vampire healing to handle.

"Please," Celia whispered, her voice broken and low. "Please, Wy. I'll do anything. Anything."

Wynona hated to do it, but she ignored her sister. Chief wasn't dying on Wynona's watch. Not now, not ever and though she hoped Celia and Chief Ligurio would eventually reconcile their differences, healing him had nothing to do with those hopes.

Chief Ligurio was her friend, a creature Wynona called family, despite his grumpy attitude and Wynona wasn't going to let this be the end of their budding relationship.

"Violet?" Wynona asked.

The mouse's tail curled tighter and her tiny paws landed directly on Wynona's skin. *Here we go.*

Wynona's face scrunched into a tight scowl as she focused every bit of energy and magic she had left into Chief Ligurio's body. There wasn't much time left. Even now, she could feel that his blood was slowing down and if she didn't get the hole stopped quickly, the flow would be completely gone.

He needs more, Violet urged.

"I'm trying," Wynona said, but her reserves were waning. She could feel the purple bubbles popping one by one as she turned everything toward the vampire on the floor. The noise grew and bodies were moving around her, but someone must have been acting as guard because Wynona wasn't being bumped or moved in any way.

At one point, she realized the room was growing quiet, which only made her focus harder. She apparently had an audience and they more than likely were all waiting to see if she would heal their boss.

"It's not enough," Wynona whispered, feeling weak and worn. She had stopped the flow of blood, but he needed help recovering and she was struggling to help rebuild his health.

"You can't quit!" Celia screamed. "Please, you can't stop."

Wynona doubled down, feeling her body sway, but refusing to give up. Her hand went numb, followed by her arm, and the feeling slowly began to leak into her chest.

Hold on, Wy! You're giving him too much! You're going to kill yourself! Violet screamed.

"WY!" Rascal shouted.

"I don't think so," said a calm, low tone.

A weight landed on Wynona's hand and her skin began to sizzle, sucking the numbness back out of her body. With it, clarity returned and Wynona gasped, bringing herself back to life in a way she hadn't realized she was losing. Her eyes popped open and she looked directly at her uncle's black eyes.

"You really need some training," he said with a smirk. "No more waiting or you're going to get someone killed." He squeezed his hand on top of hers and Wynona fed the magic he was sending through her hand and into Chief Ligurio's core.

Ten seconds passed and Wynona felt the magic slow down. She looked down just as red eyes opened and Chief Ligurio jerked upright, then put a hand to his head, groaning.

"Deverell," Celia sobbed, throwing herself at him. They fell in a heap back on the floor, Chief Ligurio moaning in pain once again.

Despite how much the landing must have hurt, his arms wrapped around Celia and he tucked his face into her neck while she cried uncontrollably.

"Come on," Rascal said, holding a hand out to Wynona. She took it and stood shakily to her feet.

"What happened?" she asked her uncle, as he climbed to his own as well.

"You were giving him your own life force," Arune said, straightening the cuffs of his shirt sleeves.

Rascal grumbled and tucked her into his chest. "How come every time I ask you to do something, you nearly kill yourself?"

"I didn't know I was," Wynona defended, leaning into his strength.

"Your reserves are more than a match for anything you needed to do today," Arune said coolly, glancing around at the bewildered crowd of officers. "But you waste it without realizing how much you're using." He turned back to her. "You need to learn to hone and focus the magic, not throw out a tsunami every time there's a problem."

Wynona sighed and nodded. "Teaching moments have been limited," she said.

Rascal rubbed her back. "You've done great," he said into her hair, kissing the top of her head. "But he's right. We need to get your settled once and for all. In fact, I think we should take you off the case until you're more in control."

Wynona leaned back, straightening her spine and shaking her head. She reached up to scratch Violet, thanking the mouse for her help. "You can't take me off the case," she argued, her voice gravelly and tired. When Rascal opened his mouth, she held up her hand. "Because I'm pretty darn sure I've figured out who the killer is."

Chapter Twenty-Four

At the rate that they were collecting creatures, Wynona was going to have to expand her house. Her small cabin had been roomy for one person. Adding Rascal had made it just about right. Now, however, they had nearly a dozen people who regularly were appearing in her living room and there simply weren't enough chairs to hold them all, let alone enough kitchen cupboard space to keep food for them.

Feed me...or die, Violet demanded from her place on the kitchen table.

Wynona raised an eyebrow. *Well, that isn't melodramatic at all.*

The purple mouse's smile was anything but sweet. *Okay...feed me...or I'll bite your face off.*

Wynona choked on her laughter and brought a muffin to the table with the wave of her hand. "Happy?"

Violet didn't respond. She was too busy stuffing pastry into her tiny mouth to acknowledge Wynona's teasing.

Shaking her head at her familiar's behavior, Wynona magically carried several trays into the sitting room where everyone was slumped around, looking as tired as Wynona felt.

Earl Grey with a Hint of Murder

"Let me help with that." Mrs. Strongclaw hurried over and grabbed one of the trays right out of the air.

"Thanks," Wynona responded, though the help had been completely unnecessary. Between Rascal and Violet, Wynona's energy and magic had come back rather quickly, which was a good thing, since Chief Ligurio and Daemon were both still as wrung out as old brooms.

The debacle at the station had everyone subdued and Wynona was sure that she couldn't have pried Celia away from Chief Ligurio if their lives depended on it.

There's something about almost losing the person you love that makes you realize just how precious time is.

Wynona turned to look at Rascal, where he stared at her from across the room. His look was steady and intense and sent a thrill through her. He'd been so upset she wasn't willing to share her thoughts on the murderer, and while she couldn't blame him, she was also grateful she had kept her thoughts to herself.

Now though, his anger seemed to be gone and he had been attentive and sweet since they'd left the station. *I promise not to keep using that tactic to keep us together,* she said, hoping he would understand the teasing.

He snorted and his eyes glowed brighter. *Thank goodness. I don't think my heart could continue to handle the stress.*

"Wynona." Chief Ligurio's words held much less snap than usual, but the room quieted just the same.

"Yes, Chief?"

"You had some thoughts for us?"

Wynona nodded, taking a deep breath. Why was this always so hard? She clasped her hands together to keep them from shaking. She had a feeling that what she had to say was going to shock the group. "Sartel did it."

For two seconds, no one spoke, then it seemed as if everyone spoke at once.

"You can't be serious."

"The girl barely speaks."

"How could you possibly think that?"

"Didn't Alpha Marcel just confess?"

Chief Ligurio climbed to his feet, slightly shaky, but tall and commanding nonetheless. "Quiet," he said. The underlying menace in his tone was enough to bring every creature to heel. He turned to Wynona. "I believe what we're all trying to say...is why do you think that?" His red eyes glared at the rest of the room. "I, for one, have seen your intuition be spot on too many times to discount your thoughts, but Ms. Gerrant seems like a spell out of left field. I'd like an explanation."

Wynona nodded, feeling every set of eyes on her and particularly those of her in-laws. Mrs. Strongclaw looked wounded, as if Wynona's declaration was a personal injury to her person.

"I know we've got more issues, with Alpha Marcel missing and tracking down whoever stabbed you, Chief, but Sartel is the common denominator in every story." Sighing, Wynona sat down on the edge of the coffee table. "The scene of the crime has bothered me this entire time and it took forever to figure out why." She looked up at Rascal. "You know how you said a small wolf can't take on a big one?"

Rascal nodded curtly, the edges of his eyes tight with tension.

"What if she caught Bermin off guard?"

Rascal frowned. "I...suppose anyone could kill with no advance notice that way."

Wynona nodded and turned back to the group. "Alpha Marcel, in the hallway, when the station broke out in chaos, shifted just his hand. He was clawing at the shield I put up." She took in a deep breath. "I believe that Bermin slipped back through the open window, after you escorted them out, Alpha Strongclaw. And I believe that Sartel followed. By this point, she knew that Opal and Barry had run away and the only way she could think to stop them was to create a situation where the law got involved."

"So she killed Bermin?" Mrs. Strongclaw said flatly. "Partially shifted and killed him."

Wynona nodded.

"Why in the world would she?" Rascal's mother continued. "Why would she care if Barry and Opal ran away?"

Wynona hesitated only a moment before replying. "Because she's in love with Barry."

The room went silent again and Wynona powered on, determined to prove her theory.

"The cuts in Bermin's neck. They were thin." Wynona shook her head. "Too thin. They wouldn't have been done by a large, male wolf whose claws are thick. But a tiny, dainty female?"

Rascal grunted and shifted his weight.

"Also, Boyer was surprised when Colby said hello to Sartel. Did you notice?"

Alpha Strongclaw scowled. "What do you mean?"

"When Colby began flirting with her, Boyer jerked back, making a face. He hadn't noticed that Sartel had followed them from the Marcel compound."

Alpha Strongclaw's brows furrowed deeper. "Okay..."

"Mrs. Strongclaw, you didn't realize that Sartel was helping the day you brought breakfast to the cabin, right?"

Mrs. Strongclaw nodded reluctantly.

"She's so small and quiet that she slips in and out without notice. Sartel realized something was going on with Opal. She followed Boyer. Then she followed Bermin back through the window. Bermin had come back because he thought you were all lying and that Opal was around somewhere." Wynona shrugged. "He probably smelled her, since Barry said he would walk around with socks and shirts in his pockets so no one would notice her scent as being abnormal when she snuck onto the compound."

Alpha Strongclaw's jaw clenched and he growled softly.

"All this time...she's been coming to see the boys..." Mrs. Strongclaw spoke slowly as if working it out while talking. "I thought she enjoyed Colby's flirtation." Her eyes were bright when she looked at Wynona. "But she was coming to see Barry?"

Wynona nodded. "Sartel told me that Opal and Barry were her best friends and she was desperate for news of them. I assumed that was why she was at the compound. Then you sent her home and later I, when I ran into Opal and Barry at the forest, Opal said she had no close friends at the Marcel compound. That's why no one knew they were planning to run away."

"That's why Sartel followed Boyer," Mrs. Strongclaw breathed. "That's what you're saying. No one sees her because of her size and how quiet she is, so she sneaks around getting answers."

"Barry was kind to her," Rascal said gruffly, his arms folded over his chest. "Barry's nice to everyone and so he was nice to her. Colby was too loud, but she tolerated him." Rascal shook his head. "I never realized that every time I saw them, Colby was always the one doing the talking. Sartel never sought him out."

"She also called Barry, Baryn," Wynona pointed out. "No one else calls him that." She gave Rascal a sad smile. "She uses a different name for him because he's precious to her."

Chief Ligurio scrubbed a hand over his face. "While your story makes sense, we still have to have a way to prove it."

"I believe we have two ways," Wynona responded. She held up a finger. "We test the rest of the hairs that were on Bermin's pants."

Chief Ligurio grunted. "Four hairs. All blond. Are you saying they were different shifters?"

Wynona nodded. "You can see through their bloodlines that the Marcel pack tends toward lighter colors. Whereas the Strongclaws are dark. All the fur was blond. It could have been multiple shifters from the Marcel pack."

Chief Ligurio put his hands on his hips. "I'm assuming your second way is more feasible since my station is in utter chaos at the moment?" He raised a dark eyebrow at her challengingly.

Wynona sucked in a breath and held it. "The other way requires a bit of subterfuge."

"I'm listening," the chief replied.

Earl Grey with a Hint of Murder

Wynona glanced at the Strongclaws, who were looking more and more stricken, the more she talked. "We set her up."

"Is that really necessary?" Alpha Strongclaw asked, stepping forward. "She's a young girl. Young, impulsive...she was orphaned as a pup. Trapping her like this feels wrong."

Wynona stood to meet the allegations head on. "While I understand your concern, we need definitive proof that she's guilty and without a lab, this is the only way I can think of that will work."

The alpha pinched the bridge of his nose, squeezing his eyes shut. When he opened them, they were begging Wynona, for what, she wasn't sure. "Are you really sure about this? Absolutely sure?"

Wynona nodded. "It couldn't have been anyone else," she replied hoarsely. "Sartel was there. She's the connecting link. She isn't interested in Colby, no one notices when she slips in and out. I *felt* Boyer's surprise at seeing her behind him." She stepped closer to her father in law. "Did you smell anyone out of place? During dinner that night?"

The alpha shook his head.

"What about afterwards? When you were looking specifically for Opal or Barry. Did you smell anything that shouldn't have been there?"

He hesitated, then shook his head again.

"What about hearing? Did you hear anything that was out of the ordinary?"

The alpha closed his eyes in defeat and again shook his head.

"She barely makes a noise," Wynona whispered. "She's small and quiet. I don't like the idea of her killing any more than you do, but she's the only one who makes sense."

"What about Alpha Marcel?" Mrs. Strongclaw argued. "I can feel your conviction, Wynona. I know you believe what you're saying, but you just don't know her like we do." Mrs. Strongclaw looked from creature to creature, seeking someone to back up her claims. "The pup is afraid of her own shadow. Alpha Marcel, on the other hand, has a temper to light the city on fire. He said it was him. Can't we use that?"

"We've got a few problems with that," Chief Ligurio said, beginning to pace the room. "One, the alpha isn't here."

"So find him!" Mrs. Strongclaw cried.

Chief Liguruio shot her a quelling glance, but Mrs. Strongclaw only tilted her chin in the air. "While we plan to do that," the vampire said in a tight voice, "I think Wynona is onto something." He turned toward her. "What is your plan for finding out Ms. Gerrant's guilt?"

Wynona looked at Rascal, who nodded encouragingly at her. She turned and walked to Mrs. Strongclaw. "I need you to call Sartel and give her a message."

The shifter didn't move.

"Please tell her that Barry made contact with Rascal and that while he's doing alright, he misses what was left behind."

Mrs. Strongclaw dropped her chin to her chest. "She'll think he was referring to her."

"And you think she'll come running?" Chief Ligurio asked.

Wynona spun. "Wouldn't you if you wanted a creature to love you?"

The room was quiet. "I would."

All eyes turned to Celia, whose red rimmed eyes told the crowd everything they needed to know.

"If I had any hope of the man I loved loving me back, I'd move heaven and earth to find him."

"Where do you think she'll come?" Chief Ligurio asked. "Where do you plan to catch her?"

Wynona spread her hands out. "I believe she'll come after Rascal."

"And that means here."

Wynona nodded. "Yes. That means here."

"Promise you won't hurt her," Mrs. Strongclaw whispered.

Wynona looked at her mother-in-law. "We won't hurt her," Wynona assured the shifter. "But we also can't let her go."

It took several long moments before Mrs. Strongclaw nodded and pulled her phone from her back pocket. The silence of the crowd was a heavy blanket as ringing came through the speaker.

"H-hello? Mrs. Strongclaw?"

"Hi, Sartel," Mrs. Strongclaw said through a tight throat. Her eyes never left Wynona's. "I, uh…have some news…and thought you'd be happy to hear it."

"Is Baryn back?" Sartel immediately pressed. "Have they found him? Is he…are he and Opal alright?"

Mrs. Strongclaw finally released Wynona by closing her eyes. "He isn't back, per se…but he made contact with Rascal."

Alpha Strongclaw put his hand on his wife's shoulder and gave her a squeeze.

"He, uh, said he was alright…but…"

"But?" Sartel asked, hope nearly tangible in her tone.

"But he missed what was left behind." Mrs. Strongclaw swallowed hard and wiped at the tears tracking down her cheeks. "I'm sure you can understand that. Leaving the way he did."

"Oh, yes," Sartel breathed excitedly. "I know exactly what he means. Thank you so much, Mrs. Strongclaw! I'm so glad you called me!"

The line cut off and Mrs. Strongclaw stared at her phone until her husband took it out of her hand and tucked it into his own pocket.

"We'd better go," he said, pulling his wife into his side. "I'm assuming you don't want us all here when it happens."

Wynona let out a sigh of relief when Chief Ligurio took charge. "That would be best, yes." He turned to Celia. "Can you port them home?"

Celia stood, nodding and still subdued. "But I'm coming back."

"I'd expect nothing less."

They shared a significant stare before Celia walked over and took the Strongclaws home.

She looked at Rascal, who looked just as sad as his parents, and Wynona wasn't sure how to comfort him, but when he walked over and wrapped his arms around her, she let him take her weight. "I'm sorry."

"Not your fault," he assured her, rubbing her back. "And I hate to say it, but she probably won't waste time." He leaned back, looking her in the face. "We need to get ready. It's going to be a long night."

Chapter Twenty-Five

"Someone's coming," Wynona whispered. She kept her vision on the life force moving through the treeline.

"How long?" Chief Ligurio asked.

Wynona tilted her head back and forth. "I don't know. She's darting between trees and looks to be in wolf form." Wynona's heart was fluttering. She had hoped to be wrong. The idea of sending quiet, small Sartel to prison was almost more than anyone could bear, Wynona included.

When the pieces of the puzzle had added up in her mind, with Alpha Marcel's partial shift clicking it all into place, Wynona had been sick to her stomach.

Chief Ligurio's near death had kept her from falling apart, but having to share her findings with everyone had been painfully difficult.

"Will she shift back?" Chief Ligurio asked. "Will she smell us here?"

"It'll be fine," Rascal offered quietly. He stretched. "Why don't you, Skymaw, and Celia wait down the hall? I think Sartel will come to the door in human form and I think she won't find it odd to have your smells here, as long as they don't smell stronger than Wynona and me."

And me. Violet sniffed, grooming her whiskers. The mouse didn't seem the least bit upset at the task ahead that night.

"And you," Rascal agreed.

Chief Ligurio took Celia's hand and began walking. "We'll come in when the time is right." Daemon followed them at a small distance, obviously keeping away from the recently affirmed couple.

They certainly got cozy quickly, Violet said with a snort. *You were right about those near-death experiences. Maybe I should fake something in order to get a date this week.*

Wynona gaped at her familiar. "You wouldn't dare."

Violet shrugged. *Why not? It seems to work for you and Celia.*

Because most mice are terrified of danger, Rascal responded. *And likely won't rescue you.*

Ah, but imagine the one that would, Violet said gleefully. *Won't he be worth it?*

Rascal put a finger to his lips and Wynona closed her eyes to realize that Sartel was almost at the doorstep. Sighing, Rascal pulled a magazine off the coffee table and flipped it open. "Sit down," he mouthed.

Wynona sat down quickly, grabbing the nearest book and opening it up.

I didn't know you could read upside down, Violet snickered.

Wynona felt her cheeks heat as she turned the book over.

Or that you were interested in police procedurals.

Wynona pinched her lips together and glared over the top of the book.

Violet snickered and went back to grooming herself.

"I don't know how you can be so calm," Wynona said in a barely audible voice.

And I don't know why you're so worried, Violet shot back.

Wynona rested the book in her lap and sighed. *I'm not nervous as much as I'm sad. I hate to see good creatures make choices like this that have such terrible consequences. Especially since this one doesn't appear to have been premeditated.*

Violet paused and gave Wynona an understanding look. *Rascal knows what he's talking about,* she said.

Wynona nodded. "I know."

The knock on the door had Wynona jumping and their conversation coming to a quick end.

Rascal stood and stepped around Wynona. "Hang here."

She heard him answer the door and soft voices made their way to the sitting room. With each moment as they grew louder, Wynona felt her heart begin to speed up, trying to climb her throat the closer they came.

"Oh, Mrs. Strongclaw!" Sartel said, rushing into the room and hugging Wynona tightly. She stepped back. "Did you see him too? I just knew you'd find Baryn...and Opal, of course," Sartel quickly corrected.

"Sartel, I..." Wynona swallowed hard. This was worse than telling the Strongclaws. "There was no message."

Sartell blinked a few times, looking confused. "I'm sorry?" she asked. "I don't understand."

Rascal came up behind the tiny woman. "Sartel, Barry didn't contact me."

Sartel spun. "But I thought..." She put a fist to her mouth. "Your mother said..."

"You love him, don't you?" Wynona asked.

Sartel paused.

"Baryn," Wynona clarified. "You love him."

Sartel slowly spun back around, her eyes wide and her face pale.

"It's why you followed Boyer," Wynona continued. "You knew something was wrong, when Opal came up missing and you heard them fighting."

Sartel's hand fell to her side and tears tracked down her cheeks.

"Once at the house, you left with the group, but snuck back in through the window when you realized that Bermin wasn't giving up." Wynona's own tears began to fall. "And then you had a thought."

Sartel put a hand in the air to stop Wynona. "Please..." She begged. "I..." Sartel sniffed and wiped at her face. "I never meant for it to go this far."

"Sartel," Rascal began. "Did you, or did you not, kill Bermin, in order to keep us looking for Barry and Opal?"

Sartel hung her head and a sob broke through. Slowly, she shook her head back and forth. "I didn't plan it," she whispered thickly. "I... I just wanted to give you a reason to stop him from leaving." She looked up, begging Wynona to understand. "He and Opal are both a- adults, and I knew that...I knew..."

"You knew that the police wouldn't go after two shifters who were old enough to make their own choices," Wynona finished for her.

Sartel closed her eyes, causing more tears to fall, and nodded. She turned to Rascal. "Do you need to take me in, now?"

"That would be my job," Chief Ligurio said, stepping out of the hallway.

Sartel jumped, but after a moment, walked over and held out her hands.

Daemon stepped forward with a hag's thread, but the chief stopped him. "I don't think that's necessary."

Daemon glanced sideways at his boss, nodded and simply put a hand on Sartel's shoulder. "This way, please, Ms. Gerrant."

Wynona wrapped her arms around herself, feeling as if a piece of her were being ripped off as she watched the young woman be escorted out.

"It was supposed to be me, you know."

Wynona forced herself to keep eye contact.

Sartel shrugged lightly and gave a wry smile. "Opal has always been so...spoiled and flighty. But Baryn is so good and down to earth." Sartel's lips trembled. "I would have been a much better match for him. Don't you think?" When Wynona couldn't answer, Sartel turned and disappeared.

Celia sent a sympathetic look over her shoulder as she followed them outside, where she would port the crew to the station.

As soon as the door was closed, Rascal closed the ten feet between them and wrapped Wynona in his arms and against his chest.

"I've helped put a lot of killers behind bars," she sobbed into his chest. "And several of them have been extremely dangerous stand-offs…but I think that might have been the worst one yet."

Rascal kissed the top of her head. "Agreed," he whispered, leaving another kiss. "Agreed."

Violet whimpered and Wynona pulled back just enough to pick up her familiar from the table. "Why, Violet…are you crying?"

Violet scrubbed at her face. *No,* she snapped. *I don't cry. I express my emotions through food consumption and what you heard was my stomach growling. There's enough drama going on in this house to cause me to eat an entire cake. It'll take me forever to fit back into my pants.*

The soft laugh Wynona gave was mostly out of politeness. Recovering from this situation was going to take time and even Violet's antics weren't enough quite yet.

Rascal rubbed her back. "We need to get Barry and Opal out of the forest." Rascal looked that direction, as if he could see through the walls of the house. "I hate to leave them in there any longer than necessary."

Wynona stepped back and wiped her face. "You're right, of course." She began walking. "I suppose there's no time like the present."

"Hang on." Rascal ran down the hall and grabbed a large flashlight out of the closet before reappearing at her side. "We might need this."

"Violet? Are you coming?"

Only if I can bring a cookie with me.

Wynona rolled her eyes, marched to the kitchen to grab one out of the jar, then picked up her familiar. "Try not to drop it."

It's hard to drop something from your mouth, Violet shot back.

Taking a deep breath, Wynona headed outside. It was cool and the sky was clear, but that did little to help her feel better. She could smell the damp earthiness of the surrounding grove and the smell was normally soothing, but the closer Wynona got to the edge of the forest, the less soothed she felt.

"It's creepy at night," Rascal stated with a shudder.

Wynona blew out the breath she'd been holding. "I guess there's nothing to do but give this a try."

"Why do you always try to kill yourself when I'm around?" Arune drawled. "I'm starting to take it personally."

Wynona spun and put a hand to her heart. "I didn't hear you."

Arune stared at the woods, his eyes glittering in the moonlight. "You were preoccupied," he muttered.

"Rayn back at the house?" Wynona asked.

"Hmm..." Arune glanced sideways at her. "She's in the middle of an experiment and I can barely get her to talk to me, let alone come out for something like this." He grinned. "Just like old times." Arune looked at Rascal. "I'm assuming everything went according to plan?"

Rascal nodded curtly. "I hate to say it was easy, but she went willingly."

Arune tsked his tongue and shook his head. "Poor creature. Hopefully the judge will go easy on her."

"So...the forest?" Wynona turned their attention back to the task at hand. She didn't want to start crying again, and the emotions were close enough to the surface that she would if they didn't move forward.

"Yes...the forest." Arune tugged at his cuffs. "What was your plan?"

"Umm..." Wynona shrugged. "Last time I built a shield around myself, as a tunnel. It held back the magic of the forest so I could actually move where I wanted."

Earl Grey with a Hint of Murder

"And you plan to do the same?"

She nodded.

Arune shrugged and waved at the forest. "Be my guest."

Frowning and feeling slightly like she was being made the fool, Wynona stepped forward.

Careful, Rascal warned her. *You've already expended yourself once today. No need to push it again.*

Acknowledging his statement, Wynona closed her eyes and began to build her magic.

"Remember," Arune said from behind her. "Focused...not flooded."

Violet wrapped her tail around Wynona's neck.

Are you sure you want to come? Wynona asked. *It could be dangerous.*

Don't make me bite your ear, Violet shot back. *I'm not being left out this time.*

"Okay..." Wynona breathed. "Here we go." Her bubble came up quickly around her body and slowly she began to push it forward, expecting a heavy resistance when she hit the line of trees.

Instead of resistance, however...she hit a brick wall and her magic bounced back, knocking her off her feet.

"Wy!" Rascal shouted, dropping to his knees beside her. "What happened?"

Wynona shook her head. "I'm not sure. The trees..."

"They remember," Arune breathed, stepping forward slightly, awe in his tone. "They know you thwarted them once before and they won't let you do it again." He reached out and his fingers jerked back when sparks shot out from an invisible barrier.

Rascal stood up, his throat rumbling as he growled. "There has to be a way." He lunged forward before Wynona could stop him, and was sent flying backward ten feet, landing with a thud on the damp night grass.

"I'm fine," he wheezed, holding up a hand as Wynona came running.

Putting a hand to his chest, she sent a quick thread of healing magic into his system. Together they climbed to their feet and faced the woods. "What are we going to do?" Wynona asked. Guilt was beginning to weigh heavy on her. If they never got Barry and Opal back out, it would be her fault. She'd left them in there when she'd had the chance to save them. How would she ever face her in-laws again?

"We have to find a way in," Rascal growled.

Arune shook his head and walked back their way. "I don't think the grove is going to relent."

"We can't just leave Barry and Opal in there forever!" Wynona shouted, panic beginning to take over her already overwrought emotions.

Arune leaned toward her. "Then use that brilliant brain of yours, dear witch…and take back what is yours."

Chapter Twenty-Six

Wynona didn't notice when she began to shiver until Rascal wrapped his arms around her from behind. "Thanks," she murmured, her eyes still on the grove. She'd been standing in the same spot for nearly an hour, studying the forest and trying to figure out how to get inside. Any spells or attempts to even touch the line of trees had sent the magic or creature bouncing back like a child's toy.

Rascal's heat helped slow down her racing heart and shaking limbs, bringing a bit of clarity to Wynona's thoughts as they continued to circle.

"No ideas, huh?" he whispered against her ear.

Wynona pushed her lips to the side. "Only one...and it's a bit crazy."

His large chest shrugged behind her. "Crazy can be good sometimes."

Wynona looked over her shoulder at him. "You really want me to give it a go?"

"Well...what are you planning to try? If it involves risking your life, I can't say I'll be fond of it."

She gave him a small smile and patted his hands where they were resting at her waist. "I can't guarantee it won't be risking my life, but...I think I'm going to talk to it."

There was a pause. "Talk to it?"

Wynona nodded. "Arune said magic was a living entity, remember?"

Rascal grunted. "So you're what? Going to negotiate entrance and exits?"

Wynona raised one shoulder. "Something like that."

"There's always a price," Arune said softly.

Wynona's head whipped to the side. Arune was sitting calmly, suit and all, on the grass, his eyes closed and his hands on his knees. He looked to be meditating, but his three piece suit was so completely out of place that Wynona wasn't sure whether to laugh or be impressed.

One eye cracked open.

"What kind of price?" Rascal demanded.

Arune opened the other eye and gave Rascal a patient look. "I cannot answer that. Only that magic, of any kind, requires a price." He looked at Wynona. "You should know that since you already paid one to the grimoire."

I totally forgot about that, Violet chittered. She laughed. *He couldn't get it to talk to him,* the mouse said. *Because the book is bound to you.*

"Well, at least we know he can't steal it," Rascal muttered.

Grumbling, Arune stood and brushed off his clothes before facing the woods as well. "That price was merely a connection of your magic. But this time...I cannot say what a being as large and old as the grove might ask."

"We'll find another way," Rascal said immediately.

Wynona slowly shook her head, a strange calm coming over her. "There isn't another way," she said. She looked at Rascal. "We both know it."

"Then I'll pay whatever it is," he said, stepping closer to her and grasping her upper arms. "You can save Barry and Opal and I'll pay whatever price those old trees want."

"Her destiny is not yet over," Arune stated. "It won't ask her life."

"There are worse things than dying," Rascal said, piercing Arune with a dark stare.

Arune nodded. "The truth of that cannot be denied. Still..." He stepped forward a few feet. "I do not think it will be as high as that."

Rascal pulled Wynona into his chest. "I don't want to risk it," he whispered, squeezing her tightly and burying his face in her hair.

"We don't have a choice," Wynona said back, grasping at his shirt and clutching it as tightly as she could. "We can't leave them in there. You know that." Pulling back, Wynona couldn't stop a couple of tears from falling. "And I'm the only one strong enough to handle this."

"My powers are growing," Rascal argued.

"They are." Wynona smiled and ran her fingers through his hair. She had no idea when he'd last cut it. It was nearly to his chin at this point. "You need a haircut."

"Stop changing the subject," Rascal grumbled. He sighed and rested his forehead against hers. "I can't stop you...can I?"

Slowly, Wynona shook her head back and forth. "It has to be done."

Rascal closed his eyes and sighed. "Why does it always have to be you?" he asked hoarsely.

She won't be alone, you know, Violet snapped. *You're acting as if this is the end of the world.*

Rascal didn't laugh. "I need her back," he told the mouse. "In one piece, body and mind."

Violet gave him a mock salute.

Rascal barked a laugh. "Like I believe that kind of submission."

Violet snickered and shrugged.

Sobering, Rascal turned back to Wynona. "I love you," he said, leaning forward to kiss her forehead. "Please come back to me." His eyes began to glow. "And don't be reckless."

Wynona nodded. "I promise." It took her a full twenty seconds before she could find the strength to turn to the forest and face what was coming. She and Rascal had had so little time together and she wanted nothing more than to be able to shut out the world and revel in each other's company.

But that dream would never come true if they didn't stop her father. And the next step was to finish the case they were on, which meant bringing Barry and Opal home. Once all that was wrapped up, Wynona and her oddly powerful band of magic users would turn their attention to the man hiding in the dark.

Slowly, she walked forward, only stopping when there was less than a foot between her and the treeline. "Hello," Wynona said softly.

Violet thumped her tail against her neck. *Are you serious? That can't be how you—*

The branches swayed and a wind hit Wynona, shutting Violet up quickly. The breeze was far from soft and caressing, but it also wasn't meant to knock her flat this time. "I, uh...I'd like to talk to you about entrance into your beautiful forest," Wynona continued.

This time Violet stayed quiet, but her paws gripped the edges of Wynona's hair.

The branches swayed again, but Wynona couldn't catch any true response. Slowly, she brought a hand up, but the zap of magic had her bringing it back to her chest quickly.

"Wynona?"

She looked over her shoulder to see Arune tapping his temple. "Not all mouths work audibly."

Blinking, Wynona turned back to the trees. "I apologize," she said sincerely. "I'm new to this and still learning." Closing her eyes, she opened her magical vision and nearly stumbled at the brightness of the life force of the forest. *It's like a forest fire,* Wynona said to Rascal. *So bright and moving, like a true, living entity.*

Try again, he urged her. *But like Arune said, try it mentally instead of out loud.*

Earl Grey with a Hint of Murder

Wynona nodded, filling her chest with a long breath. *Hello... Grove...I'm sorry. How should I address you?*

The magic swelled and grew in her mind's eyes before settling again and Wynona strained to hear an answer, but nothing was forthcoming.

I'm having trouble understanding, Wynona sent to the trees. *Can you help me learn?*

The force swelled again and this time, there was the murmured sound of chatter. Unconsciously leaning forward, Wynona strained to separate out the sounds and find a word she recognized.

We see you...

Wynona stiffened.

Well, that's not creepy at all, Violet drawled.

We see and know you.

Wynona nodded uncertainly. *Do you know who I am?*

The witch of prophecy... The voice was several layers deep, with dozens of voices mixed together from high to low, hiding any sort of categorization for gender or creature.

I'm called Wynona. What can I call you?

We are too many to name.

Wynona made a face. It would certainly make this more awkward than it already was to not have a name to call them. *Can I call you Grove? Will that suffice?*

The voices didn't answer right away. *We will answer.*

Wynona blew out a breath she had forgotten she was holding. *You have two occupants in your woods that belong out here. I'm grateful you've kept them safe, but it's time for them to return home. I'd like to negotiate bringing them here.*

Those who enter are bound by the law.

Wynona got out, you nincompoops! Violet shouted.

"Hush," Wynona urged. *I'm sorry. My familiar is protective. But if I was able to leave, why can't they? I realize there will need to be an exchange.*

And what are you willing to give, Witch?

Wynona chewed on her bottom lip. *What would benefit you? I don't understand your magic well enough to know what would be of use to you.*

Those who enter are bound by the law...your leaving broke the accord. The last words had a distinctive hissing sound to them and Wynona fought the urge to back up. The sinister tone had her stomach churning uncomfortably.

I didn't know about the...accord, Wynona offered. *I'm sorry that I broke rules.*

The law was made long ago.

What do you gain from it? Wynona asked. Maybe if she knew what the laws did in favor of the forest, she could offer something similar.

We are too many to name.

Wynona made a face and rubbed her forehead before her hand stilled. "The magic," she whispered.

"Every creature," Arune breathed. "Every single one."

If a creature crosses your border, their magic is yours, Wynona declared. *Is that the rule?*

All who enter are bound.

"That's why there are too many to name," Wynona said out loud, her eyes open with wonder. "It's the spirits of every creature who eventually passed away in there."

"We have to get them out," Rascal growled, coming up close behind her. "We can't let them become part of the forest." Her eyes narrowed as she remembered the eyes of all the wolves who had been present when she'd walked to Rayn's castle. "But some creatures live there well. Like the ones who followed me going to Rayn's." She turned to Arune.

He nodded. "I don't think the forest kills them," he mused. "But why are there so many?"

Grove...can animals leave your borders? Wynona asked as an idea sparked.

Earl Grey with a Hint of Murder

All who enter are bound.

Huffing, Wynona put her hands on her hips. "Guess that was wrong."

"Maybe not," Arune murmured. "Ask again, but change how you ask it."

"Change how I ask it?" Wynona mulled the words in her head. How could she change it? Surely the woods knew what she was getting at, Uncle Arune certainly had figured it out. *What creatures are bound by the law?*

All who enter are bound.

Wynona grunted. Maybe she should take a different route...*Can someone pay the price for another?*

The trees swayed and the wind grew and Wynona ducked her head to keep from getting dirt in her eyes.

I don't think it likes your question, Violet shouted.

Wynona kept her eyes closed and turned her magical vision back on. *Is there no way to—*

The price has been paid.

The wind stopped and the voices quieted. Cautiously, Wynona opened her eyes and straightened. "What?" she asked out loud.

Violet stood on her hind legs, nose twitching. *What did it say?*

"Wynona?" Rascal asked.

"It said the price has been paid," Wynona responded, her eyes on the trees. She took mental stock of herself, but she didn't feel anything different.

"What did you give it?" Rascal demanded.

"I didn't!" Wynona shouted back. "I just asked a question."

"I don't think it understood," Arune muttered warily. He never looked away from the forest. "It must have taken something."

"But what!" Wynona threw her arms in the air. "I don't feel any different. We didn't make a contract. I didn't agree to anything! I asked a question, it got angry and left."

"But it said the price was paid," Rascal countered. "That has to mean something."

"I don't know!" Wynona shouted, spinning to face him. "You tell me what it means! Because the voices have gone silent and I've got no answers!"

Rascal's eyes moved just slightly, going over Wynona's head before widening impossibly.

Before Wynona could ask questions, Rascal yelled, lunging forward and knocking Wynona to the ground.

She screamed and tucked into herself as she hit the ground with a heavy thud. Another scream tore over her head, but after a moment, Wynona realized she hadn't been the one screaming.

Rascal's head popped up and he cursed, jumping up from Wynona and running back the way he'd come.

Wynona climbed to her feet, gasping when she realized that Opal and Barry were tangled in the grass. She hurried over. "Is anyone hurt?"

"We're fine," Barry wheezed, helping Opal roll off of him before coming to a sitting position himself. He winced and shrugged his shoulders. "If not a bit bruised."

"What in the paranormal world happened?" Rascal shouted, his tone sharp.

Barry shook his head, as if to clear it. "One second we were trying to figure out how to find dinner, the next we were carried through the trees and spit out here." His eyes widened and he looked over at Opal, who was curled into a ball on the ground. "Aw, Opal," he breathed.

Opal's shoulders shook and Wynona watched as Barry tried to soothe her. "What's going on?" Wynona asked, kneeling next to Rascal.

He pushed his hair back and scowled. "I don't know."

Barry looked up, his face stricken. "While the wind was carrying us, we passed over..." Barry swallowed hard and looked down at the crying woman in his arms. "We passed a body, just past the tree line."

Wynona's jaw dropped open.

Earl Grey with a Hint of Murder

The price has been paid, Violet muttered. *No wonder the voices changed their minds.*

"Who was it?" Rascal asked.

Barry closed his eyes and hugged Opal tighter. "Alpha Marcel."

Chapter Twenty-Seven

Wynona fell to her backside, her inside quaking with the revelation.

"You can't be serious," Arune argued, storming their direction. "You said the *trees* were carrying you? How could you possibly have seen a body? Let alone identified it?"

Barry glared, but pointed to the woods. "He's only about fifteen feet inside, right over there."

Wynona followed his finger, then stood on shaky legs.

"Wy, wait." Rascal joined her. He took her hand, offering some much needed support and strength. "I need to see."

Wynona nodded and walked where Barry had said. Standing on tiptoe and then bending low to look through bushes, Wynona couldn't find anything.

"Barry!" Rascal shouted. "You need to come show us. I'm not finding a thing."

After a moment of quiet speaking, Opal nodded and Barry stood, trotting their way. "We saw him only a few seconds before we were spit out right at you guys." He paused. "What were you doing anyway? I thought you were going to come get us, Wynona?"

"Long story," Wynona said with a sigh. "Right now let's worry about the body. We can talk about everything else later."

Arune joined them and Barry hesitated, but turned back to the tree. "He should be right around here."

For the next twenty minutes, the group searched as best they could, Rascal even going so far as to get binoculars and to drive his truck around so they had headlights shining into the forest. The magic of the grove kept them from being as useful as Wynona would have liked, but it was the only idea they had.

"You're sure about what you saw?" Rascal asked for the hundredth time.

"I'm sure!" Barry shouted.

Wynona jerked back.

"Sorry," Barry said, bringing his voice down. He rubbed the back of his neck. "I mean...it's not like I would make something like this up. Opal saw him too. Why do you think she's been so upset?"

"He was lying on his back," Opal said, walking slowly to the group, sniffing and wiping at her face. "He was pale and his arm..." She stopped to sniffle and swallow. "His arm was across his chest." Her face crumpled. "Almost as if he was sleeping, but..." She broke off again, her tears choking the words.

Barry walked through the group, and wrapped his arms around her, turning them so he could face his audience. "But he had a... wound..." Barry said, his voice tight.

"I'm sorry, Barry," Rascal said. "But you're going to have to be more specific than that."

Barry made a face and squeezed Opal tighter. "His throat had been slit...ear to ear."

Wynona closed her eyes, her chin falling to her chest. There was no way they'd mistaken the alpha's death. Not if they both saw it.

Arune sighed and scratched at his chin. "We'll have to wait for morning," he said. "We can't see well enough now and the forest, more than likely, won't speak to Wynona a second time."

"Speak!" Barry shouted. "You *spoke* to the forest?"

Rascal stepped forward, hands in the air. "It's part of that long story that we'll talk about later."

Barry looked like he wanted to say more, but with Opal still crying into his chest, and the weariness of the group at large, there was little to do. Nodding, he followed them as they went into the cabin.

Wynona flipped on the lights as they came inside. "Does anyone want food? Or tea?" she asked. When no one responded, she turned around and gave the group a sad smile. "Come on, Barry. I'll show you the guest room."

With a quiet thank you, he followed, taking Opal with him. Once they were settled, Wynona came out to take care of Arune, but he was gone.

"He left through his portal," Rascal grunted from his place on the couch. "I think we need to discuss whether or not he can still keep it there."

Wynona nodded, sitting down next to her husband and laying her head on his shoulder. "It's been a long day," she whispered.

His arm fell down around her shoulders. "That's the understatement of the year."

Her heavy eyes fell closed and Wynona curled up a little tighter, enjoying his warmth. "What are we going to do?" she whispered.

"About?"

"About Alpha Marcel?"

Rascal didn't respond at first. "Right now the only thing we can do is wait until morning." He grunted. "Hopefully, we'll be able to handle it from there."

Wynona jerked upright. "Violet!"

Rascal shifted. "What about her?" He reached out and pulled her back down.

"I don't know where she is."

He shrugged and sunk deeper into the couch. "She'll show up. She always does." His breathing began to slow. "Besides...knowing her...she's probably in the kitchen eating something she's not supposed to have."

Wynona glanced that way, as if she could see through the wall of her home, but no noises or indication of the small creature were evident. *Violet? Where are you?*

Wynona waited, but she couldn't hear anything.

"Maybe she's with Arune," Rascal said sleepily. "Seriously, Wy. Stop thinking so loud and go to sleep."

"We should sleep in the bed," Wynona said, her mind wide awake now.

"Mm, hm..." As soon as the words were out of his mouth, Rascal was asleep, leaving Wynona to ponder the situation by herself.

"Men," she huffed, slumping against him.

"We're not so bad when you get to know us," Rascal defended, his voice husky with sleep.

"Sorry," Wynona offered. "I thought you were asleep."

He pulled her into his chest. "I'm trying. Now close your eyes and rest. We'll find the punk in the morning."

Deciding he was right, Wynona tried to relax against him. It took several long, measured breaths, but eventually the magic usage and work of the day did its own magic and pulled her into the black abyss of peace.

"Ow." Wynona sat up and rubbed her neck, which had a substantial kink in it, thanks to sleeping on the couch all night.

"You were right," Rascal muttered, shifting his shoulder. "We should have slept in the bed."

Wynona laughed softly.

"Use your magic," Rascal said as he stood and walked around, shaking out his legs.

"Violet always says that too." Wynona fixed her neck, then walked over to Rascal and took care of his aches and pains as well.

"Thanks." He kissed the tip of her nose.

Violet? Are you there?

"She'll show up," Rascal assured her. He bent over the coffee table and grabbed his phone. "Meanwhile, we're going to be invaded in about ten minutes." He looked up. "Better get ready."

"Ten minutes!" Wynona ran down the hallway and took the fastest shower known to witches, before coming back into the sitting room, shaking out her wet hair. She groaned at the full house of people.

"You made it!" Prim skipped over and gave Wynona a hug. "I can't believe I always miss all the action," she pouted. "Sometimes I think I should close the shop."

"You do and it'll be the biggest mistake of your life," Wynona said with a shake of her head. "Solving crimes isn't all it's cracked up to be."

"Says the witch who does it on a regular basis," Prim said with a raised eyebrow. "By the way...who's been running the shop? Arune said he's been helping you."

Wynona moaned and threw her head back. "I completely forgot about it," she said. "I'm not going to have a business to come back to at this rate."

"It's in good hands!" Arune called from across the room.

Wynona leaned around Prim. "You put someone else in charge? Who?"

Arune shrugged. "No one. I just left it running itself."

Wynona's jaw fell. "Excuse me?"

"Wy," Rascal interrupted. "Ream your uncle later." He raised his eyebrows and made a pointed look around the room. "One thing at a time, huh?"

Wynona nodded, but shot a nasty glare at Arune, who wasn't even looking for it to be effective. "Good morning, everyone," she said as she stepped deeper into the room. "Can I get anyone something to eat or drink?"

Earl Grey with a Hint of Murder

"Covered," Celia called out, floating a tray behind her with teacups and pots. It landed gently on the coffee table. "It's serve yourself today," Celia announced. "We've got a lot of stuff to cover and nobody's going to pander to your little requests." With a smirk, Celia threw her hair over her shoulder and strutted to Chief Ligurio's side, where she wrapped her arm around his waist and leaned in.

Well...that's new.

Rascal snorted. *I don't want to know.*

Wynona blinked and shook her head. "Chief," she began. "Why don't you start?"

Chief Ligurio cleared his throat and straightened up, but Celia didn't move from his side. "Ms. Gerrant signed a full confession last night and we have her in holding until she can see a judge."

Murmurs shot around the room and only stopped while Chief Ligurio was finishing his story.

Prim whistled low. "I never saw that one coming."

"None of us did," Arune drawled. "That's why she got away with it for so long."

I feel bad for her, Wynona told Rascal. "Wait!"

All eyes went to Wynona. "Was Violet with you last night?" she asked her uncle.

He frowned and shook his head. "No. I assumed she stayed with you."

Wynona made a face and put her hands on her hips. "Where in the world has that mouse gotten up to? I can't find her anywhere and that's not normal."

A knock on the door caught everyone's attention and Daemon, who was closest to the entryway, went to answer it.

"Good morning," Alpha Strongclaw said, followed by his wife. He nodded at the group. "I apologize for our delay."

"It's fine," Wynona assured him. "We were just getting started."

"Oh!" Mrs. Strongclaw shouted and raced past her husband, enveloping Barry in a tight hug.

Wynona was positive she could feel her own lungs being squeezed from just watching Barry.

Rascal chuckled and winked at Wynona.

Mrs. Strongclaw moved on to a still teary-eyed Opal and Barry looked at his dad.

"Hey, Dad," Barry said, hesitantly, as if unsure of his welcome.

Alpha Strongclaw gave a small smile and walked across the room, thumping his son on the back with a heavy hand. "I'm glad you're safe," he said thickly.

Wynona sniffed and wiped at her face, whacking Rascal against his chest when he laughed softly at her. "Nothing wrong with being soft-hearted," she snapped.

His hand rubbed her back. "Nope," he responded soothingly. "Nothing at all."

The room watched the reunion for a few minutes before the chatter went back to Sartel's arrest. Mrs. Strongclaw was holding onto Barry across the room, but Alpha Strongclaw came over to stand near Wynona and Rascal.

"Son?" he whispered.

Rascal raised his eyebrow in silent response.

"I don't know what it was, but as we were driving up, the forest looked like it threw an object onto your lawn. I'm not sure how else to describe it."

Wynona gasped and turned his way, but the alpha was looking at Rascal.

"It was...fairly large," the alpha finished quietly.

Rascal's jaw clenched. He looked down at Wynona. "Be right back."

"You're not going without me," she argued. "I'm the one who started this whole fiasco."

Rascal huffed, but nodded. "Then let's go."

As quietly as they could, the couple slipped out the front door and hurried around the side of the house.

"What do you think it could be?" Wynona asked, slightly out of breath from their pace.

"Part of me doesn't want to know," Rascal said harshly. "The other half thinks it can't be anything good."

Wynona made a face. "I sure wish I knew where Violet was. I can't help but think something's wrong."

Rascal skidded to a stop and Wynona nearly ran into his back. He cursed, put his hands on his hips, and cursed again.

"Rascal!" Wynona scolded, moving around him. She stopped when she finally saw what had stopped him. Her stomach churned and her breathing grew too fast.

"Get the chief," Rascal said in a low, deadly tone.

"He's on his way," Arune's voice replied.

Wynona tore her eyes from the scene and looked back to see the house emptying of its occupants. "How could this happen?" she asked Arune.

Arune put his hand on her shoulder. "Find Violet."

Wynona's heart sank. "No," she whispered, shaking her head. "No." Closing her eyes, Wynona called to her familiar over and over again, until her head hurt so badly she could hardly think straight. "She made a trade," Wynona sobbed, grabbing her uncle's shirt and giving it a shake. "Didn't she? She made a trade!"

Rascal tore Wynona away from her uncle and curled her into his chest. "Skymaw. Call the precinct. Get Azirad out here."

"On it," Daemon said, immediately pulling out his phone.

Wynona sobbed into her husband's chest, unable to breathe or hold herself up.

"No!" Barry shouted, stopping Opal from running to her father's body. "Don't, sweetheart."

Mrs. Strongclaw helped keep the girl from running the rest of the way across the yard and looked to her husband. "What can be done?" she asked.

Alpha Strongclaw shook his head. "This one is out of my hands."

He looked sick to his stomach, but he stood straight and tall as he turned to Rascal. "Just tell me how I can help."

"Just...keep everyone back," Rascal said tightly. "Chief?"

Chief Ligurio nodded and left the group, walking up to the body and kneeling down. His red eyes were bright as he turned back to Wynona. "I think we need the rest of the story, Wynona. I don't have a good feeling about any of this."

Chapter Twenty-Eight

Wynona spent the next twenty minutes going over everything that had happened after Chief Ligurio had left with Sartel in custody last night. Her words were broken and halting and she couldn't help feeling like there was a hole inside of her where her familiar used to be.

"How did I not feel it?" Wynona whispered to Rascal after her story was done and the crowd were talking about it all and offering suggestions.

Rascal shook his head. "You can't go there. What is, is. Do you really think you could have stopped Violet from offering herself up?" Rascal snorted, though Wynona could feel he wasn't as flippant as he was acting. "We both know nobody tells the little one what to do."

Wynona shook her head and wiped her cheeks. "I could have done something," she insisted. "I should have *felt* something. I don't know what she was thinking! How could she have risked herself for someone who was already dead?"

"Shhh..." Rascal cuddled her close. "Come on, Wy. I need you to breathe, okay? We'll figure this out. We don't know for sure that she's even in there. It's just a guess right now. The grove could have thrown Marcel out for a different reason, it wasn't exactly up to date on common sense."

Wynona held back another sob, but her tears wouldn't stop flowing. She buried her face in his shirt, letting it soak up the moisture as her mind spun. Violet was in there. Wynona was sure of it. But why? Why risk it?

Wynona turned her head just enough to see the trees. The longer she stared, the more angry she became. Her emotions began to form into a single army with outrage leading the charge. *How dare it.*

"Wy?" Rascal leaned back a little, but Wynona paid no attention.

"How. DARE it take HER!" Wynona shouted, all rational thought flying out the window. Pulling fully away from Wynona, she began to storm to the forest. Voices rose, but Wynona wasn't about to be deterred.

She threw her hand over her shoulder, creating a wall to keep anyone else from following.

"WYNONA!" Rascal bellowed. His fist hit the wall. *Take it down NOW!*

No.

Let me in, Rascal pleaded. *We'll do this together. I want her back too and going this alone is suicide.*

Which is exactly why I need you safe back there. Wynona's fists clenched and unclenched. Rascal had gotten strong. His pounding on the wall was almost enough to bring him through, but she was still able to hold him off...for now. If he continued to progress, she wouldn't be able to do it for much longer.

Wynona, please.

Her footsteps faltered.

I'm your soulmate. Violet is connected to me too. Do NOT ask me to sit on the sidelines. I've done far too much of it over the course of our relationship. I KNOW I'm not as strong as you, but I was chosen to be your husband for a reason and if you keep setting me aside, we'll never have the chance to see why.

Wynona let the words sink in. Rascal was right. Their pairing, especially in light of everything they were learning, had to have a reason. But...what she was about to attempt was going to be far from pretty. *You won't try to stop me?*

Not unless you're about to die. I make no promises if your life is in danger.

Wynona decided that was all she could ask for and would do no less for him. Without even bothering to consider what type of magic she needed to use, she snapped her fingers, porting Rascal to her side.

His arms flew out and he steadied himself on his feet. "What... just happened?" he croaked.

"We'll talk about it later," Wynona said, her jaw tight. "Right now I'm a little busy." The farther she walked, the calmer Wynona became and the more she felt her magic rise to meet her. She *was* the strongest witch in the world. There was no question about it. And no creature or being was allowed to take those she loved from her.

Raising her chin in the air, Wynona stopped at the tree line. *Give her back.*

The trees stirred, but barely.

Wynona tried again. *I said...give her back.*

The reaction of the forest was even less this time and Wynona's vision turned red.

Bringing her hands in front of her, she pulled her magic front and center and shot it straight into the forest, creating a shockwave through the entity. *YOU WILL LISTEN TO ME AND ANSWER WHEN I SPEAK!* Wynona screamed in her mind.

The wind began to churn and the trees swayed dangerously, bending branches until they were nearly snapping, but none of it touched Wynona or Rascal. Her own magic met it head on, feet planted, and her rational mind turned away, Wynona felt separated from the world...only she and her power remained.

I will ask one more time, Wynona thought in a low, steely tone. *Give her back.*

The price has been paid, the voices responded.

She's a MOUSE! Wynona shot back. *What price could she have possibly paid?*

The price has been paid. The voices refused to relent and Wynona found her anger growing again.

A hand on her arm brought her out of her haze just enough to recognize Rascal at her side.

"This place is ancient," he said softly, searching her eyes as if looking for something in particular. "The law it abides by is probably ancient as well. Rather than fight over Violet, why not figure out what it wants." He dropped his chin and pinned her with a glance. "And yourself is not an acceptable sacrifice."

Wynona's chest was heaving with frustration. "It wasn't alright to take her in the first place."

Rascal shook his head. "Odds are the rules were abided by," Rascal stated. "Violet would have had to offer herself. The forest couldn't simply take her, not unless she crossed the borders. And if she crossed the border without a contract, the grove wouldn't have thrown Marcel back."

Wynona closed her eyes and forced her breathing to calm down, at least a little before turning back to the forest. *I would hear your terms.*

We are too many to name.

Wynona scowled. "I KNOW that!" She put the words in her head again. *I'm not asking your NAME! I want to know what price you want for Violet?*

We are too many to name! the voice insisted.

"Arrgh!" Wynona screamed, pushing her hands through her hair. What little grip she had on reality was about to give way.

"Wy...that must mean something."

Wynona spun and snarled at Rascal. "It's simply repeating the same thing over and over again. How can that mean something?"

"Exactly," Rascal said, his tone annoyingly calm. "If it's repeating the same thing, then it must be the answer. Now...what does the answer mean?"

Earl Grey with a Hint of Murder

Wynona squeezed her eyes shut and shook her head. "We are too many to name," she muttered. "What can it mean, other than the fact that there are lots of magical spirits inside?" *There are lots of spirits inside. There are LOTS of spirits inside. There are...*

Wynona's eyes popped open. "Rascal...how big is the forest?"

Rascal groaned. "I'm not sure. A few hundred acres, I think."

Wynona spun. *I offer land,* she said hastily. *Part of my land, room, in exchange for Violet.*

Wynona's property wasn't massive, but she had space between her and the forest and she was more than willing to lose some of her yard if it meant gaining her familiar.

"Are you sure you want to do that?" Rascal warned. "That's not very...specific."

Wynona threw up her hands. "What do you suggest then?"

"Just clarify," he offered. "Give exact square footage or a point in the property line so it doesn't take too much."

Wynona considered his words, but a roaring bellow took the words out of her mouth. Looking up, Wynona caught sight of a line of fire filling the air and coming straight at her property.

Wynona quickly put another wall up, only to take it down when Rayn's dragon appeared through the flames.

Rayn landed with a heavy thud, shaking the earth and immediately blasting a bright orange flame at the trees, which remained untouched from her ire.

WY!

Wynona spun back just in time for her familiar to come flying out of the forest as well. Rascal jumped into her line of sight and caught the mouse right out of the air.

"I've gotcha," Rascal cooed, cuddling the mouse to his chest. He looked at Wynona.

Wynona stepped up. "Violet," she breathed, carefully taking the shaking body from her husband. "Violet...you're okay..."

That might be debatable, Violet said through chattering teeth. She was shaking so badly Wynona could barely understand her. Bringing

Violet to her chest, Wynona rubbed her head and tried to use her own warmth.

Slowly, Wynona's wrath slowed and her vision went back to normal, while her magic wall dissipated.

Another dragon roar, however, had them both turning to see Rayn barely being controlled by Arune.

The witch stood with his hands up. "Rayn, my love...we can't fix anything if we don't know what's wrong. Shift back and we'll talk about what happened."

Wynona walked over, but grew concerned when Rayn didn't shift. "Why isn't she turning?" she asked Arune.

"She's too angry," Arune snapped. "She's just about lost to the beast."

Rascal ducked under a wing, barely escaping one massive claw and put a hand on the dragon's side. "Shift," he said firmly, but quietly.

Wynona's eyes nearly popped out of her head when the dragon began to shrink. "How'd...you do that?" she asked hoarsely.

Rascal came back to her side, frowning. "I'm not sure. I could feel her beast and knew I could call her back."

"It's more of his alpha powers, I'm sure," Arune said as he quickly walked the distance to his soulmate. He knelt next to her on the ground. "What happened?" he demanded, while putting his arm around her. "Why did the beast go crazy?"

Rayn was breathing heavily as she looked up, her eyes still glaring with flames. "My house..." she croaked. "The forest...took...my house."

Wynona gasped, guilt swamping her immediately.

"The whole meadow has been turned into trees and the magic has taken over." Rayn's head fell, her hair wild, unkempt and smoking. "I had no warning and barely made it out before being caught inside."

Arune growled and wrapped her more fully in her arms. "What

could have possessed it to do such a thing?" he snarled. He looked up at Wynona. "Talking to it seems to have created nothing but trouble."

Wynona slowly shook her head, the tiny body of Violet her only comfort at the moment. "No..." she rasped. "It was the price."

"Price?" Arune demanded. "What price?"

"The forest," Wynona said haltingly. "It requires a price for everything it gives."

"Yes, we figured that out." His eyes landed on Violet's tiny head peeking above Wynona's hand. "Wynona," he said, his tone falling. "You didn't."

"Rayn's house isn't what I meant," Wynona replied, defending herself. "But yes...I offered a prize for Violet's return." Wynona looked at Rayn. "I'm so sorry," she whispered. "I wasn't specific enough and this is...all my fault."

Rayn looked up, her brows furrowed. "Your fault?" She clambered to her feet. "What are you talking about?" Her voice was loud and Wynona was feeling the effects of her magic having drained.

Trying not to wince, Wynona explained the situation with Violet. She barely noticed the rest of the crowd coming and gathering around them, some warily, others eagerly, but soon they were all together again.

"You gave the forest MY HOUSE for Violet?" Rayn shouted.

Wynona swallowed. "Yes." There was no way to deny it. It hadn't been on purpose and Wynona had only meant to give her own yard, but somehow, the forest had taken it another way.

Rayn shook her head and growled, smoke coming from her nostrils. "That was reckless and unbelievable, Wynona. I thought better of you."

Arune stepped between them, as Wynona's heart sank to her feet. She didn't blame Rayn, not one bit. It had been reckless, exactly what Rascal had been trying to help her avoid. There was no excuse for it. Violet gone or not, Wynona should have kept her head and dealt with the situation with caution. How she would ever make it up to Rayn, Wynona didn't know, but somehow, some way, Wynona would make it right.

"Rayn...let it go," Arune said, surprising Wynona. "None of us had any idea the forest was even sentient until last night and all things considered, we escaped the situation better than could be expected."

"I hate to be the bearer of bad news," Chief Ligurio interrupted. "But the rest of the precinct will be here any minute." He cleared his throat and looked pointedly at the body still splayed on the lawn. "We might want to shelve this conversation for later." He raised his eyebrows. "And I do believe we need to have it later. If I'm not mistaken, somewhere along the line in this investigation, we decided that we were going to run a rebellion and now several other things have been thrown in our faces." The chief took in a deep breath. "Somehow, I doubt we're going to get anywhere if we look into Marcel's murder, but we *do* need to sit down and put everything down we've learned about President Le Doux and what to do going forward." The vampire slowly shook his head. "More and more, with every passing event, I'm realizing that the time to act is here. Maybe not tonight, maybe not tomorrow, but it's coming and we're running out of excuses for putting it off." He glanced at the forest, the body and then the group. "If we don't get our act together and figure something out...our very world, as we know it...will be gone."

What's Next?

Eager for more answers?
You definitely don't want to miss
Wynona's next adventure!
Life as they know it is about to get complicated!
Check out book #10, COMING SOON!

Made in the USA
Coppell, TX
06 May 2023